GENTRY, J. E.

FIRST THING KILL THE

W9-CFI-870

2017

3756502945440 1

ROHN

Official Discard

Sonoma County Library

11/18

She'd always loved mysteries and thought investigating a murder would be a lark...until she got the note!

Clara knew she had to call Travis, and the immediate question was whether to call him now or later. She took a quick look around her, saw no one, and decided to get out of there as soon as she could. She kept looking in her rearview mirror as she drove, thinking of all those movies with somebody tailing somebody else.

How the hell do you know if the car behind you, or the one a couple of lengths back, is tailing you?

She was still shaking when she pulled into the parking garage in her own building. She didn't want to get out of her car, but she didn't want to stay in the garage either. Everything looked normal, and, finally, she grabbed her briefcase, impatiently waited for the elevator, and soon locked herself in her own place. But she didn't feel safe.

Travis picked up after the first ring, and she breathlessly told him about the note. He responded in calm, measured tones, not revealing to her more than professional concern. "You're right to be scared, Clara. You'd be a fool if you weren't. Somebody must've seen us together. It could be a sick joke, but probably not."

"Do you really think I'm in danger, Travis?"

"I'm not gonna sugarcoat this. It doesn't look good. When I told you to be careful, I didn't expect this. I was just being cautious. But now it looks like somebody thinks you're snooping into areas where he doesn't want you to snoop."

"But that sounds like there's all the more reason I should snoop. It really looks like somebody thinks I'm onto something."

Attorney Clara Quillen is stunned when she reads about the murders of three San Francisco lawyers and realizes her former boss, Bernard Kahn, is one of the victims. The lawyers were killed on the same night, in the same manner, each holding a copy of an often-misunderstood Shakespearean quote from Henry VI, Part II: "The first thing we do, let's kill all the lawyers."

When SFPD Detective Roy Travis questions members of Kahn's law firm, he recruits Clara to aid his investigation since she has access to confidential client information that may shed light on potential suspects. As a long-time mystery fan, Clara jumps at the opportunity and agrees to become an amateur sleuth, working with Travis. During the course of the investigation, the murderer strikes again. And, as the list of suspects continues to grow and Clara unearths information regarding elaborate blackmail schemes that incriminate both friends and colleagues, she receives a threat that she, herself, may the next victim unless she abandons her pursuit of the cold-blooded killer...

KUDOS for *First Thing ~ Kill the Lawyers*

In *First Thing ~ Kill the Lawyers* by J. E. Gentry, Clara Quillen is an attorney whose former boss has just been murdered. Clara left his employ because he was an unethical jerk, but she finds it hard to believe that someone hated him enough to kill him, along with two other lawyers on the same night. The detective assigned to the case is impressed with Clara's analytical abilities, and he asks for her help in figuring out who the killer is. So Clara starts investigating all of her ex-boss's clients, trying to find out who had a motive—only to discover that almost everyone did. And now whoever it is threatens to come after her. Not only is this an intriguing mystery, but with great characters, a number of interesting twists and turns, and flashes of humor, it's truly an entertaining read. ~ *Taylor Jones, The Review Team of Taylor Jones & Regan Murphy*

First Thing ~ Kill the Lawyers by J E Gentry is the story of Clara Quillen—mystery fan, wealthy widow, and retired (sort of) lawyer. Clara quit her job with Bernie Kahn because she discovered many of his practices were unethical. A month later, Bernie is murdered, along with three other lawyers on the same night. When Clara is interviewed by the detective on the case, Roy Travis, he realizes that she has access to information that he doesn't—namely confidential client information. So he enlists her aid, not to reveal privileged information, which she refuses to do, but to give him background on the clients and employees of the firm to help him narrow down the suspects. Being a lover of mysteries, Clara is thrilled. She thinks helping him find the killer will be a lark—that is, until the killer threatens to come after her if she doesn't "mind her own business." Gentry's character development is superb and the story well written. Combining mystery, suspense, a hint of romance, and a generous helping of wit, *First Thing ~ Kill the Lawyers* is one you'll enjoy reading again and again. *Regan Murphy, The Review Team of Taylor Jones & Regan Murphy*

ACKNOWLEDGMENTS

I especially appreciate the perspectives of the book group, which was an outgrowth of the Honors Seminar that I taught at a law school. I also acknowledge others who read the manuscript, and I hope you know grateful I am for your time and effort.

FIRST THING ~
KILL
THE LAWYERS

J. E. GENTRY

A Black Opal Books Publication

GENRE: MYSTERY-DETECTIVE/WOMEN SLEUTHS

This is a work of fiction. Names, places, characters and incidents are either the product of the author's imagination or are used fictitiously, and any resemblance to any actual persons, living or dead, businesses, organizations, events or locales is entirely coincidental. All trademarks, service marks, registered trademarks, and registered service marks are the property of their respective owners and are used herein for identification purposes only. The publisher does not have any control over or assume any responsibility for author or third-party websites or their contents.

FIRST THING ~ KILL THE LAWYERS
Copyright © 2014 by J. E. Gentry
Cover Design by Jackson Cover Designs
All cover art copyright © 2017
All Rights Reserved
Print ISBN: 978-1-626948-21-1

First Publication: OCTOBER 2014

All rights reserved under the International and Pan-American Copyright Conventions. No part of this book may be reproduced or transmitted in any form or by any means, electronic or mechanical, including photocopying, recording, or by any information storage and retrieval system, without permission in writing from the publisher.

WARNING: The unauthorized reproduction or distribution of this copyrighted work is illegal. Criminal copyright infringement, including infringement without monetary gain, is investigated by the FBI and is punishable by up to 5 years in federal prison and a fine of $250,000. Anyone pirating our ebooks will be prosecuted to the fullest extent of the law and may be liable for each individual download resulting therefrom.

ABOUT THE PRINT VERSION: If you purchased a print version of this book without a cover, you should be aware that the book is stolen property. It was reported as "unsold and destroyed" to the publisher, and neither the author nor the publisher has received any payment for this "stripped book."

IF YOU FIND AN EBOOK OR PRINT VERSION OF THIS BOOK BEING SOLD OR SHARED ILLEGALLY, PLEASE REPORT IT TO: lpn@blackopalbooks.com

Published by Black Opal Books **http://www.blackopalbooks.com**

DEDICATION

This book is dedicated to my husband,
who is also my best friend.
He is always devoted and supportive.

PROLOGUE

I *can't believe I did it. I really did it. At last. I killed all three of them.*

And it came off like clockwork. The perfect crime.

I feel a little queasy. I'll roll down the window some more. Get some fresh air. I thought I might feel sick. But I don't exactly feel sick. Just a little queasy. I never thought there would be so much blood.

Funny, though, I don't feel the least bit guilty. They deserved it, but I thought I might feel guilty anyway. So what is guilt? Big philosophical question.

I hate to admit it, but I feel sort of exhilarated. Probably just the adrenaline still pumping. I didn't think I'd feel this way. I actually feel sort of satisfied. I thought about it so long and wondered if I could really do it. And I did it. I got rid of the bastards.

It doesn't feel quite real, though. Mostly just kind of numb.

Hey, watch out!

That guy almost sideswiped me. Okay, so maybe I was weaving a little. I have to pick my moment to throw the gun off the bridge.

Now. Nobody close. Yeah, fine. It cleared the railing. All those practice sessions with a rock paid off. That was the last part. No one will ever find a gun under the Gold-

en Gate Bridge. Maybe it will turn up someday. Probably never. Now I can peel off these stupid gloves. Probably didn't need them anyway. Just seemed like a good idea. They can go in the trash anywhere, along with the old raincoat and shoes I got at the thrift store. Never be noticed.

The fog feels like a security blanket. It's nice coming off the bridge, back in the city. Who'd want to live in Marin County anyway? I feel like I've really gotten away with it now that I'm back in the city. This is what I've been living for—for months. I've hardly been able to think about anything else.

It was tough to keep functioning like a normal person. Not that anybody would ever suspect somebody like me could be planning a murder. That was the fun of it.

Fun? God, was it really fun, even a little bit? I never thought I was capable of killing anybody, let alone thinking it could be fun. But it was actually sort of cool watching them go down. I felt so powerful, so in control. In one instant, I snuffed out a life. Not that those guys deserved a life. They spent their lives sucking the life out of other people. I just evened the score.

Maybe I missed my calling. Maybe I could even do it again. There are plenty of bastards out there who should be wiped off the face of the earth. Maybe I'm just part of the eco-system, helping the balance of nature. Maybe I should start wearing a white hat and go around snuffing the guys in the black hats. Maybe not. I don't know.

It's all still so new. Feels really weird. I wondered what it would feel like. Now I'm not sure how I feel. Up till tonight, all that mattered was doing it. Now I just have to make sure I get away with it. But everything was perfect, with not a slip. I'll get away with it, all right.

Just find a dumpster. Then I'll be completely safe. It's over.

CHAPTER 1

Three Dead Lawyers

She got hooked on murder mysteries years ago when she was an adolescent. She'd even made up a little jingle about it.

> *Murder, murder everywhere,*
> *And what was she to think?*
> *Murder, murder everywhere,*
> *The sleuth must find the link.*

It was adapted from "The Rime of the Ancient Mariner," of course. You probably remember: "Water, water, everywhere, Nor any drop to drink." She was a model student in her English classes, but she allowed herself a minor rebellion when she hit puberty, about the same time she discovered the mystery section in the public library.

"I'd like to check these out, please," she'd said in a small voice, topping the mystery books with a poetry anthology.

The librarian had looked up over rimless glasses and smiled knowingly. Her strawberry blonde hair had contrasted with the wrinkles in her face. "These are fine," she'd said, "but come with me, and I'll help you find some really good ones."

From then on, Clara Quillen spent a lot of time at the library. She raced through her homework and then reveled in murder, mystery, and mayhem.

But that seemed like ages ago, when she'd only imagined being involved in a real murder mystery. All that would change today, when she would learn about the cold-blooded murder of someone she knew. It would be a while, though, before she would know she was already acquainted with the murderer—and ultimately would be a target herself.

The day wasn't quite ordinary to start with. Despite her eight-hour jet lag, when she woke up, she remembered that today was her birthday. Probably nobody but her mother and maybe even Jake would remember, and they were thousands of miles away. So she had written, "Happy birthday to me" on the calendar. The date was April thirtieth.

She took a long look in the mirror. Her baggy sweatsuit wasn't very flattering. She usually didn't spend a lot of time in front of a mirror, but there's something about birthdays that make you look, even if you're unsure whether you really want to—like when you pass an accident on the freeway. How bad is it?

Not bad for thirty-eight, she told herself. After all, she could pass for, hmmm, maybe thirty-seven—at least if she bothered to put on some decent clothes. She took pride in her humility—though mindful of the contradiction in terms—knowing she looked damn good for thirty-eight. She might even pass for twenty-eight—well, maybe in a dim light.

Today she'd need an extra jolt of caffeine to help get back on California time. She popped the little cup-pack of Jamaica Blue Mountain Coffee into the single-cup brewer and started it to brew while she went to the door to pick up her *San Francisco Chronicle*. Sometimes they didn't follow instructions to resume delivery after vacation hold, but she was glad to see it was there. She still liked reading a daily newspaper, even when so many had degenerated from being first-rate. Savoring the coffee, she looked out through the balcony window and saw the orange vermillion tips of the Golden Gate Bridge already peeking through the fog. It promised to be a pleasant day, not the weird day it suddenly became.

The stories above the fold weren't particularly compelling—maybe a slow news day?—but the headline at the bottom of page one caught her eye.

Three Marin Lawyers Found Shot To Death in Separate Incidents

The real jolt came at the end of the first paragraph. After she read it, she stared blankly, at first unable to breathe.

She closed her eyes a few seconds, opened them wide, and read it again. She shook herself, not quite sure she was awake yet. Maybe it was just a dream, or maybe just the jetlag after her return from London yesterday. But the words were still there.

Three Bay Area lawyers each died from a gunshot wound to the head in Marin County last night. Alvin P. Hanks, 56, a prominent divorce lawyer with two Bay Area offices, was found dead in his Mercedes sedan parked at the Lark Creek Inn restaurant in Larkspur. Richard N. Rinko, 37, a San Rafael attorney specializing in legal malpractice, was found dead in his Porsche in the parking lot of the Marin County Civic Center. Bernard C. Kahn, 44, a San Francisco attorney, was found dead on a roadside near his Mill Valley home.

Until one month ago, Clara had been an associate attorney in the law firm of Bernard C. Kahn & Associates. After weeks of pointedly ignoring his existence, she was having a hard time registering that Bernie Kahn was now dead. She shuddered, briskly rubbed the goosebumps on her arms, and read on.

The next chilling detail raised more goosebumps. At each murder scene, the same quote from Shakespeare had been found: "The first thing we do, let's kill all the lawyers."

The article said that an investigation of the killings was underway, but the police had released few details and didn't say whether they had any definite suspects. It described the discovery of Kahn's body by his wife. The "distraught widow" was quoted as saying tearfully, "I went out to look for my husband when our dog came home alone from their usual evening walk. I'm just completely devastated by the shock of it all."

Clara could just picture Charlotte saying that to some reporter and milking it for all it was worth. Of course, the quote didn't capture the nasal Texas twang in Charlotte's voice.

Clara read again about the other victims. Hanks was discovered by a waiter who had gone outside the Lark Creek Inn for a smoke. A Marin Civic Center security guard making routine rounds found Rinko slumped over his steering wheel. Although the police didn't say how the killings might be related, the fact that all three attorney-victims apparently died from similar gunshot wounds to the head, along with the same quote from Shakespeare left at the scene, made it fairly obvious that the murders were connected.

Routine murder stories generally didn't make page one of the *Chronicle,* but these execution-style killings promised elements of the sensational. So, following the skimpy details on page one, the article continued at some length on A13, although the additional information was only standard background. Most of it appeared to have come from the Martindale-Hubbell Law Directory: when and where the victims had gotten their law degrees, what their specialties were, the names of their associates, the locations of their law offices, and so on.

Clara could give them plenty of details about Bernie Kahn, far more than she cared to know. But if she'd had a choice, she wished she'd never known him at all, to say nothing of his "distraught widow." She even had a petting acquaintance with his purebred borzoi Natasha, the dog he had been walking when he was killed. She only vaguely recalled Hanks because of his rotten reputation as a ruthless divorce attorney, and she had never heard of Rinko before.

As she sat immobile with the newspaper in her hands, Clara had a nagging feeling she ought to do something or call somebody. For the moment, though, all she could do was sit and think about her seven months as an associate with Bernard C. Kahn & Associates. She could still see Bernie starting off the regular Monday morning meeting, with the support staff's veiled glances of discontent as he tossed out one of his typical snide remarks. "Well, people, do you think we can try to get through the week without any major blunders?"

After he droned on with constant criticism, Clara was pretty sure she wasn't the only one who had to bite her tongue to keep from saying, "Oh, just shut up, Bernie."

At the end of the meetings, the support staff scurried off to their tiny cubicles, like little mice fleeing from a cat, trying to avoid Bernie's wrath on whatever happened to be his hot button of the moment.

Of all the people Clara had ever known, who would be the most likely candidate for a murder victim? Yep, she thought, Kahn would be at the top of the list. She couldn't recall having known anyone else who aroused such derision, at least in those who saw through his highly polished veneer. His employees and ex-employees had several contemptuous nicknames for him, the most sarcastic being Saint Bernard. His childish tantrums usually conjured up Bernie Baby. When he was especially dictatorial, he was Genghis Kahn, and of course, the epithet earned by his dubious methods in luring new clients was The Kahn Man.

The contempt for Kahn extended to others related to him. His "lovely wife Charlotte," as he usually referred to her, had the endearing nickname of The Empress Charlotta. His parents and siblings, though no one had met them, were The Munsters. Even the borzoi Natasha, who was almost always in the office on Fridays, was surreptitiously called Timid Tasha. She was a beautiful dog, but skittish, and the general opinion was that any dog of Bernie's would have to be neurotic.

It was a fluke, of course, that Clara had gone to work for Kahn at all. She'd considered her options when she finished law school near the top of her class at the University of California's Boalt Hall. She'd decided to wait until after she took the bar exam in July to think seriously about any definite plans. During the month of August, she'd had interviews with a couple of prestigious firms. She'd had trouble seeing herself submerged in one of those big firms. So she'd been intrigued by the pitch in the *Daily Law Journal* advertisement for Bernard C. Kahn & Associates. "Greater potential for professional development than being an inconsequential cog in a huge law firm."

The ad had sought a beginning associate with "impeccable academic credentials" to do research and writing for a civil appellate practice, an area Clara had hoped to pursue. When she'd looked up the firm in Martindale-Hubbell, she found that Kahn's office also did general business law and estate planning, with related tax and probate work. She had decided she would answer the ad when she saw that the firm's two associates were women, though she'd wondered why there were no partners.

She recalled every detail of her first meeting with Kahn in what she thought of as her "true blue interview suit" with a cream-colored blouse and pearl earrings.

"Good morning, Ms. Quillen, and welcome to our little boutique firm," he'd said without apology, thirty-seven minutes after the interview was scheduled to start.

Months later, she learned he would often read the newspaper in his office while he deliberately kept people waiting, with the intent to increase their anxiety and reinforce his sense of control.

"We hope you recognize the exceptional quality of the firm we've developed. We think your excellent credentials indicate that you are the caliber of person who might fit in well here."

She'd noticed that what might have been intended to sound like a compliment just came off as pompous. She'd also noticed his use of what seemed to be the "editorial we" and had wondered whether maybe it was more like the "royal we." Even so, Kahn had an undeniable facile charm. She'd later watched him shift smoothly from urbane sophisticate to colorful good-old-boy or any other persona the occasion called for to entice a client. He'd seemed quite bright and apparently had a very successful law practice. But despite his faultless attire, he'd still given her the slightly creepy impression of a lounge lizard in a polyester suit.

Looking at her résumé, he'd said, "I'm pleased to see you were on law review. That's an exhilarating experience, isn't it?" Instead of waiting for her response, he'd launched into a story about something he had written when he was on the *Harvard Law Review*. He'd made a point of informing her that he had gone to Harvard, which of course she'd already known from preparing for the interview. Later, she observed that he typically managed to work Harvard into the first few minutes of a conversation with anyone new, especially a client.

At that point in the interview, Clara had known she could just sit back and let Kahn do the talking. Her Southern upbringing had groomed her perfectly for just how to hang onto a man's every word without being too obvious about it. And so, long after she had effectively shed her Southern accent, she took advantage of her early training—of course, she'd resisted the temptation to drawl, "Why, li'l ole me would just love to work for a big, impo'tant man like you."

After a few more of his pointed, little anecdotes, Clara had decided it was a toss-up which lacked more subtlety, Bernie or the office itself. It was ornately decorated, a feeble imitation of a small Chinese palace. There were actually a few impressive antiques—an excellent screen and some porcelain that had reminded her of some fine pieces she had seen in Beijing. The overall impression, though, like that left by Bernie's self-aggrandizing tales, was one of having been created strictly for effect. Adding to the effect was a vague aroma of incense, although Clara had wondered if she only imagined it. Maybe it was just Kahn's cloying lavender cologne that had drifted across the carved rosewood table.

Eventually, she learned Kahn had acquired the few good Chinese antiques on a honeymoon trip to Hong Kong with one of his previous wives; no one was quite sure which one or even how many wives there had been. The heavy-handed, more recent decor was the product of Kahn's current wife, The Empress Charlotta, whose part-time work as a real estate agent seemed to have given her the misguided notion that she knew something about interior decorating. Office gossip speculated about whether Kahn actually liked the decor or was merely indulging his wife.

Concerned much more with Kahn than the decor, of course, Clara had scrutinized him, while appearing to be captivated by everything he said. He was a smallish man, and she'd guessed that his pompous demeanor had evolved as compensation for his short stature. He had a boyish face embellished by a precisely groomed mustache that she'd supposed was meant to make him appear dignified or maybe dashing. But the real effect was to further weaken his doughy and slightly receding chin. His styled brown hair had just the right touch of gray at the temples. His watery gray eyes were a tad too close together, more noticeable because he had a habit of knitting his eyebrows when he wanted to appear particularly serious or concerned. His manner of dress was consistent with the rest of his personality—all image. His perfectly tailored suit camouflaged his sloping shoulders and tendency toward a middle-aged paunch.

She'd seen him as a bit of a dandy, but he'd also reminded her of a famous portrait of Napoleon she had seen in the Louvre, if one were to draw a precise facsimile of Kahn's mustache above the Little Corporal's upper lip. Later, as she gradually became aware of Kahn's more pernicious qualities, when he was being especially obnoxious in one of his long, pointless meetings, she would amuse herself by picturing him with his hand thrust into his waistcoat, sputtering orders to all who would obey. For variety, sometimes she would imagine the portrait of Napoleon with the emperor dressed in one of Kahn's fancy designer suits and Gucci loafers.

Despite her initial negative impression, the lure that

first had attracted Clara to work for Kahn came when he'd said, "I assure you that you will be able to plunge into appellate work right away—with my professional oversight, of course. Here, you will have the opportunity for immediate experience that would take years to acquire in one of the mega-firms."

He'd told her that as soon as she passed the bar exam—with July results due about Thanksgiving—she could expect to be working as a full-fledged appellate attorney.

She had to admit, he had pretty much lived up to that expectation. She didn't learn for a while that the real reason he'd allowed her so much responsibility was his own aversion to the practice of law. He preferred being the front man—the rainmaker, who was all image and no substance. He worked his associates and office staff into the ground for as little pay as he could get away with. He took all the credit, as well as the profits, and then preened when the clients observed how brilliant he was.

The salary he'd offered Clara was barely more than half of what she could get from other firms. She had not, however, let on that she happened to be in a financial position that made salary of virtually no concern to her. But just to exercise her negotiation skills, she'd nudged him up a little before she'd accepted his final offer.

What actually convinced Clara to accept the job were her potential colleagues. Whatever his faults might be, Kahn seemed to have an uncanny knack for hiring good people. She'd immediately liked the two associate attorneys he introduced her to—Katy MacLeod, who did the estate work, and Maura Grimaldi, an experienced appellate attorney and the one Clara would work with most closely. They'd talked only a few minutes, but Clara had known instinctively that she could learn a lot from Maura.

As soon as she started working at the firm, Clara had also found she liked the support staff. There were two quasi-paralegals. Francis Davis was actually a retired attorney with a wealth of knowledge and experience. He was a dear man in his early seventies who exhibited a gentle nature and a penchant for being inordinately helpful. The other one had left shortly after Clara started. She was an intelligent young woman who had a master's degree in fine arts and needed a job. The office manager, who functioned largely as Kahn's handiest scapegoat, oversaw the work of a substantial staff: three word processors, a receptionist, an accountant, a bookkeeper, a computer techie, a file clerk, and a combination copy clerk/office boy.

There were no traditional secretaries. Kahn typically said, "I don't believe in secretaries—they tend to get too proprietary." Translated, that meant he had a paranoid fear of divided loyalties.

Before long, Clara had begun to wonder why an office with only three attorneys had such a large support staff, and she'd asked Francis why.

"It's obvious after you've been here a while," he'd said. "Genghis Kahn has to have some troops to order around. There's even a sort of rank structure. It's codified in a thick manual of intricate office procedures, complete with an organizational chart for who does what, and excruciating detail for how and when every office task is to be performed. The manual even specifies the number of minutes for coffee breaks based on job description and length of employment. Any procedural infraction is cause for reprimand, regardless of whether the procedure has any practical purpose."

The enigmatic exception to the rank structure was the role of Kahn's personal assistant, a striking Asian-American woman about twenty-five named Terri Hu.

Francis had mused, "We were all curious when Terri was hired. At first, we thought Bernie might have chosen her primarily because she complemented the Chinese decor. Terri answers to no one but Bernie, and she responds to his every beck and call, which makes all of our lives easier in the office. She's very good at her job, even if it isn't always clear what her job is. She's perpetually busy, mostly from trying to keep Bernie organized, but she remains placid, no matter what office catastrophes occur— and, unfortunately, they do occur pretty often."

When a crisis did occur, Kahn's typical reaction was to impose blame and then issue an order, usually the functional equivalent of "Off with their heads!"

He never acknowledged that his laborious procedures and his own procrastination in approving work to go out were the root causes of most office problems.

As a result, the turnover among support staff was continual, and of all of them who were there when Clara started right after Labor Day, only Francis and Terri were still at the firm when she left at the end of March.

By then, Clara had learned there were as many as forty or fifty previous employees, including a few attorneys, who had formed a sort of club that had an annual party and generally kept in touch with each other. She was looking forward to becoming a member of the EKG, the Ex-Kahn Group.

She knew that the two associates, Maura and Katy, would have liked to quit, too, as Kahn didn't spare the attorneys his ill temper and demeaning management style. But they needed jobs at a time when many Bay Area law firms were downsizing, and Maura had said candidly, "I can't afford to quit because I'm still helping my husband pay off the loans that got him through medical school. Katy is a harried single mom, and I think she just can't face another job change right now. It's a mystery to me why Francis and Terri stay on."

When Clara had asked Francis why he stayed, he was uncharacteristically vague, and she never seemed to get a chance to have a really personal conversation with Terri.

The petty office problems, even Kahn's mistreatment of his employees, weren't the final impetus that drove Clara to quit. She might have tolerated his being a despotic boss, but she couldn't ignore Kahn's unethical tactics. He often expanded work needlessly to bill more hours to the clients and sometimes even flagrantly padded the bills. Several times, Clara had challenged him, trying to let him know diplomatically that she was on to him.

The first time she'd noticed it, she'd told him there was a mistake on the Fairfax bill. She'd only spent one-and-a-half hours on research, not the four-and-a-half hours that appeared on the bill. Even with her time billed as a junior associate that meant an overcharge to the client of hundreds of dollars.

He'd simply replied, "I just assumed your time sheet was erroneous, so I changed it. I thought the research must have taken over four hours."

She'd had no way of checking whether the error was corrected on the final bill to the client.

After several such incidents, though, she'd become increasingly concerned about her ethical obligation to report his conduct to the state bar. In confidence, she'd asked Francis for his advice. He'd looked dejected as he told her, "I'm sorry to disappoint you, Clara, but there really isn't much you can do about it. If Bernie adds time to what was legitimately billed to the client, it's merely his word against yours as to how much time was actually spent on the work. If he exacerbates a legal matter and unnecessarily protracts work that needs to be done for a client, he could say that you're inexperienced and don't understand the subtleties of his legal strategy. One of the harsh realities about practicing law is that it's hard to monitor anyone's ethics but your own, especially when the offender is your boss." He'd brightened a bit as he'd added, "If it's any consolation, though, I practiced law for over forty years, and I think most lawyers are honest and ethical. And the unethical ones generally get what's coming to them."

Most of the clients were wealthy and didn't question their bills, and many continued to be blinded by Kahn's charm. They loved his personal attention and responded well to his talent for stroking their egos. He had a lawyer's equivalent of a comforting bedside manner. But in the course of her work, when Clara had occasion to review old files, she was astounded to discover how many fee disputes there had been over the years, as well as a large number of clients who had abruptly dismissed Kahn with no apparent explanation.

Ironically, it was because of his murder that Clara would ultimately learn the most sinister of Kahn's schemes to bilk his clients and others. And in the process of opening the Pandora's Box of Kahn's chicanery, she had no idea how vulnerable she would become to the murderer who in one night killed three lawyers.

Clara's thoughts turned again to the murders. As she recalled her little "Murder, murder everywhere" rhyme, it set off a sort of quivering in her bone marrow. Even so, as uneasy as it made her feel, she had an irresistible urge to know every detail.

She wondered if there might be some further news and was about to turn on the television when the phone rang.

"Clara, hon, it's Maura. I wasn't sure if you were back from England yet," said a breathless voice. "Have you heard the news about Bernie? Isn't it awful? I just don't know what to think."

"Maura, hi, yeah. I just read about it in the paper. Do you know any more about it?"

"Not really. There were some short blurbs on the local morning news. I switched around the channels, but they didn't really say anything that wasn't in the paper. I called Katy, and she hadn't heard yet. She couldn't believe it. At first, she thought I was pulling her leg. You know how many times we bantered about hiring a hit man to get Bernie so we could run the firm the way it ought to be. It's a pretty sick joke now."

"God, I didn't think about that," Clara said. "What a ghoulish thought. I don't know anybody who liked Bernie much, except maybe Charlotte and the clients who only saw his charming side. I still can't imagine anybody who'd actually try to kill him. And what about the other victims? Do you know of any connection between Bernie and the other two lawyers?"

"No. As far as I know, Hanks didn't handle any of Bernie's divorces. Rinko did legal malpractice, but even with all of Bernie's faults, I don't know if anyone ever brought a formal malpractice case against him."

"What happens now? Have you been contacted by the police or anybody?"

"Matter of fact, I just had a call from a Detective Travis. He said he has a few questions. I told him I want to get into the office and figure out what needs to be done, and so does Katy. He said that's okay, he'll meet us there, and he wants to talk to everybody who worked for Bernie. I'm on my way now, as soon as I can get myself pulled together. Do you want to come in, too? I guess they'll get around to you eventually, anyway."

"Sure, I'll come in. You and Maura will undoubtedly need some help. But I don't think I'll come this morning.

I'll wait a little while and give this detective a chance to do his thing at the office. In fact, I think I'll stop by the deli and bring in some sandwiches for lunch. If it turns out you want me in sooner, just give me a call."

"One more thing, Clara. I know this may sound sort of melodramatic, but do you think we have anything to worry about? Our own safety, I mean?"

"Hey, I thought about it, too. There's no harm in being careful, at least until we know more about what happened. Everybody knows there are plenty of lunatics out there. Let's just hope three dead lawyers is the quota."

"Why do I not find that very reassuring?"

"Seriously, just take care, okay?"

"Okay. You, too, Clara. See you around noon."

But, Clara wondered, *how do you take care when you have no idea where a threat might be coming from?*

CHAPTER 2

Fractured Firm

She could think of nothing but the murders. "Murder, murder everywhere, And what was she to think?" Funny to have that little jingle running through her head after so long. Clara flipped on her CD player, barely aware of Rubinstein playing Chopin, and went out on her balcony. Even with the fog beginning to lift, the morning chill was still damp and gray, relieved only slightly by the warm mug of coffee she sipped. The coffee aroma mingled with the salt air, and in the distance, she could hear the occasional moan of the old foghorn.

The balcony of her penthouse was a great place to think. As the fog dissipated, the impressionistic canvas below evolved into discrete shapes from the Golden Gate to the Bay Bridge. It never ceased to amaze her how far she had come from her provincial upbringing in a small Kentucky town. Now, here she was, after years of reading murder mysteries for escape, curious about who had killed Bernie and the other two lawyers. She wondered where old-fashioned Miss Marple or one of the savvy modern women detectives would begin to look for the killer.

Roused by a distinctive knock at the door, Clara knew who it had to be.

When she opened it, Adrian Holt gave her an affectionate hug. "I thought I heard your lovely music from the balcony."

He shared the other penthouse on the top floor of the building with his companion Blake Erikson. They were both stockbrokers, but Adrian had stopped working sometime back to stay home and work on his gourmet cooking and try to write historic cookbooks, none of which had yet been published.

Both men were in their early forties—tall, well built, and gorgeous. Adrian was dark and swarthy, with a lithe, sinewy body. Blake had sandy blond hair, blue eyes, classic Nordic features, and muscles that attested to long hours in the gym. They both worked out with weights every morning before Blake left for work. Clara had been perfectly happy to learn that these attractive men were a couple. She didn't want any romantic complications in her life, and she welcomed the friendship that had developed, especially with Adrian. He always provided good conversation and a sympathetic ear. She sometimes confided in him when she didn't want to discuss things like office politics with her co-workers.

"Welcome home, luv," Adrian gushed. "It's been absolutely desolate here without you. But I thought you were going to take a really long holiday in England and then on to the continent."

"You know me and my old Puritan work ethic. I just decided it was time to think about doing something productive again. Besides, my old travel memories were beginning to get to me. Of course, I had no idea I'd find such sensational news when I got home. Have you heard about what happened to Bernie Kahn?"

"Yes, I saw it on the news this morning. I can hardly

believe that twit is dead. From all the things you told me about him, there must be a lot of people smiling this morning."

"Did I really make him sound that bad? Murder is pretty drastic, even for a lousy boss."

"Knowing you, he was probably even worse than you described. Anyway, people kill for all sorts of reasons. Do you have any idea who killed him?"

"None. I'm still stunned by the whole idea. The funny thing is, I was just thinking—if I were to do some sleuthing, I wonder if I could come up with any clues to help the police."

"Don't even think like that, Clara," said Adrian. "You read too many murder mysteries. In books, the amateur detective may come out on top, but in real life, you certainly don't want to go mucking about with cold-blooded killers. Isn't that why you avoided going into criminal law?"

"No, not exactly. I decided I couldn't practice criminal law when I realized that I wanted to prosecute all the bad guys and defend all the innocent ones. But that isn't very practical the way the system is set up."

"In any case, you don't want to be getting involved in real murders. There's no telling what might turn up, and I wouldn't want my favorite attorney snooping around when somebody out there is killing lawyers. You know, I'm much too fond of you to try to break in a new neighbor."

Clara smiled. "Thanks, Adrian. I can always count on you to give me good advice. I don't really know where I'd begin to snoop anyway. But as much as I disliked Bernie, I hope they find his killer soon. It's very unsettling to know some unknown entity killed somebody I knew. Enough about that. What's new with you and Blake?"

"Same old grind for Blake, but I have exciting news. My first cookbook has been accepted for publication. Wouldn't you know—I can't get anybody interested in my esoteric gourmet stuff, but they're going to publish that little thing I wrote about homey San Francisco recipes. It's called *San Francisco on a Shoestring (Potato)*. A bit corny, of course, and it's obviously the chatty vignettes that sell the inexpensive recipes."

"Still, that's great, Adrian. At least it's a start. Besides, everything you ever cooked for me was fabulous, including the simple stuff."

"Which reminds me, how about coming over for dinner tonight? You probably don't have any food in the place, and we have a lot of catching up to do. How about seven?"

"That should work. I'd better give you a call after I see how the day develops, though. You remember my former associate Maura, don't you? She called a while ago and said they're going to be questioning everybody who worked for Bernie. They'll probably get to me eventually, and meanwhile, I thought I might as well go down to the office and lend a hand. I guess I'd better be getting ready."

"Sounds like fun. I always wondered what a real interrogation would be like. Do you suppose they'll do good cop, bad cop?"

"Who knows? I admit, I'm curious."

"Remember, luv, don't be too curious. Until they catch this killer, please be extra careful," he said, as he pecked her on the cheek.

But despite Adrian's advice, after he left, she still couldn't stop thinking about how a detective would go about finding out who killed Bernie Kahn.

✆✎✆✎

"The staff meeting is supposed to start at eight-thirty, but most people are already in the conference room," said the attractive blonde receptionist to the latest arrival at the Embarcadero Center office of what used to be Bernard C. Kahn & Associates. It was a few minutes after eight a.m., but employees had started arriving about seven-thirty.

It was a nice little touch of irony. Although Bernie was habitually late for appointments, he had gotten into such a snit about any employee's occasional tardiness that he'd added another penalty to the thick procedures manual. The receptionist was required to log in everyone's arrival time in order to dock accrued vacation an hour for every five minutes they were late, even though he probably couldn't have enforced it legally. The policy was self-defeating anyway because everyone resented it so much that even when they happened to arrive early, they typically made a point of waiting outside until just before eight-thirty before they would enter the office. But this morning, everybody was early, and they had already gone through several pots of coffee.

By eight-fifteen, everybody was in the conference room, conversing in funereal tones, and Maura Grimaldi began the meeting. Maura was the "senior" attorney, who had been with the firm for three years, while Katy had been there two. Both of them had outstanding academic credentials, and Bernie had lured both of them away from dismal jobs with big firms. Maura was pretty, though prematurely gray at forty-one. At the moment, she looked slightly distraught, but still businesslike in a trim gray suit. She sat in her usual chair, to the right of the head of the long oval conference table, next to Bernie's now empty chair, the only upholstered one in the room.

Katy MacLeod, a thirty-six-year-old lanky brunette with gorgeous legs, ivory skin, and clear blue eyes sat next to Maura. Terri Hu, with her ever-present legal pad and pen, sat to the left of the empty chair, looking perfectly professional, as she always did at the regular weekly staff meetings. (No one had yet thought to wonder where Bernie's personal assistant would fit on the organizational chart now.) Francis Davis, the septuagenarian ex-lawyer/paralegal, was to her left, and the rest of the employees filled their usual spots around the table.

Conversations suspended as Maura began to speak. "It looks like everybody's here, so let's get started. I know you've all heard the news about Bernie. I don't know exactly what to say at a time like this, but despite the tragic events of last night, we have a lot of work to do. I know we were all shocked to learn about what happened to Bernie, and I imagine we're also feeling some level of anxiety. So we should try to be supportive of each other in dealing with this. It may help if we express our feelings, and we should feel free to talk about it with each other."

(Another irony, as Bernie had discouraged any socializing in the office—but for once his usually misguided paranoia had been accurate when it made him believe that much office interaction represented an almost continuous undercurrent of gossip and complaint about him.)

Maura went on, "A few clients have already started calling this morning. I'm passing out copies of a brief statement Katy and I prepared to help you with answering calls. It's probably going to be too much for one receptionist to handle, so everybody should pitch in and help as necessary. We'll notify the state bar, and we plan to continue with the legal work that's already scheduled. We'll also be reviewing all files and getting letters out as fast as possible to assure the clients that we're on top of their legal concerns. Of course, we don't know at this point exactly what the future holds for all of us here, but

Katy and I will be making the most pressing decisions and let you know as soon as possible how things stand.

"Of course, we'll do whatever we can to protect everyone's job security. For the moment, let's just assume that for the next month at least, there'll be as few changes as possible, except that Bernie won't be here." Her voice cracked ever so slightly on the last phrase, and she cleared her throat. "Now I want to introduce you to Detective Roy Travis of the San Francisco Police Department. Some of you have already met him this morning. He's coordinating with the police in Marin County in the investigation of the crimes."

❧❧❧

Travis had been sitting quietly in the back corner of the room, but there was nothing unobtrusive about him. Everybody was well aware of his presence. He was a big man, tall and beefy, in his late fifties, with thick, close-cropped, salt-and-pepper hair above a craggy face. He wore a slightly wrinkled dark blue suit, light blue shirt, and solid maroon tie. The combination gave his slate gray eyes a bluish tint, although they were bloodshot from loss of sleep the night before.

Travis rose from the chair that seemed too small for him, like a schoolboy who had outgrown his desk. He spoke from his position in the corner, requiring everyone to turn in his direction and give full attention. His voice was surprisingly gentle, slow and measured, with deep resonance and the slightest tinge of a drawl.

"I'm sorry to have to be here under circumstances like this," he said, "but I'm sure you're all as anxious for us to solve these crimes as we are, and your cooperation will be greatly appreciated. A lot of people are investigating these cases in different ways. Today, I'm going to start out talking with every one of you in the little office right next to this room. Ms. Hu has given me a list and has offered to help me keep track of everyone. I'll be going down the list, but first I want to say that if you have any information about what happened to Mr. Kahn last night, don't wait for me to get to you on the list. Come on in and talk to me right away. We want to get to the bottom of this as soon as possible, so if you know anything at all that might relate to Mr. Kahn's death, don't hesitate."

Finally, the word "death" had been uttered. Until now, everyone had avoided words like "death" or "murder" or any other term that made it seem real.

With that, Travis paused and looked from face to face around the room. There was nothing overtly intimidating about his expression—it was as inscrutable as a perfect poker face. But somehow, every person in the room felt exposed. No one stirred until he spoke again. "That's about all I have to say right now. I'm afraid I can't give you any more details about the crimes than what's already been in the news. Anything you want to add, Ms. Grimaldi?"

Maura cleared her throat. "No, I guess not. We'll let everybody know as soon as we find out about the, uh, arrangements for Bernie. Does anybody have any questions or comments?"

The only response was a ripple of movement and a couple of coughs. Katy leaned forward. "I'm sure everybody will be as helpful as possible to the police. Detective Travis, let us know what you need from us."

"I'll start with Ms. Grimaldi, then you, Ms. MacLeod. Ms. Hu will fetch everybody else in turn. Thanks for your help."

His tone and demeanor, though understated, left no doubt that he was in charge. A mere shift in his weight seemed to signal the meeting was over. There was a wave of motion toward various workstations, and a murmur of quiet conversations began as Travis followed Maura into the small room that had formerly been Clara's office.

Behind the closed door of the next office, the large corner office that had been Kahn's, an efficient female detective meticulously examined the sparse trappings. She found nothing relating to clients or anything personal, except the various framed items on Kahn's "vanity wall" and a large, flattering photo of his wife Charlotte on his desk.

Travis was an experienced homicide detective who had earned the respect of his peers and subordinates as well as superiors—a sort of cop's cop. He had a straightforward kind of toughness, tempered with innate intelligence and common sense. He had become street-wise of necessity in his early teens. His life had begun when he was born in the bedroom of a farmhouse in Ada, Oklahoma. By age twelve, he and his sister were barely subsisting on a farm with their mother, abandoned years before by their father.

Then a distant cousin who had settled in California came for a family reunion. The cousin, though much older, married their mother and brought them to Los Angeles when Travis was thirteen.

When he arrived in LA, Travis was already big for his age, and the combination of his size and wits helped the country boy survive in the city. After his stepfather died, he worked odd jobs to help support the family, served a stint in the Marine Corps, and worked while he struggled to get through college. The things he learned in the process somehow combined to make him a good cop, and he had a natural instinct for detective work. He had joined the SFPD after acquiring something of a reputation in LA—in addition to reliable routine work, he had re-

ceived several commendations, including one for his role
in apprehending a serial killer.

The initial interviews with Kahn's employees didn't
produce any particular leads to his killer, but Travis was
beginning to get a clear profile of the kind of man Kahn
had been. Travis often adopted a sort of detached
amusement at the things he learned in the course of an
investigation, a defense mechanism that helped him re-
main untouched by often gruesome details. Homicide
rarely had a pretty face.

One of the things that amused him was the predicta-
bility of what people told him. For instance, two typical
extremes he sometimes encountered about murder victims were either that "he didn't have an enemy in the
world" or "everybody hated his guts." Although Kahn's
employees took care to avoid saying anything so pointed,
this case clearly fell into the latter category. They mentioned Kahn's charm and success, but Travis had a knack
for getting people to say more than they meant to, like a
father getting his teenager to 'fess up about denting the
family car. Each employee added a shadowy nuance to an
ugly picture of Kahn, which gradually grew uglier, like
the picture of Dorian Gray.

A less experienced cop might have given no more
weight to the comments than to size up Kahn as a bad
boss, but Travis sensed that the worm inside Kahn's pol-
ished-apple exterior was truly corrupt. So, instead of having to find out who Kahn's enemies might be, this was
shaping into a who-hated-his-guts-enough-to-want-him-
dead sort of case. But complicating the puzzle, as yet not
a single clue connected Kahn's murder with the other two
lawyers killed the same way the night before.

Other detectives were investigating those two murders, along with forensics following up on details of the
crime scenes across the Golden Gate in Marin County.

There would inevitably be some jurisdictional jockeying, but, in the end, they would collaborate in trying to piece the puzzle together.

∾∾

Clara arrived at midday with a huge box of sandwiches and side dishes from the deli. After dropping most of her load in the office kitchen, she took some food and gourmet coffee to Maura's office, where she also found Katy.

"Hi, guys, how are you holding up?" asked Clara.

"Clara, come on in," said Maura. "Oh, boy, food. I hadn't realized; I'm starving. I forgot to eat this morning. This place has been a madhouse. The phone hasn't stopped ringing, and we both had to talk to that detective. We finally diverted all calls for the time being just so we'd have a chance to talk. We've got to make some decisions pretty quickly."

"So how do things look?" Clara asked.

"It's a bizarre situation any way you look at it," replied Katy. "Of course, the top priority is to take care of the clients. Maura and I were just saying, though, if it looks like enough of them will stay with us, we're going to try to make a go of it. We used to talk hypothetically about how this firm ought to be run. But it's a lot scarier to think about actually doing it."

"Does this mean you two have decided on a partnership? Sounds like a great idea to me," said Clara.

"We're thinking about it, but we have a lot of things to consider. You know we'd talked about going out on our own before, but we didn't think we had enough client base. And we knew Bernie would give us trouble if any clients decided to go with us. So, how does Grimaldi and MacLeod sound to you?" asked Maura.

"Just because you were here first?" Katy chimed in. "So what's wrong with MacLeod and Grimaldi?" She grinned. "Kidding aside, I'm really okay playing second fiddle. After all, the appellate work is really the bread and butter of the firm, and you've established a good reputation, despite Bernie's penchant for hogging all the credit." She looked a little sheepish at saying something negative about the dead but shrugged. "I should be able to keep the estate and probate work going if enough clients stay with us."

"If most of them stay, do you think the two of you can handle everything and growth, too?" asked Clara.

"We were just talking about that possibility," said Maura. "We're pretty sure Francis will be willing to stay on and help us with the legal work. You know what a sweetheart he is about sharing his expertise for very little pay, and he's so loyal. But he's also been adamant about not taking on any case responsibility since he gave up his active status as a lawyer. That brings us to you. We'll probably need another lawyer at least part-time while we're getting organized, and who knows after that. But we have no idea yet how the finances are going to work out. Are you interested?"

"I don't really know. I'd have to give it some thought," Clara replied. "This is all too new to make any decisions right now. How about this? Just count on me to help you for a while, without any formal arrangement. Let's not decide anything yet about what role I might eventually have, if any. Besides, if I don't make any definite commitment, you can use that to your advantage and not pay me until we've reached an agreement. For now, you can count on me as a friend to help you in a pinch. Later, when the dust has settled, we can see how it all works out."

"Really? Can you afford to do that?" asked Maura.

"Yeah, I can afford it," Clara replied.

As usual, she glossed over any reference to money. She had never let on just how vast her assets were, although Maura and Katy knew she lived in an upscale neighborhood. She drove a Prius that wasn't even brand new. Her clothes and minimal jewelry were of good quality, but they were more classic than high fashion.

❧❧❧

The phone rang. Maura had instructed the receptionist to withhold calls except for the police and Charlotte.

"Maura, I have Mrs. Kahn on the line. I assume you want to take the call."

"Yes, put her through," said Maura. She had tried to call Charlotte that morning, but the maid told her the doctor said she shouldn't be disturbed. "Hello, Charlotte. I have you on speakerphone with Katy and Clara. We're all so sorry to hear the tragic news. How are you holding up? Please accept our condolences," Maura said.

"Thank you, dear," Charlotte replied in a withered voice that didn't completely mask the nasal twang. "I'm just devastated, of course. I can't believe he's gone. And in such a dreadful way. It's all so horrid."

"Is there anything we can do? Do you want us to come over? Do you need help with any arrangements?"

"No, my mother and sister are on their way from Lubbock. My kindly neighbors have been good about staying with me. Several of them are here now. Of course, it's all so awful. The police questioned me last night. Dr. Ling finally gave me an herbal sedative and made them go away, but they were back with more questions this morning. I'm exhausted, of course. And I just can't stop crying." She began to whimper, as if to verify it.

Maura lifted her eyebrows, not knowing what else to say, and Katy cleared her throat. "Charlotte, hello, this is Katy. I want to extend my condolences, too. You know how sorry we all are. But don't worry about anything here at the office. Maura and I have been working on client matters all morning, and we want you to know that everything is being taken care of here."

"Yes, dear, I knew I could count on you both," said Charlotte. "I don't know a thing about the legal work, but I'm sure there are some business matters we'll have to work out. I just can't think about such things now. The funeral will be the day after tomorrow. I don't know how I'm going to get through it all."

"It's Clara, Charlotte. I just want you to know you can count on me, too. I'm here to help Maura and Katy until things settle down. And please let me know if I can help with any of the arrangements."

After an awkward moment of silence, Maura jumped in again. "Charlotte, don't hesitate to ask if there is anything at all we can do. I'll give you a call this evening. Meanwhile, try to get as much rest as possible. You'll need all your strength, and don't forget you can call on us whenever you need to."

"Thank you, dear. I'm sure I'll take you up on that." Charlotte hung up, cutting off Maura's response.

The three of them looked at each other for a few moments. Clara couldn't help wondering if Charlotte had seen some old movie where the grieving widow called everyone "dear." She was sure Charlotte hadn't done that before. "Are you thinking what I'm thinking?"

"I imagine so," said Katy. "Were you perhaps wondering how Charlotte is going to manage without her meal ticket?"

"I was trying to think of a more delicate way to put it," said Clara, "but that's about it. We all assumed Bernie picked her because she'd been a beauty queen, but haven't you always wondered what Charlotte saw in him? Even with the charm, that wears off. It had to be his money. She may not have much higher education, but she's no dummy, and she couldn't have been fooled by the charm for long."

"Who knows?" said Maura. "Far be it from me to mention she's been referred to more than once around these parts as Charlotte the Harlot. Or maybe she just wanted to get away from home. As runner-up for Miss Texas, she probably could've had her pick of a lot of rich Texans. But I realized long ago that you can never tell for sure why people decide to marry each other. And who knows what the real relationship is like in any marriage."

The comment made Clara uncomfortable. She had often wondered about Maura's marriage to the self-important doctor who never seemed to have time for her, except when he had needed her to pay off the loans that had gotten him through medical school. The uncomfortable moment was relieved by a knock at the door.

It was Terri Hu. "Hello, Clara," she said. "It's nice to see you again, but I'm sorry it had to be at a time like this. I don't mean to intrude, but Detective Travis asked if you would come in to see him now."

"Detective Travis?" she asked.

"I'm sorry. I forgot you weren't here when he was introduced. He's the police detective who's investigating Bernie's—uh, the crimes," said Terri.

"Right. Actually, Maura did mention him, but I didn't remember his name. Of course, I don't really have anything to tell him, but I guess the police have to talk to everybody. He wants me right now?"

"Yes, he's in your old office. You can just go on in. He's expecting you."

Clara was naturally curious about what Detective

Travis could expect from her, considering she hadn't even seen Bernie since she left the firm a month before. She was a bit surprised by the apprehension she felt at the prospect of being part of a real criminal investigation. Yet it was odd, at the same time, to think of it as a "real" criminal investigation when the whole thing still seemed so unreal to her. The office seemed more like when Bernie was on one of his frequent vacations—often disguised as tax-deductible professional meetings—and she half expected him to call to check up on everybody the way he usually did. But there would be no more dreaded calls from Bernie Kahn. That was the new reality.

Clara walked the familiar path from Maura's office to the one that had been hers.

"Hello, Ms. Quillen. I'm Detective Travis," he said, rising and extending a hand that seemed almost as big as a baseball glove. His handshake was firm, though awkward because his hand engulfed hers. But she liked the fact that he didn't give her hand the kind of condescending little squeeze men often give to petite women. "This isn't much of a way to be spending your birthday, is it?"

"No, I guess not." His remark was disarming, and then she looked down at her personnel file folder in front of him. "You pick up details quickly, don't you?"

"I do my best," he said, not feigning modesty.

Clara tended to size up people quickly. She sometimes had to revise a first impression, though not often. With Travis, she felt vaguely apprehensive, but at the same time, she sensed right away that she wanted to know him better.

Yet she could hardly have anticipated the impact he would have on her life.

And unlike Rick at the end of *Casablanca,* she didn't know that this was the beginning of a beautiful friendship.

CHAPTER 3

Diligent Detective

It seemed strange being back in the small office where Clara had spent so much time during the months she'd worked for Kahn. It still had the pseudo-rosewood table that had been her "desk." One of Bernie's quirks was that he didn't believe in real desks, with utilitarian drawers. Inordinately disorganized, Bernie habitually wrote cryptic notes that had often wound up stuffed uselessly into cubbyholes in his antique roll-top desk. After he married Charlotte and she redecorated the office, she convinced him that the solution was to replace his beautiful old walnut desk with an ornate, carved table. He then decreed that tables without drawers would also replace the desks in the associates' offices. The speculation was that he wanted everything out in the open because he feared the idea of anything being hidden.

The absence of useful drawers had led to a variety of devices for making the offices functional. Maura kept office supplies handy in decorative bowls, while Katy used haphazard stacks of in-out boxes.

Clara had been granted her request for a large black lacquer box that had originally been in Bernie's office before it was redecorated, but it later sat unused on a table in the firm's small law library. The box had numerous compartments and little drawers she could use for pens, paper clips, Post-its, and other handy supplies.

Clara was especially fond of the lacquer box because it somehow escaped being recognized as having the forbidden drawers, and her "Black Box" became a private joke as a symbol for circumventing Bernie.

The term could be used in a number of ways, even as a verb, such as "We Black-Boxed the brief," meaning a brief had been filed while Bernie was out of town, without his final approval, to avoid the capricious last minute changes he always insisted on making.

When Clara left the firm, Bernie had readily accepted her offer to buy the box from him for fifty dollars—before she made the offer, she had noticed a little Chinatown shop price sticker for twenty-five dollars attached to the bottom.

The box now sat in her study at home, still filled with useful office supplies, all pilfered from Bernard C. Kahn & Associates.

Another manifestation of Bernie's aversion to drawers was that there were no filing cabinets of any sort allowed in any individual office space. All files, even research notes, had to be kept in the file room. So people learned to keep materials needed for ready reference in loose-leaf binders placed on open shelves, which were permissible in offices.

The bookcase in Clara's office, now bare, was the only other piece of furniture, along with the table and two chairs, at the moment occupied by Clara and Travis.

With his customary disarming approach, Travis asked, "Do you mind if I call you by your first name?"

"Not at all. What's yours?"

Clearly taken aback, he replied, "Uh, it's Roy, but people usually call me Travis, if that's okay with you."

"Okay, Travis, and you can call me Clara or Quillen. Which do you prefer?"

"Thanks for the choice. Is the way you're addressed important to you?"

"It's not that exactly. Don't you think when a male authority figure asserts himself, a woman should try to put herself on equal footing?"

"Am I correct in getting the impression that you may be something of a feminist?"

"Is that a dirty word?" she responded, but with a smile.

"Do you always answer a question with a question?"

"Is that a problem for you?"

"Yes, as a matter of fact, I'm supposed to get answers to questions. I'm a detective, remember? Right now, I need a lot of answers."

The statement was sobering and reminded Clara of the seriousness of a murder investigation. But she couldn't help being surprised by how uncomfortable she felt at the thought of being interrogated. She couldn't figure out whether she was subconsciously mimicking the hackneyed dialogue of a television cop show or it was just natural to feel defensive when a cop asks questions. She decided probably it was just her usual feeling of insecurity when she was in an unfamiliar situation.

"I'm sorry," she said. "What do you want to know?"

The detective's first question told her Travis had decided he might as well use a direct approach with her. "Why don't you start with where you were from seven to midnight last night."

"Is that a routine question or does it mean I'm a suspect?"

"It's routine, but how about an answer instead of a question?"

"I guess I'm just a little self-conscious. I've never

been questioned by a detective before. The answer is that I was at home alone, most likely asleep, without a single witness who can corroborate it. How's that for an alibi?"

"Remember, I get to ask the questions. You were asleep at seven?"

"To be honest, I'm not exactly sure when I was awake or asleep. You see, I just got back from England yesterday afternoon. When I return from a trip abroad, I always just sort of ignore time and unpack, sleep, read, or listen to music. Then I start to get back on a local time schedule the next day. That's what I did this time, as usual."

"Why were you in England?"

"Just sort of a holiday. I actually hadn't taken a real vacation since before I went to law school, and I was getting burnt out. You probably already know I quit my job here a month ago."

Yes, Travis knew. Maura had told her he had scrutinized the term of employment of every current and recent employee of Bernard C. Kahn & Associates, and he'd tried to learn the circumstances of each departure from the firm.

"Why England?"

"A lot of reasons. Most of all, I just wanted to get away for a while, and I've always enjoyed England." She didn't mention her need to purge ghosts she had never dealt with, or her memories of traveling in England, frugally with her first husband Steve, then later more extravagantly with her second husband, Jon.

She wasn't aware of the tiny, involuntary knitting of lines between her well-groomed eyebrows.

"Tell me about your work here."

"Well, I began last September, the day after Labor Day. At first, I mostly did legal research and wrote analytical memos. I worked primarily with Maura on appellate work and also on anything else Bernie assigned to me." It dawned on her that was the first mention of his name since the interrogation began. "In November, when I got the results that I passed the bar exam, I did the briefing in a case called *Vann v. Golden Gate Hospital.* I also did the oral argument in the case in the California Court of Appeal."

"Isn't it unusual for such a new lawyer to argue in an appellate court? You must be pretty good."

"I wouldn't say that, but I knew the case thoroughly, and I'm pretty comfortable with public speaking. I was a high school teacher before I became a lawyer. Facing a classroom full of bored teenagers is much more intimidating than facing a panel of appellate justices."

While her answer was truthful, it was incomplete. The real reason Bernie had allowed her to do the oral argument was that he was afraid to do it himself because the trial record was voluminous and he didn't know the details of the case well enough. Maura could have done it but had refused to argue in court again after her last experience with Bernie's demoralizing method in practice sessions, when he ripped her to shreds and made her a nervous wreck just before oral argument. Bernie had tried the same technique with Clara, but she was unruffled. Years of dealing with her father's carping criticism had given her a tough shell even Bernie couldn't penetrate.

"So how did you do in *Vann v. Golden Gate Hospital?*" Travis asked.

"It was a solid win for our client. The opinion came down the day before I quit at the end of March."

"So why did you quit, if you were doing so well?"

"I guess you could say Bernie and I reached a point where we had irreconcilable differences—so it was time to split. It had been building up for a while. As he began to recognize the quality of my work, I was diverted more and more to working on client matters with him instead of the appellate work with Maura, which is what I really wanted to do. Bernie and I often disagreed on how various matters should be handled, but he was the boss, of course."

"Can you give me an example? You don't have to be too specific; I know you have to be careful about attorney-client privilege," Travis said.

"Okay, here's one that's typical. We had a client who had a pressing problem that needed immediate attention, and Bernie asked me to draft the necessary documents to solve the problem. I used a fairly simple, direct approach, but Bernie reamed me out, saying, in effect, that if we solved the problem too quickly, the client would have no further need for our services on the matter. He ordered me to come up with another plausible approach to stretch things out. I argued that anybody who takes a car to be repaired and gets competent service at a fair price is much more likely to return for other services. He was always annoyed when his subordinates argued with him, but I really made him mad when I told him he might be better qualified than I was to provide a long-drawn-out alternative. It was a not so subtle way of telling him I wanted no part of improperly increasing the client's bill. He gave me a lecture about this being a business and didn't like it when I retorted that I thought it was a profession, with professional ethics. He always got furious when I mentioned ethics. I also learned that the word 'integrity' really pushed his buttons."

"You said that kind of approach was typical?"

"Actually, he had a variety of approaches for increasing a client's bill. Here's another example. One time, a client called me and asked what I had learned from a particular piece of legal research. I didn't know what she was talking about and asked what she meant. She said that on her monthly statement she had been billed for some legal research I had done, but this time she hadn't gotten my usual letter explaining the effect of the research on her legal problem. I told her I didn't have her file in front of me but would check into it and call her back. When I looked at the billing records, I discovered Bernie had added several hours to her bill for some work I was purported to have done, but I knew nothing about it. So I stayed late and did the research, even though I thought it was only barely relevant to the client's problem. I wrote up the results and called the client with the answer the next morning."

"Did you ask Kahn about it?"

"Yes, the next day I confronted him, but he just dismissed it as some sort of mix-up in the billing. We locked horns several times over similar incidents."

"Did you ever consider reporting him?"

Clara winced, feeling sheepish. "To be honest, I felt pretty guilty about not reporting him to the state bar. I told myself Bernie would be too crafty for it to do any good. So finally, I just quit."

Travis wasn't surprised because the story was consistent with the other things he had heard about Kahn that day, and he suspected worse. It was always a little bothersome when he found himself developing a distaste for the victim of the crime he was trying to solve. On the other hand, when there were many negative opinions about a victim, there was also a certain pleasure in ferreting out who had sufficient motive to commit murder—detached amusement again. He always hoped it didn't turn out that he liked the murderer better than the victim. It wasn't too difficult, though, to decide that no matter what the victim was like, murder was not a socially acceptable way to rid the world of anybody, even an underhanded lawyer. Travis was a staunch law and order man.

"Was your parting with Kahn amicable?" he asked.

"From what I've heard, there's no such thing as a truly amicable parting with Bernie. In my case, he was at the least annoyed and probably angry, but then he told me he felt my work didn't measure up to his standards anyway. That was his pretty typical sour grapes reaction when anyone quit. But if he wanted to get rid of somebody, he tried to make the employee miserable enough to quit. That way he could avoid firing an employee and having to pay unemployment. Maura used to say she fantasized that at some point Bernie would drive everybody away. Then he'd be standing alone in the office with Charlotte and saying, 'See, I told you everybody was disloyal.' Unfortunately, with the job market the way it is, he never had much of a problem finding good replacements."

"Any theories about why Kahn treated people the way he did?"

"I'm almost certain it was a control thing, maybe combined with feelings of insecurity. Bernie always wanted to be in a position of power. Sometimes people mumbled CF behind his back, meaning Control Freak. He had the typical personality and faults of a control freak. You could never do anything right. If you asked for advice, he made you feel like a moron. If you didn't do the job the exact way he would've done it, he ridiculed you. It was impossible to be good enough or smart enough to please him. If you did something well, he felt threatened—so, of course, he never complimented anyone. At some point, even the best people who work for a control freak start to doubt themselves, and that's one of the ways he maintains control."

She paused and then added a related observation. "Those of us who recognized Bernie's tactics countered them by being supportive of each other. That made him suspect conspiracies among the staff, which in turn contributed to his paranoia, a vicious circle. Ironically, as far as I could tell, the people who worked for him were competent and dependable. If he'd just been a decent guy and respected his staff, control would never have been an issue."

Clara was surprised at how comfortable she was becoming as she talked with this big cop. "We all engaged in a bit of armchair psychoanalysis trying to cope with Bernie. One theory was that part of his personality may have been the result of a very repressed childhood as the son of a stern Lutheran minister. His older brother also became a minister, of some prestigious church in Philadelphia, I think. His younger sister does good works on an Indian reservation somewhere in the Southwest. We theorized that Bernie never got his father's approval as his siblings had, no matter how much money he made as a lawyer. I'm sorry if I'm rambling. I know this has nothing to do with Bernie's murder."

"That's okay. The more comprehensive picture I have of the victim, the better."

"I really would like to help. But before we go on, do you mind if I ask you a personal question?"

"That depends on the question."

"It's not too personal. It's just that, like most people, my impression of cops is based to some extent on what I see on TV. You kind of look like a cop, but you don't seem to talk like one."

Travis laughed. "You're not the first person to make that observation. I can't do much about how I look, but I tend to adjust the way I talk to the person I'm talking to. I've been referred to as a chameleon. I use street lingo or tough cop talk when the occasion calls for it. With educated people, I usually weigh my words. Now let's get back to you. Were you angry with Kahn when you quit?"

"In a sense, yes. I was angry because I'd started my legal career with such hope of doing significant work and wound up feeling compromised by a jerk. To answer your real question, though, no, I wasn't angry enough even to think about killing Bernie."

"So now you're deciding what my 'real' questions are? My real question is whether you can shed light on anybody who might have felt enough animosity toward Kahn to kill him." Travis had already tentatively decided Clara was not the homicidal type, though experience had taught him that he could never be sure until he learned more.

"I've been thinking about that ever since I first learned about the killing," Clara replied. "I've run through my mind everybody I know who knew Bernie. I can't think of anyone who actually liked him, but I also don't know of anybody who had more than fairly petty grievances against him. I don't know anything about his personal relationships, though, if he had any."

"How well did you know Mrs. Kahn?"

"I never saw her except in the office, but I think we all knew her better than we wanted to. What I mean by that is she was around the office more than any of us liked and had a tendency to poke her nose into the firm's business. I never had any direct clashes with her, but others did. For example, she got into a big argument with a nice new paralegal a few months ago about an art calendar the paralegal put up in her cubicle. The calendar had Impressionist prints, which Charlotte did not like with the Oriental decor. The argument escalated to an embarrassing decibel level, and the next day Bernie decided that the paralegal's services were no longer 'up to his standards.'

"When Bernie fired people, the reasons always seemed trivial. That hardly seems like grounds for murder, but I guess you never really know what sets people off, do you? I've been wondering how you go about in-vestigating a crime like this. I've read a lot of mystery novels, but it's really different when you don't have an author setting up the clues for you."

Travis smiled. "I thought I had you pegged for an amateur detective. Do you know about any possible link with the other two victims, the divorce lawyer Hanks, or the other one Rinko?"

His question reminded her of her little jingle from years ago. "No, not the foggiest. Have you found any connection yet?"

"There you go again with a question. Why don't you try putting some of that curiosity to good use and let me know if you pick up any clues? You'll let me know if you think of anything, won't you? You aren't planning to take off for another holiday anywhere, are you?"

"No, I'll be around. As a matter of fact, I'll be around this office. For a little while at least, I'm going to work with Maura and Katy."

"Now that's an interesting turn of events. If you hap-pen to run across anything at all that might relate to the murders, here's my card." He turned it over and wrote two numbers on the back before giving it to her. "These are my home and cell phone numbers. The printed one is my office. If I'm not there, they'll get a message to me. If you call me at home and a woman answers, don't hang up. That's no lady—that's my wife. She definitely under-stands me—and my profession," he said in a tone of af-fection. "But anyway, if you need to reach me in a hurry, I can usually answer my cell phone. Don't hesitate to call if you think of anything."

ﮩﮩﮩ

Part of Clara was intrigued at the thought of being

involved in a murder investigation, but part of her was uneasy. She took the card and nodded, but didn't make any promises.

Travis didn't press, ended the interview politely, and then asked Terri Hu to call in the next person. Clara checked in with Maura and made a note of the pending client files she was to review. She spent the rest of the afternoon in the firm library preparing letters to clients. She didn't notice the time until Maura popped in at six-thirty.

"I think it's about time to call it a day, don't you?" Maura said.

"Now that you mention it, yes," Clara responded, looking at the wall clock. "I had forgotten that my neighbors invited me to dinner." She said goodnight to Maura and called Adrian.

"Hi, Adrian, it's Clara. Are we still on for dinner?"

"I hope so. You should see the gourmet goodies I've prepared. How's your timing?"

"I was just about to leave the office. I'll slip into something a bit more festive than a boring brown business suit and pop over. Is that okay with you?"

"You bet. That's perfect," said Adrian. "I'll see you soon."

As she went by her old office on the way out, Clara was surprised to see Detective Travis still there. He was sitting alone, making notes in a small loose-leaf binder.

"Have you solved it yet?" she asked.

"Not quite. Remember, there are two other murders to contend with. This is only the beginning. I was hoping you might still be here. How would you like to go for a drink and kick around a few ideas?"

"I really can't right now. I was just about to leave for dinner with friends. How about a rain check?" she asked.

"That's fine. Nothing is very solid at this point, and

I've got a lot more work to do tonight anyway. I'll check with you tomorrow," he said.

"Fine. I'll look forward to it. Goodnight," she said, as he waved her on her way.

Clara always had her antennae up where men were concerned, but she felt reasonably sure there was nothing to worry about with this man, who wore his wedding ring and spoke fondly of his wife. She already felt too comfortable with Travis to think he had an ulterior motive. Then she was amused at the thought. Of course, he had an ulterior motive, but it was not of the licentious sort. He obviously wanted to pick her brain about Bernie. That was all right with her. She had already decided he was welcome to whatever that might be worth. She was intrigued by the prospect of talking to him more about the investigation.

Clara drove straight home. She parked in her usual space in the underground garage and took the elevator to her penthouse. She sponged off a bit, freshened her lip gloss, sprayed on a light cologne, slipped into a paisley print caftan, and soon knocked on the front door across from hers.

Blake answered the door and gave her a peck on the cheek. "Come on into the kitchen. Adrian is putting the finishing touches on dinner."

When the kitchen door opened, Clara was surprised to hear a slightly unharmonious chorus of "Happy Birthday," with Maura on soprano, Katy on alto, two tenors—Adrian and Francis—and Blake on bass.

Clara laughed to keep from crying. It was the first time in her life that anyone had ever given her a surprise party. They all chimed in to wish her a happy birthday, and Adrian shooed them out of the kitchen, asking Blake to open champagne for all.

When Blake lit the candles flanking a delicate floral

centerpiece on the dining table, Clara saw a sumptuous table setting for six.

"How did you do it? I didn't even know anyone knew it's my birthday."

"You know Adrian," Blake replied. "Remember months ago you were pooh-poohing astrology, and we all mentioned our birthdays? Of course, Adrian made a note of the date. This party was spontaneous, though, since we didn't know if you'd be back for your birthday. So Adrian just put it together. You know how creative he is. He'd often heard you speak of Maura, Katy, and Francis. So he just called Maura at the office today and set it up."

"That's why there are no presents," said Katy. "None of us had a chance to go out and get anything."

"Or we're just too cheap," Francis quipped.

Clara protested, "Hey, what better present could I possibly have than a choice gathering of my dearest friends? Nothing could please me more." After a momentary lull, she verbalized what was bothering them all. "Do you think it's proper for us to be having fun, considering what happened about twenty-four hours ago?"

Francis, typically, gave the perfect response. "It's been a very tense day for all of us, and I can't think of a better way to relieve the tension. This is the first time I've met your friends Blake and Adrian, and I think it's wonderful of them to have us all for a party. Let's toast them along with the birthday girl."

"Here, here!" they called out, with the resonant clink of Waterford crystal.

There was one birthday gift, though, which Adrian and Blake had carefully selected weeks before. It was a pair of exquisite earrings, with a gold filigree butterfly resting on a leaf. Engraved in small script on the back of one earring was an "A" for Adrian and "B" for Blake on the other. They knew Clara's penchant for butterflies, as she had used a butterfly motif in decorating her penthouse. She had always admired their beauty, and she identified with the stages of a butterfly's life, having gone through many diverse stages in her own.

For a while, the party guests talked about the events of the day, especially the investigation. Adrian and Blake were particularly interested to know if any leads had developed, and the others were eager to talk about their interrogation that day by Travis. Finally, Clara exercised her prerogative as the guest of honor and called for a shift in subject matter.

For the rest of a lovely evening, the conversation drifted among topics like travel, the arts, and Adrian's wickedly delightful knowledge of San Francisco gossip. Not a single reference was made to Bernie or the murders or anything remotely connected with the legal profession.

As much as Clara enjoyed the good conversation, though, she would have appreciated it even more, had she known that the next day would focus so intensely on Bernie Kahn.

CHAPTER 4

Mellow Widow

When Clara got home from her birthday party, she was exhausted, but too wound up to sleep. She made a cup of herbal tea, enveloped herself in a comfy robe, and sank into her buttery-soft Italian leather sofa. The music on the local jazz radio station was cool and understated. Despite herself, her thoughts kept drifting back to the murders. But she knew no more than she had that morning when she first read about them.

Finally, she willed herself to stop thinking about Bernie Kahn and began to reflect on the quirks of fate that had brought her to live alone in a penthouse in San Francisco. Sometimes she was still awed when she thought of the little Kentucky girl inside her who now lived at the edge of Pacific Heights, overlooking the white limestone Spreckels mansion reminiscent of the Grand Trianon palace at Versailles. She hadn't chosen her home because of any pretensions about the neighborhood, but simply because the place suited her so well. Her comfortable penthouse, as well as the other one on the top floor of the building, had a spectacular view of the bay and the city. The two gentle men in the adjacent penthouse were a serendipitous bonus, friends more than just neighbors. Friends were rare in the city. She felt fortunate in many ways.

Clara sometimes stepped out of her own skin and looked at herself as if she were someone else, both physically and emotionally. It had started when she was a child growing up in a small Kentucky town, when her dour father continually told her she was "plain" and "ordinary." Like most little girls, she wanted to be pretty and special. With her bedroom door closed, she would study herself in the mirror and wonder how she could be merely ordinary with burnished auburn hair, huge golden amber eyes, and freckles skipping across her nose.

Even if she had been plain before, when the freckles faded into a creamy complexion, and her figure developed as she reached her ultimate height of five feet, two inches, the attention she got from boys left no doubt—contrary to her father's put-downs—that others considered her attractive.

Thinking of Bernie's death had reminded Clara of her father and the other two men in her life who had died. The small twinge of guilt she felt because she lacked any real sense of loss over Bernie was nothing compared with the far more intense emotion she had felt when her father died. Above all, it had been an enormous, almost overwhelming sense of relief.

Avoiding unpleasant recollections of her father now, she turned her thoughts to the two men who had been most important in her life, the men she had married. For a long time, she'd tried not to think of them and bring back the pain that never completely left her. But there was a positive side, too.

In addition to the pure joy she had experienced with them, the fates that had brought them together—first Steve and later Jon—had led her to a penthouse above San Francisco Bay.

೧ನಿ೧

She met Stephen Ziarko during her senior year at the University of Virginia. One day at dusk, she was walking across campus to the library when she encountered a large boxer dog and stopped to pet him. As a child, she had begged her father for a dog, but he would never allow her to have any kind of pet. Despite the boxer's intimidating appearance, she sensed he was friendly—but not as friendly as Steve, the good-looking young man not far behind with a leash dangling in his hand.

"Aren't you supposed to keep him on that leash?" she asked.

"I usually do, but sometimes I think he deserves to run completely free. There's usually nobody around here this time of day."

"Some people might think he's threatening."

"You're the first woman who ever stopped to pet Rocky. You're not only pretty, but also fearless."

"He seems fairly harmless, except for a little excess drool," she said, as the dog licked her hand. "And who wouldn't look pretty good next to this mug? But really, isn't Rocky a sort of obvious name for a boxer?"

"You must be one of those English majors. They're always fussy about names. What would you have named him, the Marquess of Queensberry or something?"

"Guilty as charged—senior in English lit. And you must be a history major."

"A doctoral candidate in history, actually."

"I'm impressed. What's your dissertation about?"

"Are you sure a preposition is something you want to end a sentence with?"

They both laughed and, before long, were continuing the conversation over coffee, soon followed by a full-blown college romance.

Steve was from Chicago, earning his PhD with the help of a fellowship grant. They seemed to have a world of thoughts in common, as well as physical sparks that sometimes had to be doused when they really had to get their studies done. He liked her view of literature as more meaningful within a historical perspective, and she liked his literary sense of history. Without making any formal commitment, after their first date, they simply didn't want to go out with anyone else.

They had vigorous intellectual debates, but their interests and values were fundamentally compatible. Steve had been brought up Catholic, Clara Protestant, but both had abandoned organized religion in favor of secular ethics. Their political views were almost identical. Their biggest difference was sports, which she thought was a total waste of time, while he read the sports page every day right after the headlines.

The relationship deepened quickly. There was no traditional bent-knee proposal, but it came as no surprise when Steve asked casually, "What kind of wedding do you want? Do you think we should have it right after graduation or wait until later in the summer?"

When she wrote home about him, of course, Clara's provincial Southern father disapproved of her interest in some Yankee named Ziarko whose grandparents had been Polish immigrants. Her mother, as usual, was happy as long as Clara was happy. As it turned out, her father was no impediment to their marriage. Before wedding plans were set, he died from a fall down the stairs, almost surely alcohol induced, though it was never acknowledged. His death was profoundly liberating for Clara, but at the time she would never have uttered such an inappropriate thought, even to herself.

Steve further encouraged her liberation, although it had been a struggle for him to overcome his Old World upbringing. When they were married, he respected her choice to keep her own surname, which, he had to admit, went better with Clara than Ziarko. She had always liked the name Quillen because as a kid, she was the only one in school whose last name started with "Q." It also held a fond memory of her grandfather, who had told her when she was a little girl that the name was a contraction for "quill pen" and meant she would be a good writer. She never formally traced the name because she liked her grandfather's version.

After Steve received his doctorate and Clara her master's degree, they were ecstatic when he received an offer to teach at the University of California in Berkeley. They didn't have to think twice before accepting and moved their few belongings across the country and into a minuscule rented cottage in the Berkeley hills.

Clara began looking for a teaching job and was extremely lucky that the senior English teacher at nearby Piedmont High School had just given notice when Clara inquired about a job. Piedmont was a wealthy community, and the school was known for excellence. Although the principal hadn't intended to hire a young, inexperienced teacher, he was won over by Clara's enthusiasm and solid academic credentials. He decided to give her a chance, and she never gave him reason to regret the decision. Her extra income allowed her to take a brief trip to England with Steve the following summer, even though they were on a very frugal budget.

The two years of Clara's marriage to Steve were filled with work and play—newlywed joys of sharing their lives. They often talked about the things they wanted. Family was foremost, and they planned to have their first baby after Clara worked another year. She always regretted that they'd waited. Of course, they didn't know their idyll would be shattered by brutal violence.

They were saving toward a trip to Europe, and both had just started teaching summer courses to earn extra money. One night, Clara was at home alone grading papers, while Steve had stayed late on campus to work with some students. As it got later, she began to worry, and even more so at getting no answer when she tried to call him. She feared the worst when she answered the doorbell to find two uniformed Berkeley policemen with somber faces.

"Ma'am, are you Ms. Quillen, the wife of a professor named Zarko at Cal?"

"Yes, it's Ziarko, Stephen Ziarko. What's wrong? What's happened to Steve?"

"May we come in, ma'am? I think you'd better sit down and let us explain."

"I don't want to sit down. Just tell me if Steve is all right," she demanded.

"I wish we could, ma'am. I'm sorry to have to tell you—your husband died before he got to the hospital." As he said it, he reached out for her, to keep her from falling as her legs buckled.

Clara heard an anguished cry, which she only barely realized was coming from deep inside her. The policemen were patient and told her the rest when she was ready, sitting with them at the kitchen table. Steve had encountered a couple of thugs in ski masks roughing up an elderly professor in the faculty parking lot. He grabbed one assailant and never even saw the switchblade before it plunged into him, or the second knife wielded by the accomplice. The thugs fled, and Steve bled to death from massive wounds. The old professor survived, but couldn't give much of a description, and the killers were never caught.

In the weeks to come, Clara was disconsolate. She had bloody nightmares and struggled with deep depression. It frightened her that she no longer saw any point in living, and she was grateful to friends who helped her through. Eventually, she realized life would continue when she made her first conscious decision: she moved out of the cottage and into a nondescript efficiency apartment with no ghosts of Steve. She began to function again when the new school year started, and she plunged into work. She spent nearly all her waking moments preparing lessons, teaching, working with students, and grading papers. Gradually, the pain diminished, and she finally accepted that Steve was gone forever, but she still existed.

ᏴᎣᏴᎣ

It was all too easy to remember the pain that had never totally left her. Now, as she thought about Bernie's murder, she remembered the haunting blood that surrounded her memories of Steve's death. She had never been squeamish before Steve's murder, but after that, she didn't even like teaching bloody *Macbeth* in her English lit classes. And now she didn't want to think about the blood that must have spurted from Bernie's head.

She wondered if it would be so painful for Charlotte and how she would cope. For Clara, the next few years after Steve died were fulfilling professionally, though in limbo personally, as she continued to teach at Piedmont High. She was a dedicated teacher who devoted an inordinate amount of time to her students, traveled in the summers on a frugal budget, and savored the charms of San Francisco. After a while, she began to accept an occasional date, but never quite allowed herself to become seriously involved with anyone. She no longer believed Tennyson's "better to have loved and lost Than never to have loved at all" and couldn't bear the prospect of loving enough to suffer the pain of losing the love.

The dramatic change in her life began in an unexpected way one afternoon when Jake Westgate, her favorite student—though she would never have admitted having a favorite—stayed after school to talk to her on the pretext of talking about his college plans to go to Cornell. Although Jake had been in her honors English class for almost a year and they had talked on many occasions, he seemed uncharacteristically awkward.

"Ms. Quillen, I, uh, may need some more references for college. Uh, is it okay if I put your name down again?"

"Sure, Jake, I told you it's okay to use me as a reference anytime. You don't even have to ask again."

"Like, uh, I just don't want you to feel pressured or anything. I mean, I've really enjoyed your class, and uh, you're really one of my favorite teachers. Well, you know, I like a lot of my teachers, but I don't just like you as a teacher. I mean, uh, I really admire you as a person, too."

When he almost seemed to blush, Clara became uncomfortable as it dawned on her that she may have unintentionally fostered a schoolboy crush, which had happened a couple of times before in her teaching career. She was poised to handle it delicately when Jake blurted out, "So would you consider going out with my dad?"

Clara didn't fully register what she had heard until Jake calmed down enough to explain. She had chatted with Jake's father, Jonathan Westgate, at a couple of parent night meetings and remembered him as a distinguished-looking man who had shown a keen interest in Jake's progress.

It turned out that Jon was not only his father, by adoption, but also his biological uncle. Jon had adopted Jake when he was a baby, after Jon's only brother and his wife were killed by a drunk driver in an auto accident.

"Well, Dad—I mean he's both my dad and my un-cle—Dad never married" Jake explained, "and he always devoted himself to two things, me and his business. That doesn't leave much time for anything else. Oh, some-times he takes women out, but most of them seem more interested in his money than in him, and they're not over-joyed when they find out he has a teenage son. Lately, I've been thinking how lonesome Dad will be when I leave for college. So I just sort of started thinking about who would make a good companion for him, and you're the only one I could think of."

"Jake, is this your idea or your father's?"

"Uh, I admit I haven't mentioned it to Dad. But I got to thinking that time is really sort of running out because I'll be graduating next month."

"I'm really very flattered, Jake, and your father did seem very nice when I met him at school. But I'm sure you understand it really wouldn't be proper for me to go out with the father of a student."

Jake looked crestfallen but took it with good grace. Clara gave it no more thought until graduation night, when she discovered Jake was a very resourceful young man.

After the graduation ceremony, Jake approached Clara with Jon in tow and asked her to share in a small celebration. She couldn't resist and joined them for what turned out to be a turning point in her life. Jake got into Clara's car with her to show her the way to his house. Jon followed in a chauffeured black sedan, which Clara learned wasn't hired for the occasion, but instead Jon's usual mode of transportation; merely practical, he ex-plained later, so he could get work done instead of wast-ing time in traffic. They arrived at a gated Piedmont man-sion hidden behind tall hedges. Clara knew that many of her students were from wealthy families, but she had never visited any of their homes.

The house was well appointed and tasteful, though perhaps a bit on the masculine side in decor. Even though the furnishings were obviously expensive, the place still had a comfortable ambiance. A light supper of crab, artichoke hearts, other delicacies, and some more conventional fare was set out in the library. Clara tried not to covet the fine books on floor-to-ceiling shelves. The crowning touch was a perfectly chilled bottle of Dom Perignon to celebrate Jake's eighteenth birthday that had occurred a few days before. The champagne was superb and nothing like any champagne Clara had ever tasted before.

Clara was surprised to realize how much at home she felt, but she was even more surprised when Jake wolfed down a few bites of buffalo wings and said, "Uh, I hope you guys will excuse me, but I'm supposed to meet some buddies to celebrate graduation."

"I thought they were on their way here for a party," Jon said.

"We, uh, sort of had a last minute change of plans." Jake dashed off almost before Clara and Jon realized what had happened, and they both burst out laughing.

Jake's scheme, though transparent, was effective. Clara and Jon joked about Jake's matchmaking, but neither minded in the least. They talked into the wee hours, when Clara finally said she really should be going. Jon insisted on following her home, this time driving himself because the chauffeur had already gone home. He saw her to the door, where he squeezed her hand as he asked when he could see her again.

The warm glow he left with her lasted until she fell asleep, the most contented sleep she'd had in years. The courtship, which had clearly begun, continued with lunch that same day, and the days of their whirlwind courtship blended into one another.

At the end of the summer, just before Jake left for Cornell, Clara married Jon in a small ceremony in the library of what would be her home for the next three years. When she asked him how he felt about her keeping her own name, Jon replied simply, "I'm not changing my name. Why should you change yours?"

But he did make a major change, having decided he had devoted enough of his life to work. He cut back drastically on his work, and she quit her teaching job. They enjoyed the good life in the Bay Area, did some charitable work, and traveled anywhere in the world whenever it struck their fancy.

What had been a dream abruptly became a nightmare. Clara had always wanted to go to Spain, and among the wonderful places they visited together, the last was Seville. They were eager to see the cathedral, the veritable symbol of Seville, begun in 1401 and finished in a mere one hundred years. It was said that the cathedral was the world's largest Gothic building and the third largest church in Europe, ranking just behind St. Peter's in Rome and St. Paul's in London.

Clara and Jon began with a climb up the lovely tower known as the Giralda, reputedly the model on which San Francisco's Ferry Building is patterned. The structure itself was three hundred and twenty-two feet high, and the viewing area was two hundred and thirty feet up, reached by trudging up a long succession of sloping ramps. The reward for the walk was an incomparable view of the city and the Guadalquivir River.

"The climb was certainly worth it. What a view," Clara said, as they got back to ground level.

They were just about to go into the cathedral itself when Jon said, "I'm a little tired. Before we tour the cathedral, how about some tapas in the square right over there, with a view of the Giralda?"

Those were his last words. They had taken only a few steps when Jon collapsed with a massive heart attack.

What followed was a surrealistic blur. A crowd, an ambulance, a hospital, a flight home, a funeral—the first thing Clara really remembered clearly after the Giralda was holding Jake's arm tightly when he placed the simple urn in its niche in the columbarium. Jake stayed with her a while, as they consoled each other over their loss. They helped each other deal with their anger about Jon's death, especially when they learned from his doctor that Jon had been aware of his heart condition for some time, but didn't want them to know. Above all, Clara and Jake were grateful they had each other, the nucleus of a family that would always cherish how dear Jon had been to both of them.

It took some time to wind up the estate, even though Jon had left things in good order. Their attorney, Marvin Morrison, was a family friend and extremely helpful. Clara had no idea how vast Jon's fortune had been until Marvin laid everything out for her. In essence, Jon's will specified that the estate was to be equally divided between Clara and Jake, with his share in trust until he was twenty-one, and they might jointly decide the disposition of the house. After talking it over, they decided that since neither of them really wanted to live in the big house, it would be sold.

Clara gave Jake first choice of anything in the house he wanted, and most of those things went into storage. She found the penthouse in San Francisco where she would live and chose the things she wanted as furnishings for it. They gave the sedan to the chauffeur, and Clara bought a Prius for herself. The longtime housekeeper received a generous stipend and a few items from the house. Marvin helped Clara arrange for the remaining personal property to go to appropriate charities.

After Jake returned to college, she was lonely but busied herself with other decisions about Jon's estate and getting settled in her new place. Gradually, she mellowed into acceptance and began to wonder what she should do with her life. She was unsure whether she wanted to go back to teaching, but she didn't know what else to do. She couldn't see herself just living a life of luxury, although she had more money than she would ever need, even if she were to be extravagant.

One day, Marvin and Clara had lunch to discuss some details about setting up a charitable trust in Jon's memory, in particular, to consider which of his charities she wanted to continue. In the course of the conversation, Marvin asked, "Clara, have you given much thought to what you want to do now?"

"Sure, I've thought about it, Marv, but I don't really know. I guess eventually I'll want to travel again, but not for a while. I toyed with the idea of going back to work on a PhD, but I think I'm more inclined to make my further studies in English lit for pleasure and not a degree."

To her surprise, he asked, "Have you ever thought about law school? We've had many a philosophical discussion about law."

"It's interesting you should mention that. Ever since Jake started talking about Columbia Law School after he finishes at Cornell, I've had a growing fascination with the law. I find myself paying more attention to Supreme Court decisions and reading books about law and lawyers. But I've always heard how demanding law school is supposed to be, and I'm a little intimidated at the thought of law school after reading *One L.* Even so, I think I could use an absorbing mental discipline at this point in my life."

After much thought and sounding out some people whose views she respected, Clara decided that even if she never practiced, she wanted to study law, and she was happy to be accepted at the University of California's Boalt Hall. For the next three years, the study of law occupied most of her waking hours, and even her summers were filled with volunteer legal aid work.

Of course, after she finished law school, she went to work for Bernie Kahn, and now here she was back to ruminating about her murdered former boss. Finally, she drifted off into a deep and dreamless sleep.

A good night's sleep comes in handy before an unusually difficult day.

CHAPTER 5

Unlikely Liaison

The spirit of a more relaxed regime filled the office the next day. The receptionist was instructed to disregard logging in employees and other pica-yune duties, but instead to focus on being as courteous and helpful as possible to everyone. The office manager and Terri Hu began revising the employee handbook and procedures manual, with directions to streamline them in any way that made sense to them, subject to eventual oversight by Maura and Katy. It didn't take long to cut it down to a fraction of its former size, centering on employee benefits and guidelines for getting work done efficiently.

The rest of the staff continued normal functions, except the office was to be closed two hours early to allow time for condolence calls at the Cypress Lawn mortuary in Colma, and the next day the office would be closed after noon for Bernie's funeral. At first, it seemed odd that the services wouldn't be nearer Charlotte's home in Marin County, but on second thought, it seemed apropos that someone with an ego like Bernie's should have his final resting place in proximity to the likes of Crocker, Spreckels, and Hearst.

For Clara, the day whizzed by, yet all the while she felt she was moving in slow motion. Time was somehow out of joint, and it seemed to be more than just jet lag. Exhausted the night before, she had slept as motionless as a still life painting. And so, despite her odd sense of time, she felt quite productive in the newly charged atmosphere in the office. Everyone was working, and things were getting done, but employees were also talking with each other and seemed to be developing a new kind of camaraderie. A common topic of conversation was their interrogation yesterday by Detective Travis. Typically, they were impressed by his decorum in handling things, and most were surprised at how easy it was to talk to him.

Although everyone else left early, Maura, Katy, and Clara worked until seven and then headed for Cypress Lawn in Katy's car. They agreed it would be easier to face the ordeal together. When they arrived, most of the office staff had already come and gone. There were a few unfamiliar faces, some clients, and, of course, Charlotte sitting on a throne-like chair with her back to the closed coffin laden with exotic tropical flowers. Wearing a long black gown with sheer chiffon sleeves, Charlotte dabbed at her puffy eyes with a large white lace handkerchief as she held court in mournful tones.

After saying the proper and expected things to Charlotte, Clara walked as far from the coffin as the room would allow and introduced herself to the elderly man who stood by a potted palm with another man in his late forties.

The older man was a small but stately gentleman, with intelligent blue eyes and thin white hair.

"How do you do, Miss Quillen. I'm Martin Kahn, and this is my other son, also named Martin. Were you well acquainted with Bernard, Miss Quillen?" This gracious little man had a benign dignity, not at all the forbidding tyrant she had expected based on Bernie's occasional references to his austere religious father.

"I was an associate in your son's firm for seven months. He had spoken of you, and I'm so sorry to meet you under circumstances like this," Clara said. "Please accept my condolences."

Martin the younger shook his head. "We could never have imagined that God would choose to take Bernard in such a tragic way. It's difficult for us to comprehend now, but perhaps with time, greater wisdom will help us understand."

"At least it is a blessing Bernard's mother did not live to see this day," said the elder Martin. "It was heartbreaking when she passed away just before Christmas last year, but sad to say, I am grateful she's not here now."

Clara could hardly believe what she heard. Bernie had been gone most of December last year, and she recalled his talking about skiing, but she couldn't remember his saying anything about his mother's death. How very strange, even for someone as strange as Bernie.

She tried to think of something to say now. "Do I recall that you also have a daughter? Is she here?"

"No, Rebecca will not be coming," the old man replied. "I spoke with her yesterday and persuaded her it was better for her to stay in Arizona with her work. There are so many people on the reservation who depend on her, and I told her not to be concerned. I feel sure Bernard would understand. Martin and I will be leaving right after the services tomorrow, as we have duties at home as well. Charlotte has assured us there is nothing she needs, and I trust she will have assistance from her family and friends."

"And all of us from the office will do anything we can to help," Clara said.

She recalled a few spiteful remarks she had heard

Charlotte make about Bernie's family and had no doubt she would be perfectly happy to bid them a hasty farewell.

Clara was struggling to make conversation when Maura and Katy came over. After introducing them, she moved on to talk with some of the clients she knew. The quiet conversations around the room were occasionally disrupted by the braying of two strident female voices. When Clara found the source, she saw that the attire of the two women was likewise inappropriately loud, the older woman wearing a gaudy print dress and the younger one in a vivid purple pantsuit.

She watched the two women go over to reclaim the two seats flanking Charlotte's imposing chair. No doubt, they had to be the mother and sister who Charlotte had said were coming to be with her.

When Clara decided she might as well meet them and get it over with, she cringed at their cloying Texas drawl.

She was glad to see a welcome face in a corner of the room and made a beeline for Detective Travis. "Is it true detectives always attend wakes and funerals to look for suspects?" she asked.

"Do you always open a conversation with a question or only with detectives?"

"I'm just curious about how real detectives operate. Can you forgive the questions?"

Travis gave her an indulgent smile. "Sure. I'm getting used to it. I think we might even strike a deal. I want to hang around here till everybody leaves. Then how about that drink we mentioned?"

"Okay, as long as you can give me a ride back to my car at the office. I hope this thing doesn't go on too much longer. I was planning to cut out with Maura and Katy as soon as we've done our duty."

"No problem."

"Good. I'll tell them I'll stick around and talk to the rest of the clients and let them know I have a ride."

With another taxing day ahead, Katy and Maura were only too glad to leave. As the evening wore on, Clara found herself looking around to spot Travis. Several times he caught her eye and nodded reassuringly. When the callers had dwindled to a trickle, Charlotte made a grand exit with her mother and sister.

Travis escorted Clara to his very ordinary beige car, which he drove back to San Francisco to a corner bar named Take Five in a sort of middle class, mostly residential neighborhood Clara had never been to. She was pleasantly surprised there was no smoke, the conversational level was reasonable, the music was cool jazz, and the Pinot noir turned out to be drinkable, though not pretentious. Travis ordered tonic with lime from a friendly bartender named Andy, who obviously knew Travis.

"I really like the music here, Travis. I gather this place was named after "Take Five" by the Dave Brubeck Quartet."

"You know Brubeck? He's before your time, isn't he?"

"He was timeless, and Paul Desmond's alto sax work was sublime. I wore out that wonderful *Time Out* album, and I was glad to replace it with a CD. It was a loss when Brubeck died, but I'm glad he lived to a ripe old age. I don't claim to know much about jazz, but I really like cool jazz. My main preference in music is classical."

"I'm a greenhorn when it comes to classical music, but I'm often exposed to it because my wife likes it. But she's learned to like my jazz, too."

When the drinks came, Clara looked at his tonic with lime. "Are you an alcoholic?"

"No, why?"

"Most of the people I've known who don't order liquor in bars have been alcoholics, and you don't seem like the teetotaler type. I was just curious."

"So what else is new? No, I'm not an alcoholic or a teetotaler. I just don't drink when I'm working, and right now, I need to keep my head sharp enough to retain all of the information you can give me. Can we start with a rundown of all the people there tonight?"

Clara began to describe everyone she knew in as much detail as she could, and Travis responded appreciatively to her perceptive comments. He had already managed to identify everyone who had been there and also knew the names of some people Clara didn't know. He asked her to focus particularly on the clients, as they were the most difficult for him to get information about.

"You know I can't tell you anything about the clients' legal matters, though," said Clara.

"That's a given," he replied. "Just tell me what you can that doesn't come under attorney-client privilege."

"I've already told you the little I know about most of them, except for the three clients I knew best because I did quite a bit of work for them. That's Dr. Hershel Andrews, Pamela Fairfax, and Miguel Fuentes. I can talk about Dr. Andrews freely, though, because he was a defendant in an appeal I did a lot of work on, *Vann v. Golden Gate Hospital.* It's a published appellate opinion, and the case is final. So there's nothing much privileged regarding Dr. Andrews."

"I remember. That's the case you said you argued in the appellate court, isn't it? What about the other two clients?"

"You may have seen Pamela Fairfax on the society page. She's a bigwig with the symphony and the opera. Miguel Fuentes is a bit more enigmatic."

"Okay, let's start with Andrews, then the others," said Travis.

"You couldn't have missed Dr. Andrews tonight. He's a distinguished physician with great presence, the tall, silver-haired man in the perfectly-tailored slate-gray suit. He's the exact image of what you want your doctor to look like. And he not only has a gracious bedside manner, but he also seems to keep up on the very latest medical developments."

"So what was the lawsuit about? If he's so great, why was he sued?"

"Dr. Andrews wasn't sued for medical malpractice, but rather as the administrator of the hospital where Mr. Vann was treated for a rare neurological disease that causes various debilitating problems, including blindness, before the patient dies. Unfortunately, even though the hospital rendered the best treatment available, and it prolonged his life by almost a year, Mr. Vann apparently got an infection that caused his death not long before he would've succumbed to the disease. Poor Mrs. Vann was influenced by some greedy lawyer to sue the hospital and everybody else in sight for wrongful death, but she lost at trial because the jury was just not convinced that the hospital was liable for negligence."

Clara didn't notice Travis's eyes glazing over and continued describing the case. "So even if Mrs. Vann's husband had gotten the infection at the hospital, which was not established under the evidentiary standard, he was fully informed of that risk before consenting to the treatment. The appeal followed on the theory that Mr. Vann had not given his informed consent for the treatment that allegedly exposed him to the infection. The appellate court did not find any reversible error, though. The court's opinion was well written, expressing sympathy for Mr. Vann's unfortunate demise. The court decided the jury was correct in finding that all the evidence indicated, first, even if the infection had caused the death, it was within the standard of care as a recognized risk of the treatment, and second, he would not reasonably have withheld his consent, even if the infection could cause his death, because he most likely would have died even sooner, if he had not received the advanced treatment."

"I'm not sure I follow all of that," Travis said as he suppressed a yawn, "but it sounds like it means Dr. Andrews must've been very happy with your legal representation."

"I don't know if Dr. Andrews really knows how much I did on the case. I did all of the record review and legal research, as well as writing the appellate brief and presenting oral argument, with Maura overseeing my work to make sure I didn't make any mistakes. Of course, as always, Bernie's name went above mine on the brief, and he essentially took all the credit. He said the clients always had to be assured he was the responsible attorney because he had such a great reputation. My guess is Dr. Andrews really knew who did the work, though, because anytime he had a question or a problem that needed to be resolved, he dealt directly with me. And he attended the oral argument and seemed pleased with my representation."

"Do you know of any possible grievance Dr. Andrews might have against Kahn?" asked Travis.

"I hesitate to say this because I really have no idea what it was about, but I saw something peculiar one night after I'd worked late. One of Bernie's little control freak things was to give an assignment at the end of the day and say it had to be ready first thing the next morning. Sometimes he did the same thing late on a Friday, as if testing your loyalty by making you work on weekends when it really wasn't necessary. But sometimes it was just because Bernie was so disorganized he'd forget to assign something until the last minute." Clara shook her head. "I'm sorry. I know I'm digressing. It was just such an annoying way to have to work. Anyway, that night when I went to the parking garage, I heard familiar voices arguing behind a big pillar. I knew Bernie had taken Dr. Andrews out for a drink, which he frequently did to cozy up to clients. I wasn't invited, of course, even though I was doing the work on Dr. Andrews's case. I don't really know what they were talking about, although it seemed a bit heated, because as soon as they came around the pillar and saw me, they both said a jovial hello and then went toward the elevator. That was really all there was to it. I'm sorry I can't tell you more."

"That's fine, Quillen. Let's just file that away as something to find out about. One more thing, do you happen to remember where Dr. Andrews lives?"

"He lives with his wife in Berkeley, not far from the university. And I think he said he occasionally stayed with his son in the city when he had to work late. Why do you ask?"

"Just getting as full a picture as possible," he responded. "Now, what about the hoity-toity Mrs. Pamela Fairfax?"

"The thing that always puzzled me about her is why she used Bernie as her attorney at all. Her husband is Charles Fairfax of Fairfax Clothiers, which is generally considered the most exclusive purveyor of fine menswear to gentlemen in San Francisco. He seems to keep the shop as a hobby, though, as his family is old money. With their wealth, Mrs. Fairfax could afford any attorney she wanted, but for some reason, she let Bernie look after a number of her financial interests."

"She's the one who breezed in and out like she was on her way to another social event, wasn't she, that elegant woman about fifty?" asked Travis.

"Yes, but maybe closer to sixty. Even if she was on her way somewhere, she would still do the socially proper thing. She probably has a calendar conflict with the funeral tomorrow and decided to make her appearance tonight. She's very involved in a lot of cultural affairs. One reason she and I got along well is that I know a bit about classical music. She wouldn't have deigned to speak with me if she knew I'm really just a hick from Kentucky," said Clara.

"You cover it well," Travis said with a chuckle. "How was it you did legal work for her?"

"When I first started with Bernie, I made it clear I wanted to do appellate work, and I didn't think transactional work was my strong point. Katy actually enjoys it, but instead of assigning work according to inclination or even ability, Bernie exercised control by fiat. Mrs. Fairfax dealt directly with him on a regular basis until sometime about February, I think. After then, he met with her, but I did the legal work. It didn't amount to much, but still, it would've made more sense for Katy to do it. When Mrs. Fairfax quit using our legal services, he criticized me for not developing the client's need for us, but that was a familiar routine he used on all of us."

"Are you aware of any ax Mrs. Fairfax may have had to grind with Kahn?"

"No, but would you actually consider a woman like her a suspect?" Clara asked.

"Nothing can be ruled out, at this point," replied Travis. "Right now, I have to gather as much information as possible before I can start to narrow anything down. By the way, do you know where Mrs. Fairfax lives?"

"She lives in San Francisco in the most exclusive section of St. Francis Wood. It's an affluent residential neighborhood, a little west of Mt. Davidson. They can afford to live anywhere they want, of course. I think they also have a country house somewhere up in Marin County. Is that what you're really interested in?"

"I'm interested in every detail I can get. Let's go on. You also did some work for Miguel Fuentes, you said. He's that handsome Hispanic type who was talking to Terri Hu at the office yesterday. Tell me about him," Travis said.

"Miguel used Bernie as an attorney because he needed help with some international law issues. Bernie tried for a while to develop a practice in international law—I think mostly it was an excuse to finance some of the travel he wanted to do. Miguel is a naturalized American citizen, but he has family in Mexico and a lot of financial interests in Mexico City and some in other Latin American countries, too."

"Do you know how he came to use Kahn for legal work?"

"Bernie met Miguel at some function at the Mexican consulate where he was trying to promote some legal work and told Miguel we could handle any of his legal issues. In reality, Bernie didn't know much of anything about international law, but he would have me do computerized legal research in Westlaw and write detailed analytical memos that he used as the basis for the legal opinions he gave Miguel. I wasn't comfortable with it at all because I think law is so specialized that you have to practice regularly in the relevant area to be qualified to provide competent counsel. Even if you give the client the right answer based on solid research, it's too easy to miss some related element that should be considered."

"Fuentes is a handsome guy. Did you have any personal contact with him?"

"Not really. I guess he flirted a bit. I admit I thought he was attractive, but frankly, I've found extremely handsome men are often not very interesting. Anyway, I asked Terri about him, and she told me he has a beautiful blonde wife who stays home and takes care of their four children. That was certainly not a scene I wanted to interfere with. I never really found out if Miguel was inclined to play around or was just flirtatious."

"Do you know of any friction he may have had with Kahn?"

"He dropped our services quite abruptly. He called me one day and said he wanted all of his files transferred over to another attorney who was a specialist in international law. I didn't think much of it. In fact, I was relieved. I thought it was about time he realized that our firm wasn't really very well qualified to handle his legal work. That was maybe early March, not long before I left. And before you ask, Miguel lived with his family in the Peninsula area, either Atherton or Hillsborough, I think, but he always used his business address in San Francisco."

"Okay, Clara, this is a sort of blanket question, and I want you to think of it as a standing question until this case is solved. Is there anything else at all you can think of that I should know?"

"I'm not sure I'd recognize what you should know, even if I saw it," she replied.

"I understand. That's why it's a good idea to give me details whether they seem relevant or not. Sometimes a scrap of information may fit with something I've learned elsewhere that you aren't aware of," said Travis.

"I've been dying to ask you what else you've learned. Is there anything you can tell me?" Clara asked.

"Possibly. I'm about to make you an offer you can't resist. Sometimes, detective work calls for unorthodox methods, and I've learned to be creative. I'm sure you know the police use informants all the time, and I want you to be an informant for me on the clients Kahn represented."

"First of all, I thought police informants are usually sort of lowlifes who hang out with criminals. At least that's how they're usually portrayed on TV. But second, you know I'm bound by attorney-client privilege. I couldn't tell you anything about the clients."

"Okay, first you know better than to take what you see on TV as real police work. And second, I wouldn't ask you to violate confidential information. We were able to get a list of Kahn's clients from your office, and I'm pursuing other sources as well. But we don't have access to the client files because of attorney-client privilege. That's where you come in. I want you to be my eyes and ears at the office, and anywhere else you can pick up anything. It wouldn't involve any information about the clients' legal work, just peripheral information about them that could possibly relate to the murders."

"Since I can't violate client confidentiality, I don't see how I could be of much use to you."

"I understand you wouldn't violate any ethical obligations to your clients. That's exactly how I expected you to react. But you can look at internal client matters and tip me off to things I can investigate in other ways. Also, I think you're the kind of person who can get other people to let their guard down. Maybe somebody will tell you something they otherwise wouldn't let slip out."

That was true. Clara had often been amazed at the personal things people told her, and she had always felt honored when someone trusted her enough to share an innermost feeling.

But she also felt that she should never violate the trust of anyone who confided in her.

As she thought about it, Clara was conflicted at the idea of working with Travis and didn't know what to say.

Finally, she said, "What did you mean about an offer I can't resist—letting me in on things?"

This was the part Travis had thought long and hard about before approaching Clara. He had done a thorough investigation of her background and felt reasonably confident she was both reliable and trustworthy. He'd considered other members of the firm and decided Clara was his best bet—if he could convince her to work with him.

He also knew he'd have to provide her with a certain amount of undisclosed information about the investigation if she were to be helpful, but he'd still be in control of how much information to give her. Although there was always some downside to working with informants, he had a good track record of making astute judgments when he employed unusual methods. The department wouldn't even have to know because she wouldn't be a paid informant. From investigating her, he knew it wasn't money that would induce her to cooperate.

He could see the wheels turning in her head, and then he put out his best bait. "If you work with me, I'd have to let you in on some things normally not disclosed outside the official circle of the investigation. But we would have to make a pact."

"What kind of pact?"

"That's the rest of the deal. I'll tell you about other things I learn elsewhere to help you know what to look for if you become an unofficial participant in the investigation. But if you agree, everything I tell you must be held in the strictest confidence between the two of us, not revealed in any way to anyone else. And you would have to guard any information I give you just as absolutely as you would client information."

"Of course. I understand," she said softly, then hesitated. "But this is a lot to think about. Please go on."

Travis was pretty sure he had her hooked and started

to reel her in. "All right, here goes. This is the first installment. All three victims were shot in the head at point-blank range, right between the eyes, each with just one bullet from the same very ordinary type .38 caliber pistol. Kahn was shot just about half a mile from his house in Mill Valley, on the road near where it feeds onto Camino Alto that leads up toward Larkspur. We think the killer then drove up that road and shot the second victim, Alvin Hanks, in the parking lot of the Lark Creek Inn in Larkspur. Hanks was found in the driver's seat slumped over the wheel of his new Mercedes, which he had picked up from the dealership a couple of days before. The car still had that new car smell, in spite of the blood. The killer apparently drove on up to the Marin County Civic Center in San Rafael—you know, the one Frank Lloyd Wright designed. There he shot the third victim, Rinko, the same way. He was in almost the same position in his vintage Porsche as Hanks was in his Mercedes."

"Some of this was in the news," Clara said, "but it doesn't mean much to me about who killed them. You refer to the killer as 'he.' How do you even know it was a man?"

"Good point. We don't, and it could just as well have been a woman or even more than one person. There were no signs of struggle with any of them and no reason to think a woman couldn't have pulled the trigger. I say 'he' just for convenience, but I know it isn't politically correct, especially with you."

"You're forgiven. Sometimes I forget myself, even though I make a real effort to avoid sexist pronouns. That aside, what else do you know about the killer? And what about the Shakespearean quotation about killing all the lawyers?"

Travis frowned. "Frankly, we don't know much. I haven't seen many crimes with so few physical clues, especially since there were three victims in three separate locations. And the crime scene clues we did find haven't led to anything solid."

"How did the press find out about the quotation?"

"We deliberately let the news guys know about the quote from Shakespeare, in case it triggered something that might make somebody come forward with information. But we withheld the details that there were identical photocopies of the printed page where the quote appears, and in each case, it was found clutched in the victim's hand. It's usually a good idea to hold back some information, mostly because it helps in eliminating false confessions or even copycat crimes."

"Was there anything identifiable about the copies?"

"The paper was ordinary copy machine paper available in almost any office supply store. The page matches a paperback edition of *Henry VI* sold in bookstores throughout the country, including a lot of college bookstores."

As Travis talked, his voice was detached and professional, a lot like attorneys discussing the issues of a case. "What we know so far, for whatever it's worth, is that the murders seem to have been deliberately planned and methodically executed. They could have occurred within as short a time as an hour or so, but in any case probably within two hours, between eight and ten p.m. Kahn's wife discovered him just after nine, although a neighbor saw him go out about eight with the dog. Ms. Kahn said she dozed off watching television and was surprised he wasn't there when she woke up. She called a neighbor, and they went out to look for him."

"And what about the other two victims?"

"They were both found just before ten p.m., but because of the locations, we think Kahn was killed first, then Hanks, then Rinko. That allowed the killer to get on the freeway and take off for anywhere in the Bay Area, including the airports and points unknown."

"Do you think the killer may not even be in the area anymore?" Clara asked.

"No, not really, unless it was a hit man, but it's always a possibility. The odds are that the killer is someone who knew the three victims, has ties in the area and is still close by. Because of the close range, it's most likely the victims knew the killer well enough to allow him to get close without any sense of danger. They probably didn't see the gun until just before they were shot."

"You're sure it was the same gun? Have you found any trace of it?" asked Clara.

"Forensics left no doubt it was the same gun, but no, we haven't found it. Given the way this was planned, I won't be surprised if it never turns up. My guess is it's at the bottom of the bay somewhere, depending on which way the killer headed. Killers sometimes hang onto valuable guns, but thirty-eights are a dime a dozen."

"I don't know anything about guns, but I have thought about the victims. I've been mostly focused on Bernie, though. What have you found out about the other victims?"

"That's the main thing that complicates these crimes. I've been coordinating the investigation regarding Kahn, and other detectives are doing the same with Hanks and Rinko. They're turning up a lot about their families, acquaintances, clients, and other potential enemies. Hanks apparently deserved his reputation as a ruthless divorce attorney, and his clients often wound up hating him as much as his opponents and their clients did. He had a habit of making even a straightforward divorce into an ugly battle. He had only one ex-wife, who remarried — years ago and seems to live contentedly in Florida. He had no kids, numerous so-called girlfriends, and as far as we can tell, was close to no one."

Travis shrugged. "Rinko is generally described as a sleazy guy, a solo practitioner who eked out a living handling legal malpractice matters, mostly defending questionable lawyers reported to the state bar. He's never been married and was partial to one-night stands. We can't find any record of Kahn as Rinko's client, but a shady guy like Kahn might've used Rinko to help him resolve any complaints off the record without state bar discipline."

"So you haven't found any connection at all between Bernie and the others?"

"We've spent hours going over each other's investigations, but so far we've all failed to come up with anything concrete that connects the three murders. Of course, we've crosschecked all their clients, and they didn't have a single one in common, as far as we've been able to determine. The only things in common we've discovered— like professional memberships, for instance—are superficial. We haven't found any suspicious link. That's one of the main things I want you to look out for. When you go through client files, I want you to try to uncover any reference that could connect the three murder victims."

"I've been wondering about that myself," Clara said. "I tried to think of something, but so far, I've come up blank."

Travis frowned. "That's what makes these murders especially challenging—the missing links. Every murder involves a unique combination of facts, but so far, this case doesn't fit either of the two general categories. First, we can pretty well rule out robbery, random violence, or the like because it appears the attack came from someone known to the victims. In a different way, the missing link complicates the second category, someone close to the victim who had a motive for murder. The spouse is always a potential suspect, at least until ruled out, but in this case, even if Kahn's wife had a reason to kill him, what motive could she have to kill the other two lawyers?"

"You mean you haven't ruled out Charlotte?" Clara exclaimed.

"Not entirely, although we don't have any definite reason to suspect her. The traditional elements we look for, of course, are motive, means, and opportunity. I always assume a spouse may have a motive, even if I don't know what it is. I'm sure sometimes my wife could kill me, but so far she's restrained herself. The means, in this case, is pretty simple. Anybody can get a gun these days."

"But what about opportunity—Charlotte couldn't very well have committed all three murders, could she?"

"Opportunity for Ms. Kahn is slim, but not impossible. If she killed her husband about eight p.m., it's at least theoretically possible for her to have driven up to kill the other two guys and come back to 'discover' Kahn's body with her neighbor. And it's also possible she could've had an accomplice who did some or all of the killing. We don't have any leads on that possibility yet, and we also haven't found any link between her and the other two victims."

"I can hardly comprehend all this," said Clara. "I don't even know if I can think in these terms. It reminds me of what my first-year law professors kept repeating: 'Think like a lawyer.' It took me almost a year to begin to analyze things the way lawyers are supposed to. But I don't know where to begin to think like a detective."

"You already have the first qualification," said Travis. "Curiosity. You're obviously a naturally curious person."

Clara laughed. "Yeah, even when I was little, my

mother said she should've named me Pandora. My grandmother used to call me Meddlesome Maddie because I loved to snoop around the old stuff in her attic and basement. But do you really think I could be helpful in finding a murderer?"

"Believe me," said Travis. "I gave it a lot of thought before asking you to do this. But before you agree, there's something else I have to make absolutely clear. This isn't snooping around your grandmother's attic. There's a very real killer out there somewhere, and he's already killed three lawyers. You have to assume he wouldn't hesitate to make it four. You must not let a single soul know you're helping me, no matter how much you trust them, or how long the relationship has existed. Even your best friend could let something slip to the wrong person and put you in danger. I want your help, but I don't want anything to happen to you. I know this may sound sentimental for a tough old detective, but I have two terrific sons who are grown up and doing well. I never had a daughter, but if I did, I think I'd want her to be a lot like you."

Until he said the words, Travis had only thought about Clara as a useful tool in his investigation. But he'd seen plenty of informants get into tight spots, and he didn't want that to happen to Clara. When he'd read the background reports on her, the murder of her first husband and loss of her second, he'd felt a twinge of sympathy. It came as a surprise, even to himself, that he'd actually begun to care for her.

Travis had no idea how much his words meant to Clara. He would have been surprised to know she'd suddenly recognized what had been tugging at her since she had first met Travis. She'd begun to view him as something of a father figure, the kind of strong, caring man she had never had for a father. She was so touched that he might even think of her as a daughter.

She found it hard to believe that a paternal attraction had begun so soon, but she had a tendency to make quick decisions about whether she wanted to consider letting someone into her life, whether for friendship, romance, or any other reason. But this was quite a new prospect for her, and she wanted to give it a chance to see if it could possibly develop into a trusting relationship.

Clara turned her head away from him because she was afraid Travis might catch a glimpse of the moisture in her eyes. "Okay, Travis, I'll see what I can do. Where do we go from here?"

He cleared his throat. "I want you to start with the client files as soon as you can and feed me whatever information you can." He reached into the briefcase sitting at his feet, pulled out a flash drive, and handed it to Clara. "This has spreadsheets of all the clients and others we identified as having any substantial relationship with the three victims. It may help you in case you stumble across some information. Tomorrow, I want you to observe everything you can at the funeral. In general, just think like a detective. I suspect you'll find it comes pretty naturally to you. Let's meet here again tomorrow night at six. Then we can discuss anything new. But don't forget—your discretion must be absolute. And be careful!"

Travis made the last statement with an intensity that surprised Clara. She still had difficulty internalizing all of this as real, even after seeing Bernie's coffin.

സ്റ്റെ

Much later, Travis told her he knew she hadn't actually dealt with the violence of the murders yet.

Even so, he was glad he didn't have to pull out any

of the other items from his briefcase to persuade her to work with him. When he'd decided to approach her, he didn't really want to shock her into helping him by showing her the gory photos of the victims' bloody heads, photos still in his briefcase. Though he believed Clara was strong and self-reliant, he found that he wanted to protect her from any harm, even the sordid side of crime. He eased his conscience by telling himself that if she worked with him, he would be in a better position to protect her.

When he finally told her all of this months later, he admitted he wasn't sure himself how much of it had just been an excuse to look out for her.

Whatever his reasons, it had already been sealed by their bargain. He now had a novice deputy detective, and he was responsible for her. And when he dropped her off at the parking garage at her office, he waited until she was safely driving away before he took off.

એએએ

When she got home, Clara rode up in the elevator with Blake, who had just picked up his mail from the mailbox. She was on the verge of telling him all about her potential work with Travis when she remembered how strongly he had admonished her not to tell anyone she was helping him. She was good at keeping secrets, though, so even with Blake, she kept the conversation to superficial chitchat. She wondered how difficult that would be with all her friends in the days to come.

That night, Clara lay awake thinking about Travis. There was no question of her wanting to help him in the investigation, but she kept examining why. She knew it was more than just wanting to try her hand at being a detective, or even curiosity about who killed Bernie. After all, was there anything really wrong with having a father figure at long last?

Clara had always been introspective, but, eventually, she had come to avoid thoughts of her father just because they were too painful. He had been hypercritical of her as long as she could remember, with the criticism most intense during her adolescence. In high school, she had striven for the perfection that her father had demanded. When she brought home her first report card with an "A" in every subject, her father had sneered, "So, doesn't that school give A pluses?"

That became his standard remark with every report card, except the one and only time Clara brought home a "B" after having taken an algebra exam when she had the flu. Her father restricted her from all social activities until the next report card, when she again got straight As.

The constant criticism was about more than just school grades. It was everything: her hair, her make-up, her clothes, her friends, her room, even her "uppity" taste in music. He especially chided her for listening to the Metropolitan Opera broadcasts in her room on Saturdays, never aware that at first it had just been a way to avoid her father.

"You can't be a normal teenager and like classical music," he'd scoffed.

Clara had little concept of what being a "normal teenager" could actually mean. She lived in dread of her father's criticism, which was always worse when he had been drinking.

On Clara's sixteenth birthday—it was hard for her to believe that was twenty-two years ago—she recalled stepping outside her skin and looking at herself, wondering if she was really as inferior as her father tried to make her feel. It occurred to her that she could not recall ever having gotten through an entire day without her father's criticism, and she decided to try. By her seventeenth birthday, she had kept track in a journal for a full year, and indeed she had never gotten through a single day without her father's caustic criticism. Sometimes, it was a small matter, like disapproval of the shade of lipstick she happened to be wearing. Other times, it was more extensive, like the lengthy critiques of everything she'd said wrong in a telephone conversation with a friend. It was a long time before she felt at ease when she talked to people on the phone.

Clara had sought no solace from her mother, a genteel Southern lady—even though her Kentucky family history suggested some ancestors had fought for the North, some for the South. Clara had learned early that most of her mother's energy was required to cope with her father. Her foremost mission with Clara seemed to be to instill in her daughter the importance of keeping up appearances. Her mother's outlets were church and volunteer work that provided socially acceptable excuses to be out of the house as much as possible, since it would have been "unseemly" for her to work for money. Clara was pleased when, a year after her father's death, her mother had "taken up with" a nice widower from her church, whom she eventually married.

Coping with her father produced the side benefit that Clara did well in school in more than grades. She became emotionally dependent on accolades at school to counteract her feelings of inadequacy, and extra-curricular activities gave her an excuse to be away from home. She was happy at school, but at home, her only refuge was her room, where she could listen to music and read, mostly mysteries and "good" literature. She developed valuable coping mechanisms, the best of all when she finally accepted that she would never please her father, no matter how hard she tried.

That realization was the beginning of her liberation—she stopped trying.

Even so, she never fully overcame the insecurity that raised its ugly head at odd moments. But to a large extent, Clara's liberation blossomed when she escaped to college. Her father said he would not allow her to go out of state, but he relented when she earned a scholarship to the University of Virginia. It was glorious to be on the campus infused with the spirit of Thomas Jefferson. There was even a delectable irony in that history: Clara's father, a consummate Southern bigot, saw Jefferson as a slave owner and the university as a conservative Southern school. Instead, for Clara, it became a place of freedom and enlightenment, opening windows of her mind and doors into realms she had barely imagined.

By then, of course, she had realized she enjoyed learning. Besides English literature, she took a broad range of subjects and immersed herself in ideas. No longer inhibited by her father's restrictions, she made new friends who were bright and interested in the world beyond Southern provincialism. She no longer played the role of a Southern belle, which she had learned so well from her mother. If she dated a young man who seemed intimidated by her intelligence, she simply never went out with him again. That process was part of what had brought her to appreciate Steve and to know she wanted him for her husband.

She had decided long ago not to dwell on her marriage to Steve and especially its tragic end. Now, paradoxically, Steve was part of why she wanted to help solve Bernie's murder. She had always felt a certain void because Steve's killers had never been caught. Maybe now it would help a little if she could be involved in the process of catching another killer.

Whatever the reasons, she was committed now. And

it was a special bonus that she really liked Travis. Somehow, even the prospect of the funeral the next day wasn't quite so onerous knowing Travis would be on duty.

CHAPTER 6

Requiem for a Rogue

T he next morning, Clara went out to her balcony and found the bay and city shrouded in leaden mist. The little picture of today's weather in the *San Francisco Chronicle* showed the sun fully cloaked. How appropriate that the day of Bernie's funeral would be gloomy, the kind of day that had intensified his frequent melancholy moods. When she looked at the calendar above her kitchen phone, she saw it was still on April. She turned it to the next month and knew she had missed May Day altogether. It was now May second.

Clara had no trouble picking out her clothes for the day. Of course, it had to be the well-tailored black suit with the gray silk blouse and Tahitian pearls. The first funerals she had gone to as a child, those of her grandparents, had required quiet pastels for a child, but for her father's funeral, her mother had decreed black dresses for them both, with a heavy black veil for herself. Clara had not worn that black dress again until Steve's funeral, then gave it to Goodwill, along with other things too painful to keep. For Jon's funeral, she had worn a black wool challis dress he had liked on her when she wore it with a bright coral silk scarf, but, for his funeral, she wore it with the pearl brooch that had been his mother's. She gave that dress away, too.

Today, she would wear the basic black business suit, and she knew it would go right back in her closet with no emotional bonds.

At the office, she first took care of essential client matters and then began her search for anything that might help Travis find a link among the three murder victims. While she ate lunch at her desk, she compiled a list of clients who either had had fee disputes with Bernie or had dismissed his representation before their legal matters were fully resolved.

With her usual efficiency, Terri Hu had worked out a transportation plan to the funeral, and Clara would be giving a ride to three of the support staff. As she drove through the castle-like entrance to Cypress Lawn, it seemed more like entering a country estate than a cemetery. There were only a couple of cars parked by the chapel when she arrived. She had deliberately planned to arrive early to maximize her opportunity to observe all of the attendees. It turned out to be unnecessary, as the gathering was much smaller than she had expected.

When she entered, she saw Bernie's father and brother sitting in the front row, just to the left of the closed coffin, now with an even heavier layer of exotic flowers. Their expressions were stoic, with heads slightly bowed, and Bernie's father looked quite frail. Travis was sitting in an inconspicuous chair in the dimmest corner of the room, and the remainder of the office staff and a few others began to trickle in. Clara recognized several clients, including Dr. Andrews, who came in with a younger man she didn't recognize, and Miguel Fuentes. The room smelled of pungent incense, the same scent she had sometimes detected in Bernie's office.

A few minutes before two, the appointed time for the

service to begin, Charlotte and her entourage made their grand entrance. Swathed in black crepe, she came down the aisle leaning on her younger sister, who was wearing a black-and-white polka dot dress short enough to display her piano legs. On Charlotte's other side was her mother, wearing a floppy black hat and a shapeless dress of shiny black material. They were followed by Dr. Ling in a white robe and two young Asian men in saffron robes. The young men carried censers, adding to the aroma in the room, and placed them at the head and foot of the coffin. They began a somber chant punctuated by whimpers from Charlotte and her mother, now seated in the front row just to the right of the coffin.

Clara had seen Dr. Ling in the office a couple of times with Charlotte. Once, he had hung crystals in strategic areas and placed stylized pictures of eyes and hands around the support staff cubicles. Another time, he and Charlotte had a lengthy session with Bernie in his office behind the closed door. She had heard Charlotte say Dr. Ling had healing powers, but she had no idea what kind of doctor he might be.

Dr. Ling conducted the funeral service, unlike any Clara had ever attended before. There were more chants, piped-in music reminiscent of some she had heard in Tibet, and the semblance of a eulogy. Dr. Ling alluded to all sorts of lofty virtues that no one who knew Bernie well could possibly have associated with him. Of course, even a rogue is usually extolled after he dies. Those comments were interspersed with mystical phrases that were meaningless to Clara.

She looked around the room and tried to decipher individual expressions, but the faces seemed to be masks covering minds lost in their own thoughts. The good reverends in the front row, rather than reflecting the grief normally expected from a father and brother, seemed to show only a concentrated effort to conceal great discomfort.

At last, there was an awkward silence. Then the Cypress Lawn funeral director solemnly instructed the gathering about forming a processional to the burial site. The five family members and Dr. Ling filed out of the chapel into the back of a white limousine, which followed the black hearse, and Clara could only imagine the uncomfortable conversation that may have taken place during the few minutes' ride. Everyone else followed in private cars, including the two young men in saffron robes, who trailed incongruously in an old avocado green Volkswagen van.

Cypress Lawn was filled with notable San Francisco names: Hearst, Spreckels, De Young, Flood, Larkin, Coit, Crocker, Atherton, even Lefty O'Doul and Lincoln Steffens. Bernie's grave was not adjacent to any of them, however, but instead toward the outer edge of the cemetery. The graveside service was mercifully brief, the most dramatic moment being when the coffin was lowered.

As Dr. Ling dropped a handful of iridescent crystals on it, Charlotte cried out, "No, no, they can't put you in that cold ground," and began to sob.

Clara was jolted by an unexpected mental picture that popped into her head—herself at age nine burying a shoebox containing the remains of the dead parakeet her father had killed after she brought it home without his permission.

Charlotte's mother and sister led the grieving widow back to the white limousine, as others dispersed to their cars. Clara noticed that Bernie's father and brother lingered and said a prayer over the grave. Instead of getting in the limousine, they rode back to the chapel in a black car with the Cypress Lawn funeral director, presumably to their rental car and on to the airport for their flight back to a world they understood better than this bizarre California culture.

There was a little delay as people returned to their cars and waited respectfully to leave in turn. It happened that Dr. Andrews was in the car next to Clara's, and he took the opportunity to introduce her to the younger man she had noticed with him earlier.

"Clara, I want you to meet my son, Heath. He's a doctor, too, but he's a real one, not an administrator."

"Hello, Heath," she said as she shook his hand. "What kind of real doctor are you?"

"I'm an internist, with a specialty in hematology. Dad tells me you're a lawyer with Mr. Kahn's firm."

"Yes. Did you know Bernard Kahn?"

"Not really. I met him once briefly at Dad's office."

"It's generous of you to attend the funeral of a man you didn't even know."

"Not really. Dad's car is being serviced, and he and I have a meeting to attend. It's down at Stanford Medical Center, so the funeral was sort of on the way. I was also a little curious about Cypress Lawn. I've never been here before."

"Me neither. Oh, it looks as if the cars are beginning to move now. It's good to see you again, Dr. Andrews, and to meet you, Dr. Andrews."

"I hope to see you again," Heath said, with one of the warmest smiles she had ever seen.

He had perfect white teeth that set off a pleasing but not perfectly handsome face. He had thick dark hair, with the slightest sprinkle of gray, and it waved exactly like his father's silver-gray hair. Heath's eyes were dark chocolate brown framed by a few tiny lines that deepened at the corners when he smiled. He was tall and slim, wearing a dark suit and conservative tie. Clara was surprised at herself when she realized she was pleased to notice he wore no wedding ring. She hoped his "hope to see you again" was not just a polite comment.

It had been announced that condolence calls at the home of the widow would be appropriate after the funeral, and the funeral director handed out maps with directions. That translated to a command appearance, at least for the attorneys who had worked for Bernie. Clara offered to take her office staff passengers along, but they all opted to be dropped at the BART station instead. Bernie had never closed the office early, not even on Christmas Eve, and Clara certainly didn't blame them for taking this opportunity to cut out early. She drove on up to Kahn's house in Mill Valley, a place where neither she nor any of the other members of the firm had ever been invited.

The house was tucked back from the road, requiring parking along the roadway and walking the wooded path up to the house. Clara saw Charlotte's red BMW in the driveway, but there was no sign of Bernie's black Beemer. It was a nondescript house, not as large as Clara had expected, and furnished inside with the same overblown Oriental decor as the office.

In the front room, Charlotte sat on an uncomfortable-looking sofa, upholstered in garish fuchsia silk brocade, with her mother, sister, and Dr. Ling hovering about. The room seemed smaller than it really was because it was so filled with Oriental knickknacks. There was a fireplace with built-in bookshelves on either side, but oddly there were no books at all, only more bric-a-brac. A buffet table laden with food and flowers, brought and served by several neighbors, dominated the small dining room.

Clara knew Maura, Katy, Francis, and Terri from the office would be there. The other guests were neighbors and a few clients, including Miguel Fuentes, with whom Clara chatted briefly. Travis somehow managed to look unobtrusive, and Charlotte did not seem to acknowledge his presence. Clara was impressed with his social graces. He moved about the house getting the name and some identifying information about everyone present, and when appropriate, he merely said he had not known Mr. Kahn well, but just wanted to convey his condolences to the bereaved. She admired his skill in getting people to talk about themselves while preserving his own anonymity. Clara was sure he was also making mental notes of anything that might be worth knowing, anything he might have missed in his earlier investigation of the house.

Having extended her final condolences to Charlotte, Clara left for her meeting with Travis. She took a short detour off the freeway and stopped at a vista point to look back across the bay toward the city. It had remained gray all day, but the fog was only wispy now, allowing a hazy view. One of the charms of the Bay Area was to see a different perspective by looking at the stunning views from a variety of vantage points. Daily, she looked toward this shore from her balcony, and now she reversed the view. She couldn't make out the precise pinpoint of her home, but she could identify the affluent Pacific Heights neighborhood. She never lost sight of how fortunate she was to be financially independent, but often thought of the truth in the truism that money can't buy happiness.

She didn't quite think of herself as unhappy but rather felt there were things missing in her life, mostly someone to share it with. But for the moment, she was extraordinarily grateful because, for the first time in a long time, she felt she had something really useful to do: she was going to help find a killer and, in doing so, make the world a little bit safer place to be. As a kid, she had loved mystery stories on television and fantasized about doing police work.

She had never told a soul. Her mother would have thought it "unseemly," and she didn't even imagine what her father would have said. Now, she had a chance to help a police detective.

She drove across the Golden Gate Bridge, glad to be going the opposite direction from the commuters driving back to Marin. It was almost six when she pulled into a parking space, walked past the bland beige car she recognized as Travis's, and entered the inviting bar named Take Five.

She had barely sat down in the corner booth with Travis when Andy came over from the bar, greeted them, and put a glass of Pinot noir in front of her and tonic with lime for Travis. Andy disappeared as quickly as he had appeared.

"Did you learn anything helpful today?" Clara asked.

"I was about to ask you the same thing."

"Nothing that I'm aware of, I'm afraid." Clara handed Travis a flash drive with the information she had gathered. "I have a duplicate copy, and tonight I'll go over it and see if I can correlate anything with the lists you gave me. Is there anything else I can do?"

"For now, just be open to everything you can observe and let me know if you come up with anything."

They spent more time discussing the people they had seen at the funeral and afterward, but nothing concrete emerged. Clara was frustrated. "Shouldn't we be coming up with some leads?"

Travis smiled. "Just like a rookie. You want everything to fall into place right now. It almost never happens that way. One of the toughest things I had to learn about being a detective is the importance of patience. Sometimes, you gather a ton of what seems like meaningless information and then at last something clicks."

"Unfortunately, patience has never been one of my strong points. But I'll try. Just keep reminding me that patience will be rewarded in the end."

"I wish I could say it always is. In police work, most of the time patience combined with hard work pays off. But sometimes homicides are never solved. My track record is pretty good, though."

"Is that false modesty or true modesty?" Clara asked.

"I don't bother with either when I'm with someone I respect. And I admit, I wouldn't mind if you respect me as a competent detective. But I'd work just as hard if you weren't involved. There's a real challenge in solving a homicide and a terrific sense of accomplishment when you do it."

"I'd like to hear more about that, but I'm pretty bushed now. I just want to go home and get out of these pumps before I collapse."

Travis looked disappointed. "And here I had a dinner invitation for you. Tonight is the first night I've been able to go home for dinner lately, and Jo Anne said to bring you along."

"Jo Anne is your wife?"

"Yes, and she's really my better half. She's the only person I tell everything to, and I've told her about you. She wants to meet you, and she's a very good cook."

"It's definitely tempting, but I suspect she might be glad to have dinner with just the two of you for a change. Please thank her and tell her I'd love to do it another time."

Travis laughed. "Jo Anne will love this. You haven't even met, and already you're on her side." He gave her hand a spontaneous squeeze and then looked sheepish.

Clara smiled and squeezed his big hand with her small one. "I'll let you know tomorrow if I dig up anything when I crosscheck the information I have. You and Jo Anne have a nice night."

CSCS

As Clara drove home, she began to feel how tired she really was. When she stepped off the elevator, she noticed the door to Adrian and Blake's place was ajar, and she called hello into their entryway. Almost instantly Adrian appeared. "Hello, luv, how was it? Do come in and tell me all about it."

But Clara didn't go in. "It was the strangest funeral I've ever been to, but somehow that seems very appropriate for Bernie. It was sort of Eastern-mystical with touches of traditional. I'll tell you more about it later, but right now, I just want to collapse."

Blake called out, "Won't you come in for a bite? You do have to keep up your strength, you know."

"Thanks, but I munched on a few things at Charlotte's house, just to have something to do. I'm really not hungry. I'll fill you in on all the details later." Clara appreciated having solicitous neighbors, but they were mutually understanding about respecting each other's privacy as well. Once, in a discussion with Adrian about introverts and extroverts, Clara had defined herself as a "gregarious loner." He recognized this as one of those times when, after being gregarious most of the day, she now wanted to be alone.

Contented to be home, Clara slipped out of her black suit into an orange leotard and tights. She had a drawer full of them in different colors, and these were the brightest she owned. She did a few yoga exercises, made herself a cup of chamomile tea, and went out onto the balcony to look over the view she had come from earlier on the other side of the Golden Gate Bridge. It was getting dark now, and she couldn't pick out the exact spot. Even the surrounding city was mostly blotted out as the fog had grown denser. It was cozy to be inside with the lights on and a fire in the fireplace, even if it was only a gas log.

Clara's penthouse was unassuming and luxurious at

the same time. The living room was well appointed, with a distinctive, eclectic decor that reflected Clara's taste: soft Italian leather furniture in teal placed on an exquisite Persian carpet with the same shade of teal, mingled with muted shades of turquoise and coral. One wall was solid with handsomely bound books; another was covered with remarkably fine paintings, displayed as in a museum for their intrinsic quality rather than as decor. The third wall was the glass doors of the balcony, and the fourth was only a half wall, so the upper open space permitted a city view from both living and dining rooms. The kitchen was the perfect compromise between efficiency and spaciousness, with a small island in the center.

The hallway to the other three rooms was decorated with a Chinese silk wall hanging covered with embroidered butterflies in a spectrum of color. Clara's bedroom was light and airy, from the skylight during the day and indirect lighting at night, and because of the colors, predominantly peach with accents of aqua and turquoise. Besides the bed, dresser, and chest, there was a small alcove with a chaise lounge and a good reading lamp. The guest room, which was Jake's on his short visits home from college, was all in earth tones, occasionally brightened with a pastel floral comforter and pillow shams for Clara's mother's rare visits.

Clara went into the remaining room, a combination study and den. Except for the space required for the computer furniture, a leather chair, and a large television screen, the walls were solid bookshelves filled with books. Clara sat down and turned on the computer, then transferred the information from the flash drive she got from Travis to her hard drive. She named it Miscellaneous Household Expenses and buried it in a household folder.

Maybe I'm taking this cloak and dagger stuff too se-

riously, she thought, but what could it hurt to mislabel the file and put it with a bunch of others.

She made random notes on her observations of people at the funeral and other recent events. Then she spent a couple of hours manipulating data from the lists, her own and the ones from Travis. No matter what she did to the data, or how much she thought about the possible significance of the information, she couldn't come up with anything that even remotely suggested a lead. She was becoming frustrated and more than a bit annoyed with herself—she wouldn't have anything to tell Travis. She hated the thought of disappointing him.

A sudden tightness in her chest jolted her. No, she simply would not impose on Travis the features of her father. If Travis was to be her friend—or father figure or whatever—he would have to accept her as she was. She refused to strive for perfection for his sake, or anyone else's for that matter, and that would have to be okay— even if she still lived with her own residual insecurities.

At just that moment, she felt a jolt of another sort. The room started to tremble, and the lamp swayed. She had been out of the country during the last sizable earthquake in the Bay Area, but she had felt several minor earthquakes. It was always a little scary. This one lasted only a few seconds, but it was enough to cause one book to fall, the heavy *Black's Law Dictionary* that had been precariously balanced on the edge of the bookshelf above the black lacquer box. It came crashing down on the box, which shattered instantly. A picture frame with Jake's picture also fell, but the shatterproof glass was unbroken.

The room was still again, and Clara found herself automatically doing calming breathing from her yoga exercises. Within a couple of minutes, the phone rang, and she was not surprised to hear Adrian's voice.

"Everything okay over there?" he asked.

"I think so. A couple of small things fell, and I haven't checked around the rest of the place, but it didn't seem too bad. My best stuff is all anchored down. How about your place?"

"Nothing serious, but you know how nervous we get since the last big quake. That's why we moved out of the Marina district. Anyway, I'll let you go—I know you're tired—just wanted to be sure you're all right. Give us a jingle if you have any problems. 'Night, luv."

"Goodnight, Adrian. Thanks for caring." He really was a mother hen at times, but Clara found some comfort in knowing someone nearby seemed to care whether she lived or died. She thought it would be dreadful to die alone and be discovered only when the stench wafted out weeks later. *Am I really getting that morbid?*

She walked through the rest of the place and found nothing amiss, except a broken teacup she had left too close to the edge of the polished granite kitchen counter and a perfume bottle that had fallen over on her bathroom vanity. She wiped up the perfume, thinking it was a pretty expensive way to make her bathroom smell good and then went back to the study to turn off the computer and lamp. Her natural tidiness would not allow her to leave the lacquer box in shambles, and she began to put the pieces into the wastebasket.

She had hardly begun, though, when she saw something she had never seen before, a slim imitation reptile notebook at the bottom of the heap. Upon examination, she could see there had been a thin, hidden compartment in the bottom of the box that she hadn't noticed before. When she opened the notebook, she saw the familiar scrawl that had been Bernie's. The first few pages had some barely legible random notes about promotional ideas and potential clients. Then a few pages were blank, followed by eight right-hand pages similar to each other, each page headed by two large block letters, followed by a list of numbers in two columns. The letter headings were AH, DF, FM, FP, GM, HA, HT, MK.

Clara was stunned. She had gotten used to the odd sensation of running across Bernie's handwriting in the past couple of days, but that was all predictable stuff in the office. This was different. Why had he hidden the small notebook? Why had he left it in the secret compartment when the box was moved out of his office? Why hadn't he taken it out before he sold the box to her? Had he even realized it was still in the box? Was it anything important anyway? Was it just more of Bernie's big ideas? Could it possibly provide any information related to Bernie's murder?

Questions, questions, questions. She could still hear her grandmother saying, "Clara, sweetheart, don't you ever stop asking questions?"

She couldn't escape the thought that the little notebook was somehow important, first because it was hidden, and second because the eight pages seemed to be in some sort of code. But if it was really important, surely he wouldn't have left it in the box.

Clara probed her memory. The box had been in Bernie's office until about Thanksgiving, and that was around the same time he was all excited about his new upgraded tablet, which he took with him on his ski trip in December. Charlotte had just finished some redecorating in January, and the box had sat in the firm library for a while before Clara had asked if she could move it into her office.

It was possible Bernie had transferred whatever the eight-page symbols represented to his new tablet, and the little notebook had been forgotten in the shuffle. After all, his mother had died in the interim, and even Bernie might have found that unsettling. Besides, he was always juggling countless details anyway. His memory for detail was unreliable, as witness the elaborate schemes he'd devised for trying to keep himself organized. Even with computers and Terri monitoring his schedule, he still could barely keep track of things.

Clara was cautiously hopeful about her discovery and started to call Travis. No, it could wait. She hoped he and his wife were enjoying some time together. Besides, Clara had no idea about the significance of the notebook anyway. But maybe, just maybe, it could shed some light on the mystery.

Only much later did she realize that it was the key.

CHAPTER 7

Gender Identity Dysphoria

S he had a restless night. Clara normally slept without clothing, but tonight she wanted to crawl into a protective cocoon. She dug out a flannel nightgown her mother had given her. As she burrowed under the covers, she couldn't stop thinking about Bernie's notebook. She tried deep breathing, got up, made a cup of chamomile tea, and tried again to sleep. She tossed fitfully during erratic dreams in which she was chased by huge pairs of block letters that had feet, kept bumping into gnarled old men in saffron robes, and stood before the supreme court in her flannel nightgown without knowing what case she was supposed to argue.

Finally, she sank into a deep sleep and awoke more refreshed than expected, only slightly later than usual. She called Travis as soon as she got to the office and told him she had something to show him. She polished off some client matters in record time and was just returning a book to the firm library when Travis stepped out of Maura's office.

"Ms. Quillen, I'm just checking out a few details. Would this be a good time for you?"

"Sure, come on in my office." Clara had moved back

into her old office, and it was already taking on some of her personality. Instead of the Oriental prints that had hung on the walls and one of Charlotte's cheap vases on the bookcase, she had brought in some good etchings, a couple of her favorite plants, and an antique scale that was her stepson Jake's present for her graduation from law school.

"What were you talking to Maura about, Travis?" she asked.

"Nothing really. But I didn't want it to look like I came just to see you. I'll chat with a couple of other people before I leave."

"You think of everything, don't you? Do we really have to be so careful in this office?"

"You never know. The rule of thumb is to think of the person you're talking to as the guilty party, but never make it appear you think so unless it serves your purpose. By the way, you need a code name for me to keep others from suspecting we're in cahoots. If I call, I'll say I'm Mr. Powell."

"Any special reason you picked the name Powell?"

Travis almost blushed. "You're too young to remember, but it was William Powell who played the detective in *The Thin Man.*"

"Hey, you're not old enough to remember that either. But even if they made those old movies before I was born, I love all the *Thin Man* flicks, and I adore William Powell."

"So does my wife. She even has some of Myrna Loy's barbed wit. It's one of the ways she keeps me in line. Now, want to get down to business? What do you have for me?"

Clara took out the imitation lizard notebook and explained how she found it, along with every related detail she could think of. Travis pulled thin white gloves out of his inside pocket and put them on before examining the book carefully, holding it by the edges.

"I'm sorry. I didn't think about fingerprints or anything," Clara said.

"Don't worry about it. This is just force of habit. If there are any fingerprints, they're probably just Kahn's. It's what's written inside that's most likely to be useful. What do you make of it?"

"The notes at the beginning are probably inconsequential. They're similar to notes Bernie often made on legal pads when he tried to come up with ideas for business promotion, and sometimes he'd flesh them out as memos to chide us for not being rainmakers. It's the cryptic eight pages that I hope may mean something. The two block letters look like initials. The first one is AH, and I immediately thought of Alvin Hanks, the divorce lawyer who was killed the same night as Bernie. But none of the initials match the other victim, Rinko. Then I tried comparing the initials with our client list. The only one that matched was from a closed file of a client who died years ago. And I have no idea what the numbers mean."

Travis gave her a knowing look. "I can get you started on that. Over the years I've seen variations of lists like this kept for any number of devious reasons. The most typical are bookies and blackmailers, and I have a hard time seeing Kahn as a bookie. The numbers in the left column appear to be a reverse date—just read the numbers backward. The right column is probably payments. I would've expected a more sophisticated code from Kahn. This is pretty simplistic."

Once he explained it, the numbers seemed obvious, and even without dollar signs or decimal points, it was clear that the payments were pretty substantial. The dates went up to last November, but some stopped sooner.

"Since the date numbers are reversed, could it be that the initials are reversed, too?" asked Clara.

"Give it a try. You can see they're in alphabetical order by the initial that comes first, which could stand for the last name: AH, DF, FM, FP, GM, HA, HT, MK."

Clara retrieved the client list on her computer screen. In no time, she found three matches, AH = Andrews, Hershel; FM = Fuentes, Miguel; and FP = Fairfax, Pamela. Clara frowned. "Three out of eight still isn't very good. And I can hardly think of any clients less likely to have sinister characteristics than those three."

"Sorry to keep repeating a cliché, Clara, but you never know. The initials could be for them, but they could just as well be somebody else. You have to keep an open mind and follow every lead. It's too easy to miss something otherwise. And we have to keep an eye out to identify the other initials."

Just then, Terri Hu knocked on the door and came in to ask if Travis wanted her to arrange for him to talk with any other staff members.

"I'm just about through here. I'll be with you in a minute."

She had barely closed the door behind her when they said, almost simultaneously, "HT! Hu, Terri!"

"Could it be?" Clara grabbed the list of employee extension numbers next to her telephone. "That's it. DF is Davis, Francis; GM is Grimaldi, Maura; HT is Hu, Terri; and MK is MacLeod, Katy. The only one missing is HA. Maybe that one really is Hanks, Alvin, the other victim."

"Could be. You never know. Okay, we have a start, and now we have to think what to do about it. I'll see if the lab can come up with anything on the book. Meanwhile, let it simmer a while, and I'll call you at home tonight."

"Okay. I'll see what I can come up with. I made photocopies of the pages of the notebook."

"Don't forget to keep it well concealed."

"I know, Travis. You never know."

After Travis left, she had a hard time concentrating on her work and made little headway. The receptionist buzzed. "Dr. Andrews is on the line, Clara. Do you want to take the call?"

She looked at the doodles on her legal pad. AH—Andrews, Hershel. She shivered involuntarily. "Yes, please, put him on."

"Clara, I hope you remember me." The voice was not the one she'd expected.

"Oh, you're *that* Dr. Andrews—Heath. I thought it was your father. What can I do for you?"

"You've already made my day just by remembering my name. I'm sorry we didn't have more time to get acquainted yesterday. I expect to be near your office around midday, and I wondered if you might have time for lunch."

"Actually, I've already ordered a sandwich from the deli. I have a ton of work to do." She bit her lip and thought, *Say yes, you idiot.* "On second thought, an extra sandwich never goes begging around this office, and I could use a break, as long as we go somewhere nearby. Where shall we meet?"

"You name the time and place. I'll be there."

"How about the Boulevard on Mission Street at one? It's by the Embarcadero. Do you know it?"

"I'll find it. That sounds great. See you then."

She could hardly believe the flutter she felt. She tried to remember how long it had been since she'd had a date, even a casual lunch date.

Of all times to be wearing casual clothes. Bernie had refused to adopt Fridays as a casual dress day at the office, as many San Francisco offices had done, but Maura and Katy wasted no time changing that policy.

But maybe it's better than a business suit, she thought. She was wearing perfectly fitted taupe slacks with a soft silk blouse in a multi-colored impressionistic print, colors that complemented her shiny auburn hair and fair skin. Her jewelry was a simple gold chain and the gold butterfly earrings Blake and Adrian had given her on her birthday. *Yes, you'll do*, she thought. Still, she found herself taking extra time to primp before going to meet Heath.

The restaurant was crowded, but Heath was easy to spot near the entrance, and they were steered to the quietest corner. She wondered how he had managed that on a busy Friday. They ordered—a salad Niçoise for her and sea scallops for him—and began to chat.

"So, what brings you to Embarcadero Center, Heath?"

He hesitated ever so slightly before answering, "Honestly? You do. I started asking Dad about you after we met yesterday, and he teased me unmercifully all the way to Stanford. He said if I didn't ask you out I was no son of his. Frankly, I'd never try to match his charm with the ladies. Even my mother admires it. Anyway, I have to go to a conference in Los Angeles this weekend, so I thought I'd at least try to catch you for lunch before I leave. Am I babbling? I'm usually not so verbose. I guess that's a lot more of an answer than you bargained for, isn't it?"

She was definitely amused by his candor. "It's not exactly the answer I expected. I haven't been out much lately, but I seem to recall that most men tend to be a bit cagey about expressing interest in a woman."

"Now who's being cagey? Or should I say coy? It's hard to believe you haven't been out much lately."

"As long as we're being so candid, the truth is, I hadn't really noticed not being out much lately until you asked. When I thought about it, I realized that I just got back from a solitary trip to England less than a week ago to find my former employer murdered. Before the trip, I was working hard at my new job, before that law school, and before that…"

Heath stuck to a neutral subject. "You were in England? That's one of my favorite places, as you might guess from my name."

"I wondered about your name. I've never known anyone named Heath before. I like it. How did you come by it?"

"The official story, from my ladylike mother, is that she was always fascinated by Heathcliff in *Wuthering Heights.* She figured that was a pretty hefty name to hang on an innocent baby and settled on Heath. Dad's version is a little more risqué, something about being with Mother on a heath on their honeymoon, which was exactly nine months before I was born. Anyway, I'm glad you like it. What about your name? How did you wind up being Clara?"

"It has a literary history, too, but not as classic as *Wuthering Heights.* My father was a very domineering man, and my name is the only instance I know of when my mother triumphed over his authoritarianism. She was enamored with *Gone with the Wind,* both the book and the movie, and she wanted to name me Melanie. She thought Melanie Quillen sounded quite romantic and genteel. My father wouldn't hear of it—if the baby was a boy, it was to be named after him, but if the baby was a mere girl, he would allow my mother to name it, as long as it wasn't a character from *Gone with the Wind.*

"So she got away with naming me Clara, which was her own little secret. She named me for Clark Gable, but he never guessed it because she told him it was for Clara, the little girl in the *Nutcracker* ballet. When I was little, before I knew my mother's secret coup, I didn't much like my name, but ever since she told me the real story, I've been very fond of it. I guess I'm the one who's babbling now, and I generally don't like to talk about myself. Tell me, have you spent much time in England?"

"Not as much as I'd like. Mostly just around London. I never seem to have enough free time for travel, except when it's combined with professional trips. My work is pretty demanding."

"I'm interested in knowing more about your work."

"I started as an internist, and I'm on the staff at San Francisco General. As the AIDS epidemic became more and more significant, I became particularly interested in studying about its transmission as a blood-borne disease and, in particular, how to protect the blood supply. So I did specialty training in hematology and have been doing research, consulting, and writing ever since."

They continued talking about their work and other interests, as they nibbled at lunch. Heath looked at his watch. "Oops, I hate to eat and run, but it's nearly three, and I was supposed to be on a plane at four. I'm sure I can get on another flight, but I'm one of the after-dinner speakers tonight. Can we continue this conversation later?"

"Sounds good to me." They exchanged cards, with home phone numbers written on the back, and he walked her back to the office before heading to the airport.

As she entered, the receptionist grinned. "Have a nice lunch, Clara?" She giggled and added, "He's kinda cute for an old guy." The receptionist was a very young blonde, who never seemed to have a shortage of "cute" guys, mostly young and muscular.

Clara blushed slightly and smiled. "You're the expert. Did anyone miss me?"

"I'm sure they didn't. There's been a lot of stuff going on inside. Mrs. Kahn is here to pack up the crown jewels."

Indeed, there was a flurry of activity. Clara recognized the two young men who had worn saffron robes and carried censers at the funeral. Now in jeans and T-shirts, they were packing up the Chinese screen and the few good porcelain pieces. Charlotte herself was rolling up the scrolls that had adorned Bernie's office and the conference room. His diplomas and other items from the "vanity wall" in his office were already packed in boxes. Clara went the other direction, toward the firm's law library, and worked on some research until the commotion subsided.

When Clara ventured out, Charlotte and her companions were gone, along with the boxes and bundles. She could hear a buzz of conversations from the cubicles and laughter from Maura's office, where she found Katy with Maura. She could hardly wait to hear the details.

"It was hysterical," Katy said. "She came bursting in and announced she wanted to make sure Bernie's personal effects didn't get 'misplaced.' She ordered her lackeys to start packing up and said she'd be out soon to check on things. Then she came in to talk to Maura and me about the disposition of the firm. Can you believe, she actually tried to sell us the name 'Bernard C. Kahn and Associates' for alleged goodwill."

"You can imagine how that went over with us," Maura cut in. "Anyway, we haggled a bit over how to handle the office furniture and equipment and pick up the lease for the space. There's no way she could have any claim on the clients, but you know we'd never hold back on anything Bernie had earned up to his untimely demise.

We should be able to work things out with her lawyer without too much trouble. He had already called this morning and informed us that Bernie left everything to Charlotte. He seems like a reasonable guy to deal with, and I think he deserves a purple heart just for being her lawyer."

"Among the other benefits of our new law firm, now we can get rid of these stupid tables and get some real desks," Katy said. "We plan to decorate simply, at least at first, with just traditional, dignified law office stuff. Pretty radical, huh? And of course, the staff can decorate their own workspaces any way they like. They can even keep the crystals and evil eyes if they want them. For some reason, Charlotte didn't take any of that stuff."

Clara laughed. "Are you sure you can handle such anarchy? You may have noticed I didn't wait for permission. I already brought in some of my personal stuff. Then again, I didn't have as long to become intimidated here as you two did."

"Yeah," said Katy, "but I don't think we'll have too much trouble changing our ways. Starting this afternoon, we're going to try to let everybody off at four-thirty every day. And we hope to gradually cut back to noon on Fridays, if we can afford it with no cut in pay for anybody. Of course, we'll work as long as necessary to get the work done, and Francis has already offered to fill in as much as we need him for anything. He said he knows we couldn't get along without him, and he refuses to leave the office early."

"Do you know yet how well the client base will hold up?" Clara asked.

"It's looking even better than we hoped," Maura responded. "We've only lost a couple of Bernie's real old cronies, who are male chauvinists anyway, and we can live without them. And now we're starting to get a few calls about new legal work for former clients, especially from some of the sharper women who had figured out Bernie was a closet sexist despite his charm."

"Good for you," Clara said, as Francis came in.

"Everybody's gone but us chickens," he said. "Anything, in particular, you want to make sure gets done before Monday morning?"

"No, I don't think so," said Maura. "Why don't we call it a day?"

"Yes, quite a day and quite a week. How about the four of us going for a drink?" said Francis. "My treat."

"Thanks, Francis," Katy said, "but this will be the first time in ages I've had a chance to pick Jennifer up from daycare without having to pay late sitting charges. I'd really like to spend some time with her."

"And I wouldn't mind being home in time to give my husband a little attention," Maura said. "There's been a bottle of good champagne in the back of the fridge ever since I worked late on our anniversary a couple of weeks ago. I think it's about time to open it. I may even slip into something slinky."

"Then I guess it's just the two of us, Francis," Clara said. She went to get her handbag and jacket. But despite being exceedingly fond of Francis, she couldn't stop herself from thinking DF—Davis, Francis.

Surely DF must mean something else, not this dear old man, Clara thought. She didn't know how she could have gotten through the first couple of months working for Bernie without his help. Like all new lawyers, she didn't know a lot of things that only experience teaches, and she could go to Francis without fear of exposing her ignorance. He always reassured her, reminding her that ignorance was not the same as stupidity, and competence would grow with experience. She was so grateful for his help, and she liked him enormously as a person. But as she thought about it, except professionally, she realized she didn't really know him very well. Could he have some deep, dark secret? Could he be Mr. Hyde instead of Dr. Jekyll? Questions again. "You never know," she could hear Travis saying.

Being on the early side of the Friday evening crowd, Clara and Francis were able to slip into a booth at a near-by bar. Martinis were already flowing freely, at a special happy hour rate, and Francis was ordering his second one while Clara still had half a glass of Pinot noir. She had her car in the parking garage, but he would be taking BART home to the Glen Park area of the city. So she wasn't overly concerned about how much he drank. She also knew he was lonely and had no one to go home to since his wife had died sometime last year.

They chatted about the events of the week, with some special barbs aimed at Charlotte's mission to re-move the valuables from the office this afternoon, a scant twenty-four hours after her beloved husband's funeral. They agreed that it would never have occurred to anyone at the office to deprive her of Bernie's personal property.

As Francis slowly downed more martinis, his usual sharp wit gradually devolved into sloppy sentimentality. He began talking about ambitions never pursued and dreams never realized. He sighed. "At last I can be the woman I always wanted to be."

"You're getting sloshed, Francis. Don't you mean you can be the man you always wanted to be?"

"No," he said firmly, as he fluffed his wavy white hair and straightened the collar of his pink and mauve flowered shirt. "Don't you like my shirt? I would never have dared to wear it while Bernie was around."

"It's very nice, Francis, and I think we were all com-fortable being able to wear casual clothes today."

"It's much more than that for me. I've decided I'm going to come out of the closet."

Clara blinked and took another sip of wine. "You mean you're gay? I had no idea. But why didn't you ever mention it? Nobody at the office would have a problem with that."

"No, I'm not gay. My closet is more literally like a clothes closet. I'm a crossdresser."

Clara almost choked on a pistachio.

"Some people are even more prejudiced against crossdressers than gays," he continued. "But with me, there's actually more to it than that. My shrink's term is 'gender identity dysphoria.' I'm actually transsexual at heart, but I decided I'm too old now to undergo sex-change surgery. Basically, I prefer to think of myself as female. Bernie made my life hell because of it, but now I've decided I don't want to hide any longer. I really just want to be one of the girls."

Clara was stunned. Although Francis was in his seventies, he still had a good physique for his age and had always appeared very masculine to her. She didn't know what to say and sipped thoughtfully on her glass of wine that was now nearly empty.

He pulled out his wallet and showed her a picture of himself in full feminine attire, complete with wig and makeup. He was obviously pleased with the look, but it was all she could do to keep a straight face—he looked for all the world like Mrs. Doubtfire!

"I'm sorry, Clara. I didn't mean to shock you. Are you okay with this?"

"Sure, Francis. It's just such a surprise. Excuse me, I guess I should've said Fran. You mentioned that you preferred to be called Fran, but it never occurred to me there was any special reason for it."

"The truth is, I would prefer Francine, but I never

had the nerve to ask anybody to call me that, especially with Bernie around."

"Did you say Bernie knew? What did you mean about his making your life hell because of it? You always seemed to get along better with him than anyone else in the office did. You were the only one he would admit knew more about law than he did."

"I really hated his guts, and I had no respect for him as a lawyer."

"I had no idea. You never let on. Was there more to it than the things we all disliked about the little dictator?"

"Yes, I'm ashamed to admit. For a long time, he was blackmailing me. Of course, he didn't call it that. He referred to it as enhancing my legal services. It's the only unethical thing I ever did in more than forty years of practicing law. It was not only unethical, but it also totally violated the agreement we had when he hired me."

"What was that?" Clara asked.

He took another swallow of his martini and continued. "When I retired, I found I missed working, but I didn't want to be the responsible attorney on anything ever again. In fact, I never much liked being a lawyer at all. What I would really have loved was to be a legal secretary to be able to work in a feminine role. Bernie came across as very domineering, and I liked that. When he hired me, I told him I was willing to work as his paralegal as long as I didn't have any case responsibility. But I really fantasized I was an old-fashioned legal secretary, subordinate to the boss's every whim. In my mind, I came to work dressed like those nice prim secretaries they used to have in the nineteen-forties' movies, with a perky little hat and white gloves."

"So what was the problem with Bernie?"

"One weekend when my wife was out of town, I was dressed in my secret wardrobe at home when Bernie showed up unexpectedly with a file he wanted me to re-view that he needed right away. I opened the door only a crack to take the file, but he saw my painted fingernails. He pushed the door open, and you can't imagine the ex-pression on his face. I was in full drag—wig, makeup, dress, high heels, and all. I made him a drink, and by the time he got over the initial shock, he'd probably already recognized his opportunity. The next day, he told me I was to beef up every minute I worked on something from then on. I was to bill minor paralegal work under my name and prepare additional timesheets for him to submit at his higher rate as an attorney. He insisted I had to word most of my straight paralegal work to sound like Bernie's work because he could bill nearly four times the rate for me as a paralegal."

"After all the talks you and I had about ethics, I'm surprised you agreed to it."

"It wasn't by choice, I assure you. Bernie threatened to tell my wife, who had a serious heart condition. If I showed any signs of balking, he would say something like, 'Now, Frannie, you don't want to be troublesome, do you? How's your wife these days?' After she died, I was going to quit and report him to the state bar. Just as I was about to march into his office, you came up to me almost in tears because you were having trouble with an issue in the Vann case."

"I remember. You took me under your wing and gave me one of the best legal lessons I ever had. You looked over my research and told me it was valid. You said I should be more confident in my own ability and just ignore Bernie's demand for decisive legal precedent when it simply didn't exist. You pointed me in the right direction with the analysis, then I went back and figured out the arguments by analogy that I needed for the brief. That's when I started to develop the self-confidence to believe I could be a really good attorney."

"And I felt terrific because I could help you, just the way women are supposed to help each other—unlike the testosterone prone. That's when I decided I would stand up for myself as a woman. Instead of quitting, I went into Bernie's office and told him, in no uncertain terms that I would never again assist him in cheating a client, and if I ever caught him at it, I'd report him to the state bar. From then on, I did straight paralegal work. Just for the fun of it, sometimes I under-billed my time, especially when I did Bernie's legal work for him. And I kept on helping you and the other girls in the office. He didn't dare complain. I never expected to tell anyone about it, but frankly, it feels great to get it off my chest."

"And a nice chest it is, too," Clara said with a smile. "It's always good to make a clean breast of things, but take my word for it—it's just as hard to bare your soul as your breast in our society. Our laws are very sexist you know."

They both laughed.

❧❧❧

When Clara got home, the first thing she did was pull out the photocopy of Bernie's notebook and look at the entries under DF. They seemed to bear out everything that Francis—that is, Fran or maybe Francine—had told her. The last date was about the time of his wife's death last year. The numbers were different from the numbers under the other initials, significantly smaller, without zeros. It made sense that they referred to hours of phony billing, rather than amounts of money, which was probably the significance of the right-hand columns under the other initials.

She went to call Travis, but first listened to the messages on her voicemail. The first message had airport noises in the background. "Hi, it's Heath. I just wanted to tell you I really enjoyed lunch with you, and I'd like to try dinner next time. I'm not sure what time I'll be able to get back on Sunday, but I'll give you a call. Meanwhile, hope you have a good weekend."

She played it again and savored it a moment before playing the second message. "Ms. Quillen, this is Mr. Powell. I have a question about my case. I expect to be working late at my office. Please give me a call." She wondered who else he thought might listen to her messages. *You never know.*

She dialed his office number. "Travis," he answered.

"Sorry, wrong number. I was trying to reach Nick Charles. He's a charming man with a sophisticated wife."

"Nope, nobody that urbane here—just a plain old Oakie. How're you doing, Quillen?"

"Great, as a matter of fact. I have a piece to our puzzle, though I don't know how much it helps. But first I need to get something absolutely straight with you. You know I'm willing to give you information about possible suspects, but I want to you to promise to keep some things strictly confidential. You won't violate anyone's privacy, will you?"

"I can promise not to compromise anybody's privacy unless it's necessary to convict the killer. You have my word on that, but it's the best I can do."

"I guess that's the most I can expect. At some point, I suppose I just have to trust you."

"I'll try to earn that trust, Clara. Now tell me, what have you found out?"

"You'll never believe it. I can hardly believe it myself." She went on to tell him all of the details about Francis and Bernie's blackmail.

"That's quite a tale," Travis responded. "It looks like

we're on the right track about the blackmail record in Kahn's book, and the good news is it doesn't sound like your friend Francis had that much of a motive for murder. I warn you, though, you never know what will turn up in an investigation. That's why I'm still at the office. I've been digging deeper into the names we identified."

"I wondered why you were still there. Don't you think you should be getting home to your wife?"

"I always think that. I just don't always do it. But you've inspired me with this new information. It can wait till tomorrow, though. I have some ideas for you, too. How does your weekend look?"

"Pretty clear."

"So what about Dr. Andrews the younger?"

"How do you know about that?"

"I'm a detective, remember. Did you have a nice lunch?"

"Yes, if it's any of your business. Let's not get too nosy, Travis. He's out of town until Sunday."

"Good, then maybe you can do some more detective work tomorrow. Are you up for it?"

"Yeah, I think so. I can't imagine anyone could have a bigger surprise for me than Francis, though."

"That's what worries me," Travis said. "If one of the people on that list is the killer, I don't want you to be in for any big surprises. Do you think you can find out some more secrets discreetly?"

"Just try to stop me. Do you have any special order you want me to follow in checking out our list?"

"Who's the easiest for you to approach next?"

"Well, since tomorrow is Saturday, I could try Katy. It's been a while, but we used to go on outings with her little girl. She's a doll, but she's a typical two-year-old. It's easier for two grown-ups to handle her. I'll see what I can do."

"Okay, Quillen, but remember to be careful. And report to me as soon as you learn anything. Or if you don't learn anything. Or if you even have a feeling about something. Or don't have a feeling."

"You're beginning to sound overly protective, Travis."

"Clara, trust me. In this line of work, it is impossible to be too careful. Okay? Promise?"

"Okay, Travis. Brownie's honor. Sorry, I got bored in the Brownies and never went on to be a Girl Scout. I'll call you, even if I completely strike out."

"That sounds better. But don't be surprised if I remind you again if I catch you backsliding."

"Now that's a nice Bible Belt word. No wonder we're on the same wavelength. Don't worry. I'll keep the faith. 'Bye, Travis. Go home."

"Okay, kid. Talk to you tomorrow. G'night."

∽◦∾

Another Friday night. A light snack. A good book. A fire in the fireplace. A glass of cream sherry in fine crystal. A CD of Itzhak Perlman playing Beethoven's violin concerto superbly. Clara was content.

No, Clara was lonely.

Maybe playing detective would get her mind off it.

Anything but, she learned when she answered the phone. She was surprised because she didn't expect to hear Travis's voice again that night.

"Clara, are you sitting down?"

"Yes, but why do I have a feeling that's not going to help? What's up, Travis?"

"I wanted to tell you before you hear it on the news. Brace yourself. Another lawyer has been murdered, this time a woman."

The tightness in her chest was back again. "Who was she?"

"She's a deputy DA named Alice Garrett."

Clara took a deep breath. "Tell me about it, Travis."

"We don't know much yet. She was found in the parking garage of her office building. She was slumped over the steering wheel of her car with several bullet holes in her. On the seat beside her was a printed message in capital letters: FIRST THING LET'S KILL THE LAWYERS."

"That's a little different from the others. Do you think it's the same killer?"

"No way to know yet. I gotta go now, but I'll let you know when we learn more. But, Clara, take this seriously. Be careful and don't do anything foolish."

CHAPTER 8

More Secrets

Sleep didn't come easily to Clara that night. She couldn't stop thinking about the new murder. Was this some demented serial killer or something entirely different? A variety of scenarios ran through her head, and they didn't stop when she finally fell into a fitful sleep. She dreamed of faceless killers and guns and blood, and when she tried to run, she was unable to move.

When she awoke, tired and groggy, her first thought was about the murdered deputy DA. It was the featured story on all of the local morning news channels, but there was no significant new information to add to what Travis had told her the night before, just the usual banal comments from people who knew the victim. Alice Garrett, from those accounts, was well liked and respected for her diligent prosecutorial work.

Clara again evaluated her own role in the murder investigation. She wondered if it was fruitless to pursue Bernie's list, at least until some kind of link emerged. And, of course, she questioned whether she wanted to continue at all.

As she sorted through her thoughts, Clara finally decided there would be no harm in continuing more or less as planned. At the very least, she could help Travis figure out why the names were on the list. In the process, she'd help him eliminate friends who she was convinced had no connection to the other murders, even if they had an ax to grind with Bernie.

After coffee and a few yoga asanas, she felt ready to take the next step.

"Hi, Katy, it's Clara. Hope I didn't call too early."

"No problem. Jennifer was up at the crack of dawn. Oops, hold the phone a sec—No, Jennifer, we can't take Magilla Gorilla to the zoo with us. He's too big. There'll be plenty of animals at the zoo. Now go see if you can find your red tennies—Sorry, Clara, I'm trying to make a list of errands and cope with two-year-old logic at the same time."

"I guess my timing *is* bad. I was hoping we could get together sometime this weekend."

"Can I interest you in a trip to the zoo? Much as I love doing stuff with Jennifer, I know it would be more fun with you along."

"Sure, sounds good. I haven't seen Jennifer for months. And I've never been to the San Francisco Zoo. When are you going?"

"I have some errands to run first. How about meeting us at the entrance to the zoo at one?"

"Fine. See you then."

Clara treated herself to a leisurely morning. She made herself a mushroom and olive omelet while listening to Placido Domingo singing Mozart arias then took a long, warm shower. She hated the California droughts that made her feel guilty about luxuriating in the shower, and she limited her extravagant use of water to once a week.

It was a bright morning, the fog having lifted earlier than usual, and the weather forecast said it would be in the seventies. It would be nice to have enough warmth for short sleeves, even though that meant sunscreen and a big hat, which Clara wore faithfully in the sun, even though the biopsy a year before had shown the suspicious mole on her back to be benign. Her fair skin burned too easily for comfort.

Katy arrived at the zoo fifteen minutes late with Jennifer in tow. "I'm sorry to keep you waiting, but trying to run errands with Jennifer is like shaking hands with an octopus. She's been up since six, and I'm already bushed."

"What's boosht, Mommy?"

It was obvious that Jennifer did not lack energy, as she tugged at her mother and babbled with sometimes intelligible words and phrases. Clara was amazed at how much she had developed in just the two months since she had seen her on her second birthday. She was as beautiful as ever, of course—a perfect Asian child with glossy black hair and almond-shaped eyes. Today she was adorable, dressed in rugged overalls with a matching denim hat that had a flower the same shade of red as her shirt and shoes. Katy, in faded T-shirt, cutoffs, and sneakers was not as nattily dressed, but as usual, nothing detracted from her gorgeous, long, Cyd Charisse legs.

Except for their dark hair, Katy and her child had no other physical characteristics in common. Katy's complexion was fair, almost as light as Clara's, and her eyes were a startling cobalt blue. Jennifer was a delicate miniature, like a flawlessly painted Oriental doll, while Katy's long, lanky frame made her look as if she could leap tall buildings, no doubt enhanced by her customary air of self-confidence.

After years in the Bay Area, Clara no longer noticed ethnically mixed families as she had when she first arrived from the South, but she found herself looking at

Katy and Jennifer with fresh eyes. She seemed to be doing that with a lot of things lately. She now had the same feeling she had had with Francis—the realization of not really knowing very well a person she had thought of as a good friend.

The afternoon was great fun. They made no attempt to lead Jennifer through the zoo in any organized way, but let her imagination carry them along. When she was excited about the chimpanzees or the elephants, Katy took opportunities to educate her little girl. But when Jennifer's young mind flitted to the next thought, Katy encouraged her ingenuous enthusiasm. Clara had observed Katy with her child before and marveled at what a natural this single woman was as a mother.

Clara had some pangs of regret that she had never borne a child of her own, and she thought wistfully of her stepson in college. She could not love him more if she had given birth to him, and Jon had gone to great lengths to tell her details of raising Jake. She knew Jake loved her, but it seemed that he loved her more because of how she had enriched his and Jon's life than because of any particularly filial feelings toward her. She didn't really mind that. She was only two years older than Katy, but her stepson was nearly two decades older than Katy's child.

After over an hour of seemingly boundless energy, Jennifer started to get cranky, which Katy said was a clear sign she was tired, even if she would fight any overt attempt to get her to take a nap. Following a variation of their usual weekend ritual, Katy told her daughter they were going to the park for story time. They drove up the Great Highway the short distance from the zoo to Golden Gate Park, where they found a quiet place in a grassy meadow, surrounded by tall trees. Katy spread a blanket and gave Clara the privilege of reading a story to Jennifer. She had barely begun before Jennifer was sound asleep, with her mother stroking her shiny hair.

"You're so good with her, Katy. Motherhood agrees with you. I'm amazed that you can keep up with the demands of your job and be a single mom at the same time. It can't be easy."

"No, it isn't, but I don't regret a single sleepless night. I wanted so much to be a mother, and not a day goes by that I'm not grateful for this wondrous child. It's a struggle, though, to be enough for her, with the demands of work."

"I don't mean to pry, but do you get any help from her father?" Clara asked, knowing full well Katy had never made even the slightest reference to him.

Katy paused for some time before replying, "No." She took a deep breath, as if weighing whether to go on, then said, "I decided not to offer any explanations to people, but it's about time I told you. Jennifer is adopted. I've never borne a child, never even been married. Eventually, I'll have to be more open about it, though, because I think it's important for Jennifer to grow up knowing, not to spring it on her at some point, or even worse, have her discover it in some traumatic way."

"That's undoubtedly the right way to handle it, and you're such a good mother, I can't imagine Jennifer will ever have any real concerns about being adopted."

There was still a deep reflection of melancholy in Katy's clear blue eyes. "Yeah, I'm pretty sure of that."

Clara had a feeling Katy wanted to say something more, but for some reason was ambivalent about going on. The conversation that followed was the most awkward they had ever had.

Clara hadn't thought much about it before, but now she realized that outside of work, they didn't have much in common to talk about. She didn't share Katy's taste for pop music and sports. They had had long discussions about legal technicalities that related to clients, and occasionally they had discussed philosophical aspects of the law. Sometimes, these would be triggered by popular topics they had discussed in law school, like the OJ Simpson trials, or more weighty topics, like the role of the United Nations in the development of war crimes tribunals. But they had never discussed anything very personal.

Today, though, they seemed to be in some sort of approach-avoidance mode, and Clara had already felt that the tension intensified when they touched on Bernie Kahn. It was not the usual banter they used to indulge in when they spoke of coping with his foibles. During the awkward pauses, Clara thought about her inner conflict and recognized her own discomfort in dealing with MK—MacLeod, Katy. Finding out Francis's secret had been a surprise, of course, but it wasn't anything really disturbing after all. She was far more shocked about his participating, even unwillingly, in anything unethical than his being an emotional transsexual. And it was so like him, with his strong sense of integrity, to insist on scrupulously honest billing after he no longer had to be concerned about his wife's wellbeing.

But again, what was really bothering her was that if Katy had a secret Bernie had known about, it might be something far worse than Francis's secret. Worst of all, could it possibly be sufficient motive for murder?

Clara had always believed, no matter what the motive, cold-blooded murderers still deserved justice under the law. While she had no reservations about the legitimacy of killing in self-defense or in the defense of someone else, she had a hard time imagining any real excuse or justification for premeditated murder. She had often thought about it since she had decided to study law, especially as exemplified by some of the sensational cases.

She thought about some of the historic cases that had been discussed in her Crim-law class to examine the concept of justification for a criminal act. She could understand—and maybe even have some sympathy for—Betty Broderick's mental state because of the humiliation ostensibly inflicted by her ex-husband, but in Clara's mind that could never justify killing him and his new wife. Likewise, she could feel some sympathy for the Menendez brothers if they were as outrageously abused by their parents as they claimed, but again she could find no way to condone their apparent cold-blooded murder of their parents.

She also thought about the victims of more recent occurrences of highly publicized murders: the dozen people shot down in a Colorado movie theater, the twenty children and six adults massacred at Sandy Hook Elementary School, the loss of life during the dramatic manhunt for Southern California ex-cop Christopher Dorner, and the shootings at Fort Hood.

Clara thought about all those guns—and all the rhetoric about gun control—and wondered if there was any way America could ever become a less violent place. Even in the Bay Area, the beautiful place she had chosen as her home, how could it be that four lawyers had recently been shot to death?

There seemed to be no doubt Bernie and the other three lawyers were victims of calculated, premeditated murder. And even if Clara couldn't think of any truly positive character traits possessed by the three male victims, they had been living human beings. Although they might have deserved some appropriate punishment for their own misdeeds, she still could think of no reason their killer should escape the consequences of committing murder.

Clara had gone over and over those thoughts and variations on the theme since she had agreed to help Travis. She had read about the havoc wreaked decades ago by the Unabomber, Ted Kaczynski, and thought about how difficult it must have been for his brother to provide information to the authorities that could identify him. Could she be as courageous if she learned someone she cared for was a murderer? What if she did discover facts that would point to someone on the list as the killer? What if it turned out to be this person sitting on the blanket with her? Could she be responsible for depriving this sleeping child of her loving mother? Could she live with herself if she used friendship as a means of incriminating someone?

No matter where her thoughts led her, she always came back to the one overriding principle: the fundamental right to life. Anyone—anyone—who takes a person's life should have to take responsibility for the act.

As Clara tried to think of a way to approach the foreboding task, after the long silence Katy unexpectedly provided the opening. "Clara, did you find yourself in a way being glad Bernie was dead?" she asked hesitantly and then hastily tried to explain. "That's not what I mean, of course. I know that no decent person could be glad he was murdered. All I mean is, wouldn't a lot of people who knew him have been sort of relieved if he got hit by a truck or something?"

"I know what you mean, Katy. It's like a woman in a bad marriage. She might never seriously consider killing her husband, but she could very well wish he would be struck by lightning or fall off a cliff. Then she could have the dignity of being the grieving widow and gain her freedom at the same time."

"Yes, that's what I mean. Everybody at the office can go on with their work now. And we can do it better and with more integrity than we would ever have been able to if Bernie were still alive. I even envision a time when the practice is strong enough that we can do some pro bono work. I always meant to do some volunteer work for deserving clients, instead of always worrying about the bottom line."

Clara tried to draw the focus back to Bernie's murder. "I was just thinking about what you said, that a lot of people are better off with Bernie dead. Have you wondered who might have had enough reason to kill him?"

Katy looked away, across the meadow, into the trees. Her gaze drifted back to her sleeping child. She stroked Jennifer and then looked right into Clara's eyes. Tears rose, making watery blue pools, and in an almost inaudible voice Katy said, "I doubt if anyone had a better reason to kill him than I did."

As much as she didn't want to unearth it, this was what Clara had been digging for. As with the delicate butterfly she had been admiring in the meadow, she did not want to scare this moment away. Ever so gently, she asked, "Want to tell me about it, Katy?"

"Yeah, I really do." Katy sniffed and dug into her pocket for a tissue. "It's very hard to talk about. It doesn't just implicate me, but Maura, too. I was much more vulnerable to Bernie than Maura was, though. He controlled her with threats of ruining her career, but for me, it was even worse. He threatened to take my baby away from me."

Clara winced. "How could he do such a thing?"

"I'll start back at the beginning. Maura and I met at a women's professional meeting not long after she started working for Bernie. He still treated her like his golden girl then, the way he did all of us when we first started. She was glad to be out from under the pressures of a big firm and hopeful about doing appellate work with Bernie. Maura and I hit it off at first because I was also disenchanted with working for a big firm and was thinking about making a change. As we became closer friends, I confided in her about wanting a child and reducing my workload to be compatible with motherhood. I thought about artificial insemination but, finally, decided adoption was a better choice for me. It can be difficult, though, for a single woman to adopt. Maura had heard Bernie refer obliquely to assisting in some unconventional adoptions, and of course, I was very interested in exploring the subject with him."

"I know the adoption process can be pretty daunting," said Clara. "I can understand your turning to anyone you thought could help."

"Neither of us really knew a lot about Bernie," Katy continued, "except by then we knew that he seemed to go through associates like somebody with a cold going through Kleenex. His former associates had all been men, and we eventually learned that there had been some short-lived partnerships, too. Anyway, none of that is really very relevant. The point is, Bernie arranged for my adoption of Jennifer at the same time he persuaded me to come to work for him, and he got Maura to do all the paperwork. Now, here's the bad part. Maura and I had never done any family law before. We didn't recognize, at first, that what Bernie represented as fees I had to pay really amounted to the equivalent of buying a baby. That was an odious concept to both of us, but by the time we realized it, I wanted a baby so much that I couldn't sort out my ethics from my emotions. Maura had trouble with it, too, since she really empathized with my desire to be a mother. She and her husband Tony had agonized over their decision against parenthood because of the demands of their careers."

Katy paused again as Jennifer stirred on the blanket. "We actually didn't ever really face up to the moral dilemma, thanks to Bernie's devious ways. He said he could ruin both of us with the documentation he had accumulated on the adoption that implicated us in an illegal baby transaction, but made no reference to him, of course. And I was especially susceptible to his threats because he insinuated that Jennifer might be taken away from me. To add insult to injury, Bernie gave us a cock-'n'-bull story about the firm being on shaky ground financially and demanded a kickback on our salaries every month from both of us. Maura and I talked about it long and hard. We finally agreed that until she and Tony reached a point where they could pay off all of their medical and law school loans, and I could find another job to support myself and the baby, we'd just go along and hope for the best.

"We were pretty miserable, as you can imagine, and we tried to ignore the threat," Katy said. "But it was always hanging there, like the sword of Damocles. When we heard the news of Bernie's demise, the only tears we shed were tears of joy. We were both out from under financially, and for Maura, it had another benefit. She and Tony had had bitter arguments about the whole mess, and she says she already thinks things are getting better between them. It's been a real relief for them."

"I'm glad to hear something good came of the murder. And I really hope things get better for Maura," Clara said. "I only met Tony a couple of times, but I didn't much like him. He always seemed a little arrogant."

"I don't think that was arrogance. I think it was anger. He was really resentful of Bernie's scheme that kept us in indentured servitude. When I first knew him, he was a real sweetheart, and he and Maura seemed so much in love. I hope that comes back." Katy dabbed her eyes as tears began to well up again. "But we don't feel totally out of the woods yet."

"How do you mean?" Clara asked.

"We're worried that in the course of the murder in-vestigation, something might come to light about his hold over us. Fortunately, Maura has a good alibi for the night of the killings. She was at a dinner with Tony and a bunch of other doctors. But I was at home with Jennifer, so I could be a suspect if this ever comes out. I talked to Maura about it briefly, but it was clear to me that she didn't want to even think about it anymore. She just wants to pretend it never happened and get on with her life. I can't blame her, of course, but I really needed to talk about it." She shook her head, looking down at her sleeping daughter, then glanced up. "I just don't know what to do, Clara. I was on the verge of telling Detective Travis everything, and I'm still thinking about it because I'm afraid it'll look even worse if it's discovered. Still, I don't want to expose us unnecessarily, and I feel really bad about getting Maura into this mess in the first place. Please, Clara, what do you think I should do?"

"The first thing that comes to mind is that you've overlooked one big point in your favor. There were three murders. What motive could you have for killing Hanks and Rinko?"

Katy smiled for the first time since Jennifer went to sleep. "None whatever. I never had even the slightest connection with either guy."

"I admit I don't really know what the best thing to do is, but I think I'd be inclined to stay mum. After all, you have a constitutional right to avoid providing any incrim-inating evidence against yourself."

"I think that's what I wanted you to say," Katy re-sponded. "You know how open I am about most things. It's been so hard to hold this in, especially when the monthly payments to Bernie reinforced it as such a dirty little secret. Now that I'm free of it, I really don't want to do anything to complicate my life again. For the first time in ages, I'm beginning to enjoy my work again. I also feel that I can keep a better balance in my life and be a decent mother. I could even get around to having a social life. Who knows, I might find a good father for Jennifer eventually. But even if I don't, we'll be fine."

"That's what I like to hear. That's the most positive thing you've said since you started to tell me all of this. And you have every reason to be optimistic now."

The most important reason was beginning to stir. Jennifer opened her beautiful eyes, smiled brightly, and said, "Eye cream, Mommy?"

"Let's have some juice now," Katy said, "but I think we can have some ice cream after dinner. Want to help Clara and Mommy fold up the blanket so we can go get some dinner, Jen?"

They packed up and headed for a homey family restaurant. During dinner, Katy looked more relaxed than she had all day long. After ice cream, Clara decided it was time to head home and make her report to Travis. She was not surprised to have a message from "Mr. Powell" on her machine, saying he could be reached at his office.

"What's a suave guy like Mr. Powell doing at the office on a Saturday night?"

"What's a foxy doll like you doing at home alone on a Saturday night?"

"How do you know I'm alone?"

"Because you wouldn't be calling me if you weren't. But I know you want to know more about the new murder last night."

"Of course. What's the latest?"

"Sorry, Clara, but I don't have much to tell you at this point. We've started all the preliminary work on the investigation, but there's nothing very clear-cut right now. We're still trying to find out if the victim had any connection with Kahn and the other two guys. So far, we've drawn a blank."

"You'll keep me informed, won't you, Travis?"

"Yeah, sure, you know I will, especially if we find any connection with Kahn. Now tell me, how did your day go?"

Clara was hesitant to fill him in on what she'd learned from Katy. She essentially trusted him, but worried about betraying her friends. Finally, she decided it was better to tell him, as she thought it would be worse if he found out some other way. So she said, "Well, Bernie the Blackmailer rides again. I found out how he was putting the screws to both Katy and Maura, but I'm absolutely convinced they had nothing to do with the murders."

"I'm inclined to agree. You probably don't have to worry about them as suspects," said Travis. "I'll tell you why in a minute, but first, tell me what you found out."

"Same caveat about protecting their privacy?"

"Same caveat. And for the record, Clara, you don't need to reinforce it. I meant it when I said I will use your information only to find the killer and for no other purpose."

"Sorry, Travis. I just get very uncomfortable ratting on my friends." Putting everything in the most positive light, she went on to tell Travis everything she had learned from Katy, at the same time emphasizing her belief in Katy's innocence.

His comment at the end was, "That Kahn really was a piece of work, wasn't he? I have the feeling that whoever did him in had a very good reason, but I don't think it was your friends Maura or Katy."

"Okay, Travis, tell me. Why not?" she asked eagerly.

"Katy was right about Maura's alibi. All evening, she was with her husband, Dr. Anthony Grimaldi, who was at a dinner in honor of several promotions, including his own. There are plenty of witnesses. And Katy has a better alibi than she realizes, we discovered. We deliberately withheld details about the timing of the murders so as not to reveal any information in the wrong places, but Katy is completely clear for the relevant time. She worked late on the night of the murders and then picked up her little girl at daycare. The daycare worker remembered, and it's logged in as well. She stopped by a grocery store on the way home, and the checker remembered her with her daughter in the cart. One neighbor saw her drive in and park in her usual spot, and another saw her car there during the relevant time. Her mother in Denver said she called about ten-thirty p.m., an hour earlier here on Pacific Time, and the telephone bill shows a twenty-seven-minute call. So, because of the timing, both of your friends look like they're in the clear."

"You have done your homework, haven't you, Detective? I'm relieved, but I'm also impressed. I thought the idea was to find clues to incriminate the murderer, not to exonerate the suspects."

"The point is to find the real killer, not just pin the crime on somebody. At least that's the way it's supposed to be. And along that line, I have some other good news. You'll also be relieved to know Terri Hu is probably off the hook, too, even though she was also being blackmailed by your charming former boss."

"Really? Tell me more. What was her secret, and why isn't she a suspect?"

"I'll start with the alibi. Ms. Hu is a very studious young woman who was working on her MBA at night. She was in a class at San Francisco State, giving a presentation at the time of the murders. Get this—the subject of her presentation was Techniques for Dealing with a Dictatorial Boss."

"Oh, that's truly wonderful. She was always quiet and very composed. I had a feeling there's more to her than meets the eye. But I can't imagine why Bernie could've been blackmailing her."

"It had to do with immigration problems related to a couple of her relatives. Apparently, that's how she became involved with Kahn in the first place. Kahn hired her brother as a junior associate when he was fresh out of law school, and Kahn tried to get him mixed up in some under-the-table immigration work. As soon as her brother figured out what Kahn was up to, he quit immediately, but not before Kahn had learned about a few questionable immigration matters that threatened some members of Terri Hu's family. She came to work for him at a low salary to keep him from exposing the matter, and her family was making regular payments to Kahn through her as well."

"I knew Bernie was a jerk, but I'm still amazed at how low he would stoop. I'm glad to know Terri is in the clear."

"There could still be a problem, but I don't think so."

"What do you mean?" asked Clara.

"It's clear that she couldn't have killed Kahn, but it's still possible someone in her family might have arranged it. One of our Chinese-American detectives is still working on it, but it's very tough to investigate in Chinatown. Odds are, though, this will be a dead end anyway. We still haven't found any link with the other two murders."

"I get so immersed in thinking about Bernie's murder that I tend to forget the others. Have you come up with anything at all?"

"Not really. We've been on a few wild goose chases, and we've turned up a lot of unsavory activities by both Hanks and Rinko. Of course, we also considered an angle related to organized crime. The method of the killings can be viewed as execution style, though not necessarily. It could just as easily be an amateur who decided to do it that way for whatever reasons of his own. He may have wanted it to have the appearance of a dispassionate crime. The method can help find a killer, but sometimes it isn't until we find the killer that we understand the method. Also, the killer may complicate matters by planting false clues. I don't know if you'd remember, but the Unabomber did that."

"Does that tell you anything about the new murder, the woman DA? What about the method compared with the other murders?"

"It has a basic similarity to the others, but there are some differences. The weapon wasn't the same as the other three, but that doesn't tell us it wasn't the same shooter. There were multiple wounds, not just one like the others. And the quote from Shakespeare wasn't exact. It was printed version on a computer in block letters, not photocopied from a book. And it was found on the seat beside the victim, not clutched in her hand like the others."

"What does all that mean to you?"

"There could be logical explanations for the differences. Then again, it could be a copycat. The parts that were similar could've been from the news that's been released. We're still waiting on testing of all the physical evidence from the scene."

"So at this point, you're saying we still don't know anything very definite, do we? Shouldn't we be turning up some stronger leads by now?"

"Don't be discouraged, Clara. Perseverance is the bulwark of detective work, and we're still in the early stages. We're eliminating, or at least minimizing, the list of suspects on the first murders, even though the new one opens up a whole new can of worms. There's always the possibility something entirely new will turn up. You never know."

"Yeah, I know, Travis. You never know. So what do I do next?"

"We still have three names on your blackmail list to check out—Fuentes, Fairfax, and Andrews. I've been working on a lot of background stuff, but can you think of a way to tackle them on a personal level?"

"I'm not sure how, but I think I can come up with something. I probably can't do anything until Monday, though."

"That's fine, Clara. You should take a day off anyway. I'm even going to try to enjoy a little personal time myself tomorrow. Check in with me if you need to. Otherwise, I'll talk to you on Monday. And meanwhile, just be careful."

"Okay, Travis, sounds like a plan—or a plan to make a plan anyway. May I politely suggest that Saturday night would not be a bad time to start your off-duty time?"

"I was just packing up my stuff as we spoke. I'm outta here."

"Say hi to Jo Anne for me."

"Will do. G'night, kid."

"G'night, Travis."

ℰ∽ℰ∽

Somewhere in her head, she could hear Frank Sinatra singing, "Saturday night is the loneliest night of the week." Clara couldn't remember if it was on that wonderful old Sinatra album, *Only the Lonely*. Sometimes she thought she got caught up in a nostalgia time warp, even remembering things before her time.

Offhand, she couldn't remember the last time she'd had a Saturday night date, but whenever it was, it obviously hadn't been very memorable. Again, she reminded herself how fortunate she was. Certainly, she did not lack for any creature comforts. Even with her uneasy thoughts of the ominous new murder, tonight she was feeling a little less burdened, because it appeared that some people she really cared about were not involved in murder, even if they still harbored some heavy concerns.

Thinking about people she cared about, she realized she hadn't seen her neighbors for a couple of days and rang Blake and Adrian's number.

Blake answered. "Hi, Clara. We were wondering how you're doing. Adrian saw you go out today and said we should check on you. You know what a mother hen he can be."

"He's the nicest mother hen I know. It's been a busy week, but it seems to be calming down now. I was wondering if you two might be free for brunch tomorrow. We've hardly had a chance to catch up."

"Of course, we'd love to have brunch with you, but we already have plans with some people for the day. How about next weekend?"

"It's fine for me. Shall we try for next Saturday?"

"Yes, I think that's good, but I'll check with Adrian and confirm. He's deep in his headphones at the moment."

"Okay, talk to you later. 'Night, Blake."

"Goodnight, Clara. I'll talk to you tomorrow."

It was not yet eleven when Clara had finished her going-to-bed preparations and climbed under her down comforter with a good murder mystery. *Should I really be reading something like this now? How silly.* She had often read murder mysteries before going to sleep. Still, she jumped when the phone rang.

She had occasionally received obscene phone calls late at night and decided to let it go to voicemail. After the beep, a deep, pleasant voice said, "I guess it was pretty presumptuous of me to try to call you on a Saturday night. Oh, hi, this is Heath. I guess it was also pretty presumptuous not to identify myself. Anyway, I just thought I'd—"

Clara picked up the phone.

"Hi, I'm here. You do put a woman in an awkward position when she's at home alone and isn't sure if she wants to admit it."

"In your case, if you're alone, I'm sure it's by your own choice. But I hope you'll consider another choice. It looks as if I'll be able to get away from here on the noon flight tomorrow. I was hoping I could persuade you to spend some time with me after I get back."

"Yes, I'd like that. I'd planned to catch up on some things here at home tomorrow anyway. Why don't you just give me a call when you're back."

"Sounds good. I'll call you tomorrow afternoon then. Goodnight, Clara. Sweet dreams."

"Goodnight, Heath."

Another tune started running through her head. At first, she didn't notice. Then it surfaced to her consciousness, and she tried to identify it. It was from *The Music Man* and began, "Goodnight, my someone..." She could remember the tune, but not the rest of the words.

Clara was humming the tune as she put her murder mystery on the nightstand and went to the living room to retrieve one of the fine leather-bound books, one she hadn't read it since college. She began reading. *I have just returned from a visit to my landlord—the solitary neighbor that I shall be troubled with,* the opening line of *Wuthering Heights.* She read until she fell into a deep, restful sleep and dreamed of being on a heath in England. It was the first erotic dream she'd had in a long time.

CHAPTER 9

Romance at First Blush

Although Clara hadn't consciously thought about it, her penthouse home served the same psychological function as her room when she was growing up. Despite the seeming contradiction, it was both a spur to her imagination and her anchor to reality. This morning it was her safe haven, a place where she could isolate herself in her own world, a world that made sense, without any expectations or demands on her from anyone else.

She had always responded to the expectations and demands of others, especially, but not only, her father. Becoming her own person had meant that she no longer fixated on what others wanted from her, or even for her, but instead she listened to her inner self.

Only then did she realize that her own expectations and demands had really been the primary driving force of her life all along.

She knew it more than ever now because she didn't have to prove anything to anybody. Above all, although she aspired to be a basically good person, she did not have to be perfect—and despite her lingering insecurities, it was even okay to be selfish sometimes, as long as it was within boundaries she could live with.

She didn't have to work. She didn't have to contribute to charities. She didn't have to be kind, or considerate, or honest, or smart, or cheerful, or productive. These were things she wanted from herself because of who she was, not because someone expected them of her.

She didn't have to work for no pay to help her friends establish their practice. No one expected her to give up her free time to try to find a killer. She paid taxes for people like Travis to do that, people who were trained to know what they were doing. But passing up the chance to do this was as impossible for Clara as for a little girl to pass up a chance to go through Disneyland with her favorite Disney character as her guide. She couldn't pass up the chance to work through a real murder mystery with a real detective.

So here she was, not having champagne and caviar on a yacht drifting on the lustrous bay below her, not attending some tony social event, not driving a Ferrari in Italy—all of which she could afford without a second thought. Instead, she was sitting in front of her computer screen making up scenarios to try to fit the facts of the murders of three lawyers, one of whom she had come to despise and two others she had not even met.

She had been through the lists so many times now the names were becoming familiar. Travis had provided her with brief sketches of dozens of business contacts, acquaintances, relatives, and intimates of all three victims, as well as client lists with case names. She massaged the information and manipulated the data, but she still came up with zero.

Would she ever have entertained thoughts of becoming a detective if she had known how frustrating it could be? On top of that, one of the things she disliked about being an attorney was how much time she spent in front of a computer screen. And it definitely didn't help that coming up empty handed touched the nerve of those old self-doubts and feelings of inadequacy.

She had lost track of time when she realized that she hadn't even taken her morning shower. She could use a break, but she decided instead to start with a long, warm soak in her huge roman bathtub, which she seldom used. It would ease the stiff muscles that kinked up when she sat too long in front of her computer. She filled the tub with bubbles from a set of fragrant stuff her mother had sent for her birthday. After soaking a while, she turned on the jets of the Jacuzzi and luxuriated in the pulsating water. Complete relaxation was a rare treat. She finished up and washed her hair, showering away all but the herbal-floral scent that clung to her body.

Her body—most of the time she took good care of her body, but she hadn't paid much attention to it lately. She dried off with a gigantic terrycloth towel, which she then spread on the rack to dry. She caught a glimpse of herself in the full-length, three-way mirror. She paid little attention to it normally, except to check the final result of her appearance when she was about to go out, to make sure she didn't have lipstick on her teeth or a piece of toilet paper stuck to her shoe.

It had been a while since she had really scrutinized her naked body. She allowed herself to smile as she remembered her birthday thought—Not bad for thirty-eight, wouldn't even be bad for twenty-eight. She was compact and well proportioned. Her face was reasonably pleasing, and without make-up, her golden brown eyes looked even larger than usual. Maybe she'd never considered herself a great beauty, but her looks were quite adequate. *Yeah, not bad at all.*

She decided to use some of the body cream and splash from the assortment her mother had sent and was in the process when the phone rang. When she heard Heath's voice, she was surprised to find herself feeling a trifle self-conscious being naked. "Are you back already?"

"That doesn't sound as if you were waiting eagerly for my return."

She looked at the clock, and it was after three. "I didn't mean it that way. I just didn't realize what time it is. Did you have a good trip?"

"Yes, it was very good. I'll tell you more about it if you're up for it. Can I pick you up in about an hour to enjoy what's left of the weekend and then have some dinner? Nothing too fancy."

"Sounds fine." She gave him her address.

Nothing too fancy—good. She liked an occasional dinner at some of San Francisco's finer restaurants, but she didn't feel like anything formal and stuffy tonight.

So what should she wear? In her large, walk-in closet she surveyed her carefully arranged selection of clothes—sporty and casual clothes on the left, business clothes in the middle, and social event clothes on the right, all with appropriate shoes below and handbags and a few hats above. Within each category, her clothes were subdivided by color and type. She wouldn't dream of letting her friends know about her closet. She already took enough ribbing about her penchant for being so well organized.

The number of choices in each category wasn't large, even though she had clothes for almost any type of event. The section of the clothes for social occasions consisted of a variety of casual silks, followed by a few dressier cocktail dresses, then a couple of full-length ball gowns on the far right. She had always preferred being ready for any occasion rather than having to go out and shop for something on the spur of the moment.

Usually, she just went to the appropriate section of the closet for what she needed and picked something to suit the occasion. This time, she went through the casual-dressy section numerous times before settling on an aqua raw silk skirt and matching long sleeve shirt with an aqua-turquoise print knit top patterned after the lovely marbleized paper made in Florence. To go with it, she decided on gold and turquoise earrings and a matching ring she had bargained for in the Isphahan bazaar.

She started her usual simple makeup routine, with the goal of enhancing her face as much as possible without looking as if she were wearing a lot of make-up. She found herself taking more time than usual, though, outlining her full lips with coral before blending the peach. She applied a little blush and then decided to tone it down. The brows were left natural. She decided against eye shadow but added a touch of velvety brown mascara to enhance her lighter-colored lashes. She always tried to appear well groomed, but it told her something that she was paying such close attention to every detail.

From the lobby intercom, the doorman announced Dr. Andrews, and Clara said she would be right down. She had thought about asking him up first for a drink, but it seemed too early. Or was it that maybe it was too soon? For some reason, she wasn't ready to have him in her inner sanctum.

The smile on his face told her instantly that he was very glad to see her. He was wearing a well-tailored navy blazer—Brooks Brothers, she guessed—with a light blue Oxford shirt, no tie, and khaki slacks. *The thinking man's casual uniform*, she thought. They exchanged greetings and climbed into his two-year-old Infiniti. She was pleased when he turned on the ignition, and classical music played from a very good sound system.

"You look, uh, smashing," he said, stammering a little. "It's easy to see why Dad picked you as his lawyer. He always had an eye for the ladies."

"As much as I appreciate your compliment, your father didn't pick me at all. His professional liability insurance company picked our firm because we have a reputation for doing high-quality appellate work. I didn't even meet your father until I had already started working on his case. But he was a pleasure to work with, almost courtly in a way."

"That's Dad, all right. Even though he never pushed me, I've had a hard time living up to him as a doctor, but I don't think I'll ever live up to his genteel manners."

"You seem to do all right with your humble Jimmy Stewart style."

"Uh-oh. Is it that obvious? I thought I had my aw-shucks-ma'am routine down pretty well. Truth is, it isn't really a routine. When I'm doing things professionally, I'm confident, but I get a little tongue-tied with women. And I haven't had much practice lately."

"At least you do better than the old western movie image. 'Well, ma'am I don't talk much around women folk.'"

He started to drive west on Washington, past the Spreckels mansion and Lafayette Park. "I have a sort of loose plan, but I'm open to suggestions. Is there anywhere special you'd like to go?"

"How about the view from Fort Point? It's one of my favorite spots in San Francisco. Do you know it?"

"Sure. That's where Jimmy Stewart fished Kim Novak out of the bay in *Vertigo.*"

"A man after my own heart. So you're a movie buff?"

"You bet. You, too? What are some of your favorites?"

They had barely gotten started on the Hitchcock

films when they reached the marvelous view of the Golden Gate Bridge from Fort Point. They walked along the water, enjoyed the view from various vantage points, and climbed the steep stairs to the top of the old fort. Clara held her skirt as the wind whipped around her shapely legs, and she was aware Heath didn't fail to notice them.

When they returned to the car, she said, "Okay, that's my contribution to the itinerary. I'll leave the rest of the entertainment up to you."

"I can't top this, but it's not hard to find pretty places around San Francisco Bay. How about Marin?"

Until a week ago, Marin had meant little more to Clara than the scenic, affluent county on the other side of the Golden Gate. Now the word conjured up thoughts of murder and mystery. She hesitated only a second, though, before replying, "Fine. Marin's always great." But after crossing the bridge, she was enormously relieved when, instead of continuing in the direction of the crime scenes in Mill Valley, Larkspur, and San Rafael, he took the turnoff to Sausalito.

He parked, and they took a long stroll around the town and along the water. As they walked, they admired the scenery and chatted about the meeting he had just come from at the UCLA medical school. It was a preliminary meeting regarding some topics for the global AIDS conference scheduled for Vancouver in a couple of months.

They were near the bayside restaurants when he asked, "Are you about ready for something to eat? How about some seafood?"

She realized she had munched on things like carrots and celery through the day and was ravenous now. "Sounds great. This bay breeze definitely stimulates my appetite for seafood."

He had made it sound like a casual choice, but it was

obviously planned. When they walked into the Spinnaker restaurant, they were shown to the best table, overlooking the bay, reserved and waiting for them.

They started with a good bottle of Napa Valley wine and worked their way through appetizers, salads, and delicately flavored crab Newburg. In the course of the conversation, she learned the basic facts of his life, starting with growing up in Berkeley, then undergrad at Columbia, Harvard med, return to the Bay Area for internship and residency, and now the staff at San Francisco General. He had married his college sweetheart and divorced three years ago when his daughter was four. His ex-wife now lived in Los Angeles, and he had been with his daughter that morning.

Between the lines, Clara read twinges of guilt about not seeing his daughter more often. She studied the small furrows in his brow as she looked at the overall pleasing effect of his face, with his intense eyes and strong chin.

By the end of dinner, Clara had given him a brief outline of her life, but she really didn't want to go into detail. She was glad to shift their attention to dessert and coffee as they shared a sinfully rich chocolate mousse.

Before leaving the restaurant, Clara made a trip to the restroom and, on her way, was startled to see two familiar faces close together at a corner table. There was no doubt about it—Charlotte Kahn was very cozy with the inimitable Dr. Ling.

Clara was reasonably certain Charlotte had seen her just before she turned her head and raised her menu, hiding her face.

For a moment, Clara toyed with the idea of stopping to say hello, just for the fun of seeing how uncomfortable Charlotte might be, but she thought better of it. Even so, it was amusing that Charlotte apparently thought she shouldn't be seen, somehow giving more significance to her being with Dr. Ling than it would have had if she hadn't tried to conceal it.

When Heath and Clara went out into the night air, the fog had completely rolled in. It was chilly, making it perfectly natural for him to put his arm around her and pull her close to him as they walked to the car. On the way, they passed the bright red BMW that Clara recognized as Charlotte's, unmistakable with her vanity license plate, *4 RE C ME*. Clara wondered if Charlotte would be expanding her work in real estate or doing something else now that her life had changed so drastically. Charlotte had been vague about any future plans.

When they reached Heath's car, Clara was beginning to feel comfortable with his arm around her waist, but she was almost relieved to fasten her seatbelt and begin chattering about music. It turned out that in the past season he'd had tickets to the symphony and she'd had season tickets to the opera, and the conversation remained impersonal. Heath noticed.

They had reached the San Francisco side of the Golden Gate Bridge when his cell phone went off. "Damn," he said as he looked at the call number, then answered and listened intently. "Are you sure? Okay, just keep monitoring the vital signs. I'll be there soon."

Before he could say anything, Clara said, "Do you need to drop me nearby? I can get a cab home."

"No, it's not that urgent. But I'm sorry. I really do have to go to the hospital. We still have a lot to talk about. When can we continue the conversation?"

She had been thinking about it on and off all evening. Heath was the first man she had really been attracted to in a long time, and she was feeling very unsure of herself. He had to be aware of her lengthy pause before she replied, "Could we sort of take it slow and easy? I don't want us to run out of conversation too soon."

He got the message.

When he pulled in front of her building, he started to get out, but she said, "No, don't bother. You need to get to your patient." She turned to open her door but didn't resist when he took her hand and pulled gently. She leaned close enough for a light goodnight kiss on the lips. She hurried inside, but looked back through the intricate grillwork of the front door and watched him drive away.

She wondered if he felt the same lingering sensation of their lips touching, as soft as the wings of a butterfly. The kiss was so fleeting, she had to stop and think to make sure it was real and not just wishful thinking.

She would have been disappointed if she'd known that the closer he got to the hospital, the more his feeling faded, and by the time he pulled into his reserved parking place, it was completely displaced by his professional persona. Heath was again Dr. Andrews.

❧❦❧

Clara didn't want to think about anything that night. She didn't want to listen to music or read, but she wasn't quite ready to go to sleep either. She took off her clothes, climbed into bed, and reached for the remote control of the television set. She watched a couple of minutes of headline news, then surfed around the channels and stopped abruptly on TCM, her favorite channel for old movies. There he was, Robert Preston in *The Music Man,* bounding into River City to con the local folks with his imaginary marching band.

Good, she thought. She wouldn't have to think any-more tonight—about whether she wanted to become in-volved with a man again, whether she was doing the right thing in helping Travis, or anything else that she didn't want to deal with right now. She had started going to movies early in life with her mother and realized only much later that her mother used movies as a way to escape an emotionally abusive husband, much like the waitress in *The Purple Rose of Cairo.*

Without realizing it, Clara had taken advantage of the same sublimation to avoid unpleasantness or pain, or sometimes to postpone making a decision she didn't want to face. Whenever she didn't want to think about her real world, she submerged herself in a movie world, which had become much easier with the advent of DVDs, streaming videos, and cable television.

She set the timer on the television set, hoping she would fall asleep by the time the movie was over. She had begun to doze when Shirley Jones was singing "Goodnight, my someone, Goodnight, my love" and barely heard the rest of the words she had tried to remember just the night before.

She was sound asleep, and the television timer had clicked off before the seventy-six glorious trombones led the big parade.

⌘⌘⌘

On Monday morning, Maura provided Clara with the perfect opportunity to approach Miguel Fuentes. She explained to Clara the legal problem that concerned him.

"Fuentes was involved in a lawsuit with a result that may be a proper case for appeal. I had a call from the trial counsel on the case who was a fellow student of mine in law school. He's exploring the possibility of appealing the decision on Fuentes's behalf, and he called me for advice on some fine points of procedure and the feasibility of success on appeal. I'm up to my eyebrows in the work we already have. How would you like the experience of evaluating a new appeal? If you can do the legwork on it, I can help you evaluate the options for appealable issues."

"Sure, I'd like to work on an appeal from the ground up. Is it an interesting case?"

"The case itself is a pretty ordinary business dispute, but the judgment is for a fairly substantial sum of money, almost half a million dollars. What makes it interesting is that the potential issues for appeal involve alleged jury misconduct."

Clara would have been interested in the legal issues anyway, but of course, she had her own reasons for wanting to have a good excuse to get together with Miguel Fuentes.

Maura filled her in on the details. "In a ten-to-two split verdict, the jury decided in favor of Fuentes in a dispute with his former business partner. After the trial, counsel for the losing party learned from the two disgruntled jurors who'd voted against Fuentes that there'd been some questionable activities in the jury room that might have constituted jury misconduct. This was disputed when the other jurors were questioned. They claimed the two dissenters were just biased against Fuentes because he was Hispanic and that there'd been no misconduct in the course of the deliberations.

"But the losing party brought a motion for a new trial based on jury misconduct, and it was granted by the trial judge," she continued. "So, of course, it could be much to Fuentes's advantage if he could successfully appeal that decision, in order to avoid another trial and enable the verdict to stand. Because the judgment in favor of Fuentes is sizeable, it is well worth considering an appeal to preserve that judgment if the chances of success on appeal are good. What you need to do is get all of the juror affidavits and try to determine what the real issues are, based on the facts as alleged in the affidavits. Then

you'll have to research the current law on jury misconduct to see if the alleged activity amounts to jury misconduct as the California courts have interpreted the statutory
law. Do you think you'd like to handle it?"

"Sure," Clara replied. "It's the kind of thing I like to
sink my teeth into."

"I was pretty sure you'd like to do this, but there's a
preliminary snag. When my friend called with his questions about appellate procedure, he didn't know we had
represented Miguel Fuentes before in other matters. He
asked about any prior representation, as Fuentes would,
of course, have to agree to our associating in as appellate
counsel. I told him I wasn't sure why Fuentes had ceased
using the firm, but he had no objection to our contacting
Fuentes about the possibility of an appeal. I know you did
some work on his file. Do you know of any problems
about the prior representation?"

"Not really," Clara responded. "About the only thing
I did was some research in international law, and I wrote
some legal memos based on what I found. I met him a
couple of times, but Bernie had most of the direct client
contact with Fuentes. So far as I know, it had nothing to
do with this current lawsuit."

"Okay, then this will also give you some good client
contact experience. Before we start any research or analysis of the appeal, you'll need to find out if Fuentes is
agreeable to using our services as appellate counsel. If he
agrees, you should get him to sign our standard retainer
agreement to that effect. Then you can go ahead with the
evaluation of the appeal. Do your best to let him know
what to expect, like how much time it'll take, and, therefore, what our fees are likely to be."

Clara nodded. "Since this will be my first experience
with evaluating the validity of the appeal, I assume I can

count on you to check my work to be sure my advice is sound."

"Of course. I think you can handle this on your own, but until you've done a few of these, you'll always have the benefit of my experience. The client won't be charged for that because it's just part of the business expense of developing expertise in a new attorney. You should also feel free to consult Francis and use his paralegal services as well. That's another way to take advantage of his vast experience, but keep the cost low for the client."

"Okay, I think I have my marching orders. I'll call Fuentes."

Miguel Fuentes was as receptive on the phone as Clara could have hoped. She explained to him the importance of considering an appeal of the new trial order, and he readily agreed to come in the next morning to go into more detail.

As soon as the appointment was set, Clara called Travis to let him know. "That's great," he said. "We definitely need to find out more about his relationship with Kahn. Do you think you can parlay this into getting more information?"

"Probably, but now I'm faced with a new ethical dilemma. If he agrees to my working on the evaluation of the appeal, I should have plenty of excuses to talk with him as I report on my progress. But the problem is, as his lawyer, I doubt that I can ethically divulge any information I gain in the course of my legal representation if it implicates him in the murders."

"You worry too much, Quillen. Just go along and see how things develop. If you reach a point you have to pull back, you'll do the right thing."

"I like to think so. I guess I just have to take it a step at a time. But I can't forget memorizing one of the duties of an attorney under the California Code: 'To maintain inviolate the confidence, and at every peril to himself or herself to preserve the secrets, of his or her client.' It's almost like a mantra to me."

"Okay, I'm forewarned that you may bow out. Any other nagging doubts?"

"It's more in the category of something I've been wondering about. I've been thinking about the fact that you let me go ahead and probe things about Maura and Katy when you already were pretty sure they were in the clear because of their alibis. Why did you do that?"

"It wasn't meant to mislead you. I thought it was important to pursue the blackmail theory after what you learned about Francis Davis. I thought maybe if you knew up front that Maura and Katy had good alibis, you might not dig quite as hard."

"In other words, you were manipulating me?"

"No—not that I'm above manipulating anyone if it helps catch a killer. In your case, I meant it more as maximizing your effectiveness."

"Okay, I agreed to do what I could to help. I guess I'll just have to trust your methods."

"My methods vary according to the demands of the situation, but you can trust me that we're essentially working toward the same goal."

"I hope you're not implying that the end always justifies the means," Clara said earnestly.

"No, never. The end always has to be a valid goal, but, once in a blue moon, the price is too high to reach it. So far, that hasn't been a problem in this case. Routine deception is pretty much par for the course, though."

"I'm beginning to get used to that, up to a point. I think I can live with a modicum of deception, as long as I don't wind up with some kind of ethical dilemma. I guess I'm just trying to look out for that."

"Sometimes you think too much, Quillen. But then

again, that's not always a bad thing. Anyway, try to find out if Kahn knew some incriminating secret about Fuentes. And for whatever it's worth, Fuentes does not have a solid alibi for the time of the murders."

"Oh…" was all she could say.

"Good luck, Clara. And don't forget to be careful."

"You're starting to sound like the duty sergeant on the old *Hill Street Blues* series. He always ended the morning briefing with something like 'Let's be careful out there.'"

"Yeah, Esterhaus was his name, I think. I liked that character. Anyway, goodbye, for now, kid. Be careful out there."

"Don't worry. Travis, I will."

ৎৠৎৠ

Clara put the Fuentes file in her briefcase and headed for the parking garage. Before she got into her car, she reached out to remove a piece of paper lodged under the windshield wiper. *Probably for Chinese takeout or pizza.*

She began to shake as she read the message printed in large bold Comic Sans MS font.

Keep your nose out of where it doesn't belong, or there will be another dead lady lawyer.

CHAPTER 10

Marital Malady

Clara knew she had to call Travis, and the immediate question was whether to call him now or later. She took a quick look around her, saw no one, and decided to get out of there as soon as she could. She kept looking in her rearview mirror as she drove, thinking of all those movies with somebody tailing somebody else.

How the hell do you know if the car behind you, or the one a couple of lengths back, is tailing you?

She was still shaking when she pulled into the parking garage in her own building. She didn't want to get out of her car, but she didn't want to stay in the garage either. Everything looked normal, and, finally, she grabbed her briefcase, impatiently waited for the elevator, and soon locked herself in her own place. But she didn't feel safe.

Travis picked up after the first ring, and she breathlessly told him about the note. He responded in calm, measured tones, not revealing to her more than professional concern. "You're right to be scared, Clara. You'd be a fool if you weren't. Somebody must've seen us together. It could be a sick joke, but probably not."

"Do you really think I'm in danger, Travis?"

"I'm not gonna sugarcoat this. It doesn't look good.

When I told you to be careful, I didn't expect this. I was just being cautious. But now it looks like somebody thinks you're snooping into areas where he doesn't want you to snoop."

"But that sounds like there's all the more reason I should snoop. It really looks like somebody thinks I'm onto something."

"Maybe so, Clara, but you can't always tell what this kind of stuff means. One thing it means, though, is it may be a real threat, and you should consider cutting yourself off from me. In fact, that's what I advise you to do. As of now, you're off the case, Clara."

"I'm not sure I want to be off the case. Remember I told you my mother said she should've named me Pandora. I feel better knowing than not knowing, even if knowing is scary."

"I guess that doesn't surprise me. There's also the argument that if we keep in close touch, I'll be in a better position to know what kind of threat you may be facing. Meanwhile, though, we should minimize our face-to-face contact and make sure we're especially cautious if we do meet."

"Yeah, that makes sense. If I'm being watched, I should try to look like I'm just sticking to routine activities."

"We should keep in touch mostly by phone, but not e-mail—too easy to hack in. And I can see you at the office and tie it in with the routine investigation. I'll do that in the morning when I come by to pick up the note that was on your car. It probably won't tell us anything, but I'll see what the lab says."

"Okay, Travis. If nothing else, I'll feel better if I think I'm contributing to winding this up sooner rather than later."

"Just don't forget. Anytime you want to get off this

merry-go-round, all you have to do is say the word. You don't owe me or anybody else…"

"Got it. But for now, I'm still in."

ભ૭ભ૭

"Come in, Mr. Fuentes. It's nice to see you again, but I'm sorry it's because your trial resulted in more legal complications."

"Please do not be so formal. Call me Miguel."

"Of course. First names are easier. And I'm Clara."

She suddenly realized, although she thought she was just being professional, the real reason for the formality was that Miguel was even more attractive than she remembered. Even though she had seen him at the various funeral rituals for Bernie, she had been so distracted by other thoughts that his animal magnetism hadn't really registered.

As he sat across from her now, well mannered and well dressed, as usual, she observed his classic good looks, the epitome of tall, dark, and handsome. More than that, he had the imposing carriage and grace of a matador. She could almost imagine him in a suit of lights, ready to meet the bull.

Get a grip, she reminded herself. *You have work to do for the firm, and you have work to do for Travis. Besides, he's married and has kids*. She couldn't help wondering if Heath had stimulated some long dormant hormones.

She adopted a tone of friendly professionalism. Fuentes was receptive to the idea of an appeal.

"I hated the whole unpleasantness with my former business partner. It was such a shock when the man I had considered a friend, as well as a partner, refused every attempt to work out our differences agreeably," he explained. "I am not litigious by nature. I could hardly believe it when he brought a totally frivolous lawsuit against me. I pride myself on being a man of honor. The idea of having to resort to the courts to resolve a matter between gentlemen is as loathsome to me as failing to pay a debt or cheating at cards. I certainly do not want to face the ordeal of another trial, even though I am certain I am in the right. Ten of the twelve of the jurors in the original trial vindicated me. But the judge made that awful decision that there must be a new trial because two of the jurors said someone misbehaved, and unfortunately, one can never be sure what the next jury would do. I find the legal system itself unpredictable and sometimes even bewildering."

Clara explained the status of his case clearly and without condescension. "The first step in the firm's services would be to evaluate your chances of success on appeal. You need to understand that the civil appellate process is very different from the trial process. It's not to determine the merits of the case itself, but instead, it's to determine whether there was a legal error at the trial that's sufficient to justify overturning the trial court's decision. The appellate court's function is not to second-guess the facts about who should've won at the trial. Deciding the facts is the jury's responsibility. In this case, the appellate court would decide whether applicable law says that the trial judge failed to properly exercise his discretion in granting a new trial because of the alleged jury misconduct."

In addition to explaining the appellate process, she also explained the firm's services. "If you retain us, it would first be only to evaluate the validity of an appeal and whether the law favors your position. Then it would be your decision whether to proceed with the appeal. It would be a costly process, and you'd want to weigh that against the alternative of going back to retry the case."

"I am inclined to go ahead and have your firm evaluate the appeal," he said. "Then after I consider the alternatives, I can make a more informed decision."

They agreed that he should think over everything she had told him and meet the next afternoon.

❧❧❧

When they met again, Fuentes had a few questions, but then readily signed the retainer agreement for the firm, now Grimaldi & MacLeod, to evaluate his appeal. After he left, Clara followed the office routine for opening a new file: providing the description of the scope of the work and generally checking over the information for accuracy. She was surprised to see Fuentes's home address was no longer in the Peninsula, but instead in the Marina district. It didn't seem likely he had moved into the city with his wife and four children. It wasn't long before she learned that they were still at the family home in Hillsborough, but he was no longer living with them.

Clara had always been particularly conscientious about keeping clients informed regarding any developments, but in Fuentes's case, she had even more reason to establish a regular dialogue. She was soon rewarded with more than a professional relationship, as he became more and more comfortable with her as a person.

A couple of days later, when they had conferred at the end of the workday, somewhat haltingly he cleared his throat. "It is becoming rather late. Would you, uh, like to continue our talk over dinner?"

She was pleased at the opening, but slightly apprehensive, although their contacts had been quite business-like. She noticed there wasn't any trace of the flirtatious behavior he had exhibited some months before. His man-

ner was extremely courteous, almost prim, and he scrupulously avoided crossing any professional boundaries. She
would be on her guard, but she had to seize the opportunity to try to know him better.

As it turned out, it could not have been better if she
had engineered it herself.

After they ordered drinks in the restaurant, Miguel
relieved the tension they both felt. He began in a very
formal tone. "This is somewhat awkward, and I do hope
you will not be offended in any way, but I feel I must say
this to be sure you do not misunderstand my intentions. I
have been wanting to see you on a personal basis, but I
want it to be in the nature of friendship only. I would not
want you to think I have any improper designs, which
would be easy for you to assume, as you are such an attractive woman."

Clara had to suppress a smile, but she was impressed
by the gentlemanly way he had managed to tell her he
wasn't romantically interested, while flattering her at the
same time. She tried to match his gallantry while keeping
the formal tone. "I'm very grateful for your frankness.
You're an attractive man, of course, and I'm relieved to
know that you're interested in friendship and nothing
more. I wouldn't want to jeopardize our professional relationship, and I'm pleased to be considered a friend."

She also liked the idea Miguel had made clear this
was not related to her legal representation on his case. If
this was a purely social contact, it would not be protected
by attorney-client privilege.

During the course of dinner, the conversation turned
to personal but "safe" subjects. They talked about travel
and different cultures, especially Miguel's bicultural
background.

He was born in Mexico but had come to the States
legally when he was a teenager. His father had estab-

lished a successful business, which Miguel eventually inherited and expanded.

She amused him when she said her background was almost as bi-cultural as his, considering the differences between her Southern upbringing and her preference for the atmosphere of San Francisco.

Finally, he broached the subject that was really on his mind. "I have a certain ambivalence typical of someone like me—my roots are Hispanic, but I have been fortunate in being quite successful in the Anglo culture. I think that was probably a factor in my marrying a beautiful blonde woman to be the mother of my children." He said it with a tone of melancholy, but Clara had already noticed he was still wearing his wedding ring.

He took out a picture of his wife Grace, along with pictures of their four young children. He told her their names and ages—Michael, ten; Donna, seven; and four-year-old twins Joe and Zoe. Each child was a uniquely beautiful combination of the genes of the parents.

At last, he told her, with sadness, "I see my children only on alternate weekends, unfortunately, as they live with their mother, and I live here in the city. But we're working on our relationship. I feel I must confess that is my ulterior motive for wanting you to be my friend."

"I'm not sure I understand what you mean, Miguel."

"My wife and I were on the verge of divorce, but now we are hoping to reconcile. We have been seeing a marriage counselor, and it seems to have helped somewhat. But I am afraid I am too much a product of the machismo of my cultural background. There are things I need to understand better about a modern American woman, and I thought you might be willing to help."

"I'm not sure what I can do, but of course, I'd be happy to help if I can. It sounds as if you really want to get back together."

"Yes, more than anything. And I hope if I can understand her needs better, it may help to make that possible."

His approach seemed touchingly naive, and it brought to mind her own early attempts to understand racial prejudice. Her father had been a consummate bigot, and her mother had taught her Christian charity toward the "less fortunate races." Clara had also been naive, thinking that if she could get really close to one black person, she would be able to understand racial problems.

Although her high school was ostensibly integrated, there were only a few black students, and they kept very much to themselves. When she tried to befriend one of the black girls, her efforts were rebuffed, apparently because of pressure from the girl's own friends. Only after years of mature exposure to different people and ideas did Clara feel she had some understanding of racial barriers, and sometimes when she was being brutally honest, she admitted to herself that she might never fully understand.

Her concern was different now, although the question of her moral responsibility nagged. Even if she could justify taking advantage of information acquired outside the scope of her legal representation, was she doing the right thing? At the very least, was she being a hypocrite to sit here with a man who approached her on a personal level if she tried to find out under the guise of friendship if he was a murderer?

In a way, though, it wasn't much different from what she'd done with Francis and Katy. By seeking the truth related to a crime, maybe there was no real conflict if using subterfuge meant protecting society from a murderer. If Miguel was innocent, she would do him no harm, but rather would make every effort to do him some good by clearing him. If he was guilty, she had no qualms about being instrumental in making him face the consequences of his own acts. Still, she questioned herself.

That night she called Travis and told him about the development. "It looks as if I'll be in a position to learn more about Miguel, but I'm having some concerns about the ethics of what I'm doing."

"What could be more ethical than looking for the truth about who committed a murder, Clara?"

She knew Travis had no reservations about getting information by stealth. Ultimately, she accepted her own conviction she was doing the right thing, and that kept her going. She reported her progress to him regularly.

ɔ ɔ

At the same time, Clara was developing her relationship with Miguel, she was laying the foundation for her next target, the socially prominent Mrs. Fairfax. She started working on the premier opera committee chaired by Mrs. Fairfax. It was relatively easy to work her way in because of Jon's significant contributions to the opera, which his foundation continued after he died. She couldn't help being amused by the social strata that permeated what was supposed to be a volunteer effort to promote the opera. Clara didn't know how much success she'd have with Mrs. Fairfax, but she was pretty sure a subtle approach was the only one that had a chance.

ɔ ɔ

The first stage of her friendship with Miguel was to learn more about his marriage. She was surprised to discover Grace was a feminist, having assumed she was a traditional stay-at-home wife and mother supported by a wealthy husband. Clara was embarrassed by her own prejudice in making that assumption about women who didn't choose careers outside the home, as she had. Even if Grace looked like a beautiful blonde trophy wife, Clara discovered there was much more depth to her than met the eye.

Miguel became starry-eyed when he spoke of his wife. He often referred to her as Graciela instead of Grace.

"I admit I was first attracted to her because she was beautiful and talented. She is a gifted artist, and I met her at her first exhibition. I bought one of her paintings, partially because I liked it, but more as an excuse to get to know her. As a rule, I had little difficulty attracting women, but Grace did not respond to the approaches that had always been successful for me. When I came to pick up the painting, I drew her into conversation, but she still would not go out with me. She said she did not like playboys.

"I had not thought of myself as a playboy. I did not just go around seducing women. I love women and enjoy their company, but I pride myself on being a gentleman, not the stereotypical macho Mexican. But then I started to reflect on my so-called relationships and realized I had never had more than a superficial relationship with any woman. I began to be more thoughtful about my own views, and I was not pleased with what I saw. But I also learned some things about myself—for example, after my mother died when I was thirteen, I was reluctant to become close to any of the females in my life." Miguel turned away from Clara. Even now, after all these years, it was hard for him to think of his beloved mother without a tear in his eye. "I eventually knew I wanted a home and family and the right woman to share it with me. That woman turned out to be Grace, the woman I wanted for my wife. After she first refused to go out with me, I sent her two roses, one red and one yellow. The message with it said, *These will wither, but the memory of their beauty need not fade. Beauty is in the mind, and I cannot get you out of mine.* She told me later she thought it was corny, but she was intrigued and agreed to go out with me.

"When I asked her for the next date, she said she would accept only if I did not go out with anyone else as long as I was seeing her. I did not hesitate, but I realized it was the first time I had ever gone with anyone exclusively. Within a month, I asked her to marry me, but she kept me waiting almost a year. By that time, we knew each other well. She accepted my flirtatious nature, but she demanded absolute fidelity. I was happy to agree. As long as I had my Graciela, I wanted no other woman."

During their early talks, Miguel told Clara more about his idyllic marriage. She was anxious to press forward, but she had to let Miguel unfold his story in his own way. At the same time, she did not like the fact she was developing a phobia about parking garages. She began to use more public transportation and always looked over her shoulder when she was in an underground garage.

When she reported her progress to Travis, she let him know she thought it would take a while for Miguel to open up to her completely. Meanwhile, she found that her friendship with Miguel was becoming real, and she even began telling him a little about her happy marriages, explaining only that both of her husbands had died, without dwelling on the loss.

Miguel's pain was almost palpable because it was more recent and was still being resolved. He talked about his children, whom he spoke with daily and spent time with on weekends.

He continued to marvel at Grace and her many fine qualities. She was a devoted mother, who also worked tirelessly to promote projects in support of the arts in schools, not just in her affluent community, but also in needier school districts.

Clara found herself enjoying time with her new friend and tried to repress the ambivalent pangs that still hit her at unexpected moments.

Meanwhile, things were developing more slowly with Pamela Fairfax, and Clara began to wonder whether she'd be able to break through to any useful information.

But with Miguel, Clara was getting close, living up to her pact with Travis, even though she hoped she would not learn anything that would hurt Miguel or his family. Ironically, one meeting with him had an unexpected side effect on her own life.

She had been having frequent phone conversations with Heath, but their crowded schedules had allowed them only a few casual dates. In addition to increasing work at the office, it became time-consuming for Clara to be more involved with the opera committee work in her attempt to get closer to Pamela Fairfax. And besides being otherwise absorbed, Clara didn't mind the slow pace with Heath, unsure about how involved she really wanted to become with a busy doctor.

One night, she had a tentative date for dinner with Heath when he called. "I'm sorry about dinner, but I won't finish the analysis of the research project I'm working on for hours yet. I'll probably be tied up in the lab most of the night."

"No problem, Heath. I'm tired anyway. It's been a long week, and I can use a quiet evening at home."

After the call, she remembered Miguel had mentioned dinner, but she had declined because of the tentative date with Heath. So she called Miguel, and they went to dinner at a restaurant she'd been to with Heath, not far from San Francisco General Hospital. They were deep in conversation when Heath walked by their table, but she didn't see him until later—across the room, engrossed with a good-looking woman.

Clara and Heath both saw each other with an attractive dinner companion, but neither one was aware of having been seen by the other.

She, of course, did not know that the woman with Heath was one of the doctors who had been collaborating with him on his research project. He, of course, saw only that Clara seemed to be absorbed with a handsome man. Their phone conversations were strained in the days after, and neither seemed inclined to take the initiative in getting together. Instead, they turned their attention to other things, except when they were occasionally blindsided by thoughts of each other.

Clara continued to talk to Miguel, sometimes in person, but more often in long phone conversations at night. He was lonely without his family, and sometimes it was easier for him to talk about sensitive matters on the phone. At last, Miguel reached the level of trust he needed to discuss his paramount problem with Clara. In all their discussions, she had kept in mind what he had said about needing to understand certain things, but he still had not mentioned the subject directly. Now the time was ripe.

They were sitting in a quiet corner of a coffee house, with a Mozart *divertimento* playing in the background. "Clara, do you think it is possible ever to regain the trust of someone you have hurt very deeply?"

"Is that the problem with you and Grace?"

"Yes. I did something so terrible to her that it is unspeakable."

"But at least you are communicating with each other. Doesn't that give you hope?"

"Maybe a little, but we still seem far apart. We do talk about the children, running the house, and other things of mutual interest. But we do not talk about the things close to our hearts."

"Don't you do that in the counseling sessions?"

"I suppose we have discussed many of the problems, but in more or less clinical terms. The counselor has given us some exercises to work on, which are supposed to help us reestablish trust. But I am not sure I can see anything happening."

"Miguel, you know I'm sympathetic, but I'm just not sure what I can do to help."

"It is so much to ask of you, and it is more humiliating for me than you can imagine. You may hate me if you know the truth. But I am desperate, and I want my family back."

"It must be very hard for you, but you'll have to tell me everything, Miguel. How can I respond if I don't know the real nature of the problem? I promise I'll try to understand anything you could possibly tell me, and I won't be your judge." She had chosen her words carefully, so she could encourage him to go on without her having to lie.

"When I tell you, at least you'll understand better why I chose to involve you. It is more than just feeling you are an intelligent and understanding woman, although that is important. The other part is that if anyone could understand, it would have to be someone who knew Bernard Kahn."

Clara was startled. In subtle ways, she had tried to bring up matters from their prior legal representation to get him to talk about Bernie. But he had never taken the bait. She had even imagined he deliberately changed the subject whenever it got close to Bernie, but Miguel was such a polished conversationalist she was never quite sure. She was certain, though, that he had never before deliberately mentioned Bernie.

With the very mention of his name, Miguel seemed to undergo a transformation, so striking she couldn't help thinking of the melodramatic change in the old Wolfman movies. His handsome face was first clouded, then contorted with pain.

"I am not sure how you will feel about my telling you that I abhorred your former boss, Mr. Bernard Kahn, Esquire." Although there was a distinct edge to his voice, he said it hesitantly, waiting for her reaction before going on.

The muscles in his face eased a fraction when she said, "You needn't be concerned about that. Many people found Bernie contemptible, and I was one of them."

He looked relieved. "I could never get used to a grown man encouraging people to call him Bernie. I knew a boy in high school who was called Nerdy Bernie."

Sensing his digression as reluctance, Clara waited until he was ready to continue.

"As you may know, when I met Kahn, he jumped on me like a dog on a bone, hoping for my legal business. After our initial meeting at that event at the consulate, he called and suggested a dinner meeting. He said he would be bringing a client who could attest to the quality of his work in international law. To my surprise, the so-called client was a gorgeous French woman, whom he introduced as Colette D'Orsay. She supposedly engaged in importing French cheeses and other products, and she raved about Kahn's legal services. It was not until much later, when I knew I had been duped, that I realized she did very little talking about business."

"Do you mean she was only posing as a client? I don't remember any client by that name."

"Exactly. But it was much worse than being tricked into retaining Kahn's legal services. This is the difficult part to tell you, but I am committed to do it now. After dinner, Kahn said his wife was expecting him at home and would I be so kind as to see Colette to her hotel. It seemed like the gentlemanly thing to do, but I must admit I was enjoying her company." He looked away before going on. "I hope you will permit me to avoid going into explicit detail. It is exceedingly embarrassing even to admit I was seduced and carried on a brief affair with the woman. I was riddled with guilt and knew I had betrayed my wife. At times, I rationalized and told myself that wives of Hispanic men had always looked away from their husbands' philandering, but I knew very well that I'd broken my vow of fidelity to my wife, which I had always intended to keep. I was greatly relieved when Colette told me she had to go back to France, and I had no intention of ever seeing her again.

"That's when my wonderful family life collapsed, thanks to Bernard Kahn. He came to my office late one afternoon and made me a proposition. I was to continue his legal services at an exorbitant sum to be paid regularly in cash. In return, he would not show a certain collection of pictures to my wife. He showed me a set of appalling photos of me with Colette in very compromising situations. My first reaction was to throw him out on his ear, which he seemed to anticipate and made a hasty retreat. But that night he called me at home, and I decided I could not risk losing my family for a meaningless indiscretion. Kahn obviously knew he had me hooked, and I made my first payment the next day.

"After a few weeks, though, I knew I could not continue living a lie. I had so many conflicting feelings, but the prospect of losing the love of my wife and children was my greatest fear. I also knew that anyone so despicable as to create such a scheme would never let me rest. It was not just the money, but it was also the humiliation of having allowed myself to be deceived in such a foolish manner. I had thought of myself as a sophisticated man of the world, and there I was, merely a gullible fool."

It was clear he appreciated her sympathetic response when she said, "You're too hard on yourself, Miguel. You're not the first person I've known to be taken in by Bernie's deception." She paused, hoping he'd continue, but when he didn't, she asked, "What did you do about it?"

"I decided there was only one honorable thing to do, and I told Grace. I tried to explain how I had been tricked, that it was completely over, that I understood the gravity of my transgression. I begged her forgiveness. She is a wonderful woman, but she reacted much as might be expected. She was angry and hurt. She told me to leave her alone for a while to sort out how she could deal with it. The next day, she discussed it with her closest friend, who had recently gone through a dreadful divorce. Her friend advised her to contact the attorney who had obtained a large settlement for her. It was Alvin Hanks, the lawyer who was killed the same night as Kahn."

Clara could not repress a gasp. It was the first link. But why hadn't she seen Grace Fuentes among the names on the list of Hanks's clients? She soon learned why.

Miguel misunderstood her reaction. "I see I have shocked you with all of this. I should have known it was not appropriate to involve you. Please forgive me."

She recovered sufficiently to say, "No, no, it's all right. I'm just concerned about the gravity of the situation. And believe me, I truly understand how easy it is to be duped by Bernie Kahn. I'm really more than willing to hear more. Please go on." She tried to make her voice as sympathetic as possible, and he continued.

"Mr. Hanks's reputation as an unscrupulous divorce

lawyer is apparently warranted. It is somewhat ironic that his obnoxious personality gave me something of a reprieve. Grace went to see him and was thoroughly disgusted with his greedy attitude. She told him she wanted no more than her fair share of our property and enough support to provide for the children and educate them with as little disruption to their lives as possible. She emphasized she wanted a stable home for the children with my continued involvement as their father.

"Hanks started playing on her emotions, telling her she should ruin me for the terrible things I had done to her, and so on. Instead of seeing the real Grace, he apparently saw a proverbial dumb blonde with a rich husband and thought he had hooked a live one, with every intention of maximizing his legal fees. The more he ranted, the more she realized that was not what she wanted. So she never retained him as her attorney. And fortunately, it also spurred her to think about what she really did want. She is a sensitive woman, but she is also intelligent and very rational. She decided that if I agreed to move out for a while and see a marriage counselor with her, she would give us some time before she made any permanent decision."

"So where are you in your relationship now?"

"Grace seems to have accepted the fact that I had a despicable affair and has forgiven me. But there is still the matter of trust. I have to travel quite a bit in my work, several trips to Mexico every year and many overnight stays in Southern California. She had never expressed concern about my being away before, but I have learned that she felt some resentment I was not aware of. We have reached a sort of plateau in the counseling sessions. That is why I finally approached you. Even though I had thought of Grace as a traditional homemaker, I began to realize she is really a very liberated woman. She chose motherhood as her primary career while the children are young, but she also still paints and is involved in several art education projects. I thought maybe a career woman like yourself might help me understand Grace better, help me know what she wants and how I can fit into that."

"That's a tall order," Clara said. "Actually, I've had some thoughts about it as we've been talking, and I'd be pleased to give my viewpoint, for whatever help that may provide. I think it might be a good idea to let me think about all of this and let's talk again soon. I'm curious about something, though, if you don't mind telling me."

"Of course. What is it?"

"Considering all the anguish you've suffered because of Bernie, why did you attend his funeral and take the trouble to extend your condolences to his widow?"

"Under normal circumstances, the answer would simply be my breeding—it was good manners. But Kahn was a special case. I just wanted to be sure the bastard was really dead!"

Clara had never heard Miguel use a word like bastard before. His use of language had always been somewhat formal and precise, but now there wasn't a hint of apology in his tone.

After they parted that evening, Clara wondered if Miguel had misgivings about baring his soul to someone else, especially a woman. She hoped that now he felt more at ease, knowing he had taken positive steps toward understanding his wife. Clara's heart was lighter that night, and she hoped his was, too.

Even though it was after eleven and she was concerned it was too late to be calling Travis, she could hardly wait to call as soon as she got home. She told him all about the blackmail scheme, as Miguel had told it to her, and he listened without interrupting. She pinpointed the relevant dates based on what Miguel had told her and on her own recollection of the work she had done for him some months before.

"So what's your take on the credibility of the witness, counselor?" he asked.

"Well, except for the tendency to downplay his own responsibility for the affair, which I guess is a typical male reaction, it was all pretty believable. I can't think of any reason he'd share such secrets with me if he wasn't telling the truth. Of course, I don't see him as a complete innocent seduced by a gorgeous woman. I hardly think she dragged him kicking and screaming to her hotel room. No doubt there was at least some male ego involved. But even so, everything he said seems credible. On top of that, on a personal level, I feel that he's sincere. He really seems to care very much about his family. What do you think?"

"It all seems to fit. I can check out the details, like his wife's appointment with the divorce lawyer and the timing. It seems consistent with the schedule of payments in Kahn's notebook. If it all hangs together, it sounds as if his only motive to kill Kahn would've been some sort of vengeance. With this one, Kahn went even beyond the blackmail we've discovered with his employees—here he apparently created the whole scenario for the blackmail himself, using this French woman. I wonder if she was even French. Anyway, if Fuentes really cares about regaining his family, murder wouldn't have helped him reach that goal. If everything checks out, he's probably off the hook. And meanwhile, we still have the others in the notebook to follow up on."

"Whatta ya mean 'we,' white man? Hasn't your faithful Indian scout been doing the legwork?"

"Yeah, Tonto. Did I forget to tell you, you done good, kid?"

"Thanks, pal, I needed that. This hasn't been easy for me, you know."

"I know, Clara, and you really have been a big help. I've been working on other leads, and I'm glad you just kept plugging along on the notebook stuff. One way or another, I think we'll be able to crack this."

This time she liked his reference to "we."

"Don't be annoyed with me, Travis, but right now I feel more concerned about fixing Miguel's marriage than finding Bernie's killer."

"I understand. It's a good thing to hang onto your humanity in this line of work. In fact, it may surprise you that I might be able to shed a little light on the marital problem myself."

"How so?"

"Well, it's common knowledge that being married to a cop is tough, at best. Jo Anne and I have been through our trials and tribulations, too. She's a wonderful mother and a rock as a wife, but she wouldn't settle for half a husband. She looked after the boys when they were little and went back to teaching only when they were both in school. She held down the fort while I spent more and more hours on the job, and even when I came home, my head was still at work. She reached a point where she just got plain fed up with being married to me when I was married to the job. Finally, she gave me an ultimatum and said it was being a cop or having a family. I'd have to choose."

"But you seem to have managed both."

"Only because she softened on the ultimatum, and we eventually worked out some compromises. I cut back on the hours and learned how to distance myself from the job, and she decided she still wanted to be my wife, as long as I kept my end of the bargain. It's one of the reasons I'm still a mere detective."

"You think it affected your career?"

"Probably, but I'm not sorry about that. There was a time when I thought I had what it takes to be chief, but the price was too high. Giving up my family wasn't worth it. But my job is part of me, and Jo Anne understands that, too. As long as I don't abuse the privilege, she lets me keep being a cop." He chuckled. "You should see her face right now. She walked into the room a minute ago and has been smirking at me. I was in the middle of going over some household bills when you called. Guess I'd better get back to my husbandly duties."

"Sounds like a good idea, Travis. Thank Jo Anne for me."

"Huh?"

"She'll understand."

"Yeah, but I'll never understand women."

"We try to keep it that way with all you guys, Travis."

"Okay, one more thing, Clara. Are you making any progress with the Fairfax woman?"

"So far, it's mostly been a lot of pretty boring committee meetings. I think Mrs. Fairfax may be warming to me a little, though. She's starting to chat with me for a few minutes after the meetings instead of heading off to lunch with her regular cronies."

"Keep at it. I think you have a real knack for getting people to trust you and open up to you."

"We'll see. I'll keep you posted, Travis."

ട൚ട

Clara continued her talks with Miguel. She told him what she could about what women want from men in a general sense, but stressed that generalities must fit individual cases and sometimes don't apply at all. They talked at length about Grace's and Miguel's individual needs and how important it was to communicate them to each other.

She thought about what Travis had said about his marriage. She talked to Miguel about compromise, especially how he might cut down his travel, even if it meant being less successful in business. Influenced by their talks, he discussed with Grace whether she could accept fewer luxuries as a result of making changes in the way he conducted business, and she assured him she valued her husband much more than material things. Finally, Miguel moved back home.

Clara was very pleased.

She also admitted to herself that she liked learning the intimate secrets of other people's private lives.

Little did she know she was about to learn some bizarre details about someone else's private life.

CHAPTER 11

Elegant Victim

She expected Pamela Fairfax to be a particularly difficult nut to crack, and Mrs. Fairfax lived up to expectations. While Clara had been developing her friendship with Miguel, she'd managed to establish her niche on the opera committee chaired by Mrs. Fairfax. She was glad she had made the loose arrangement for her work at the firm, with no definite commitment or pay, which gave her the flexibility to go to committee meetings with the moneyed set, who didn't have to be bothered with the inconvenience of anything so mundane as having to work regular hours.

The committee work helped Clara get around the impediment that she and Mrs. Fairfax didn't normally travel in the same circles. Her husband Charles Fairfax was old money, and Pamela Worthington Fairfax had come from old money herself, although the Worthingtons had lost most of theirs in bad investments. Old money was reputed to reproduce spontaneously, something like wire coat hangers regenerating in a closet.

Although the current Fairfaxes still had some old money, they had not produced any offspring and, based on local gossip, it was difficult to imagine them in any sort of reproductive activity, at least not with each other.

On the other hand, it was not difficult to imagine them having carnal knowledge of others. The speculation was that Charles and Pamela Fairfax had similar tastes in certain things other than the arts, both having a proclivity for attractive men, usually young, muscular, and not qualified for Mensa. The Fairfaxes were seen together at all the appropriate social functions, from the opening of the opera season to the inauguration of the mayor—whoever it happened to be—but they were rarely seen in closer proximity than necessary on such occasions. Their pictures were a regular feature in the society columns of the *Chronicle,* and years ago they had been on hand for the ceremonies to christen Herb Caen Way, the new promenade along the Embarcadero that honored the beloved old gossip columnist.

Clara heard most of the gossip about the Fairfaxes from Adrian, who was a native San Franciscan and a history buff. He always seemed to know about everyone from the hoi polloi to the pseudo-aristocracy. Clara often had tea with Adrian when she got home and loved listening to his colorful stories, from old San Francisco to the current crop of roués and other riffraff. He summed up Charles Fairfax as "the kind of pansy that gives gay men a bad name," and he was glad Mrs. Fairfax was straight because her reputation was even worse. "She collects men the way some women collect shoes but doesn't generally keep them around as long."

On top of all that, Clara found it difficult to relate to anyone who insisted on using the name "Mrs. Charles Fairfax" for formal purposes, such as when it was etched into the plaque of big contributors to the symphony. After all, even if it was originally his money, she still had a first name. For direct address, she was always "Mrs. Fairfax," and in the social columns, she was usually "the elegant

Mrs. Fairfax." Clara couldn't help wondering if her lovers referred to her as the elegant Mrs. Fairfax.

She could almost hear Robin Williams doing a comedy routine with a pseudo upper-crust accent, something like, "Chauncey, old boy, have you had the pleasure of screwing the elegant Mrs. Fairfax?" Only Williams could make a line like that seem funny—what a sad loss. Clara also wondered how much truth there was to the rumors, especially now that Mrs. Fairfax was sixty years old. But her age was hardly a hindrance—most women would be thrilled to look as good at forty as Mrs. Fairfax did at sixty.

Clara did some research in old newspaper files and was amazed to see how little Mrs. Fairfax had changed over the years. Thirty years ago she had ash blonde hair, usually worn in some chic variation of a French twist or chignon. Now her hair was silver gray, but with the same effect. Her flawless skin as a young woman had given in only to tiny lines, but still had a firm, dewy texture. Her eyes were periwinkle blue, if eyes could be such a color, and her cheekbones and other facial features were classic—perhaps not perfect, but as nearly perfect as one is likely to see in a flesh-and-blood person, untouched by a photographer's airbrush.

Her body, always elegantly attired—what else for the elegant Mrs. Fairfax?—showed almost no outward signs of age and reminded the observer that before she was Mrs. Fairfax, she had studied to be a ballet dancer. She still had the lithe grace that testified to her having spent no less than an hour a day at the ballet barre nearly every day since her wedding. It was not surprising, of course, that Mrs. Fairfax was also active in promoting the San Francisco Ballet. The Fairfaxes attended the ballet regularly, especially the opening of each season, and their names always appeared as large contributors.

Adrian quipped that the Fairfaxes supported the ballet in their own special way, especially with the most promising new male dancers.

When Clara had first volunteered for the opera committee work, she was politely ignored, but she was welcomed with open arms after she let it be known she was the widow of Jon Westgate. His contributions to the arts were known to the inner circle, though he had chosen not to have his name etched on any plaques. As much as he loved the arts, he had been much prouder of his efforts to help needier causes, but even for them, he remained anonymous. Those who worked on the committees because they loved opera were pleased to know Clara Quillen was the person who continued contributions in the name of the Westgate Trust; those who worked on the committees for pretentious purposes accepted her for their own snobbish reasons.

At first, Mrs. Fairfax kept a polite distance from Clara, but often Clara thought she caught a sidelong glance and an occasional impression of rapt attention when she made a suggestion. Then one day Mrs. Fairfax invited her to lunch after a committee meeting to "discuss some ideas."

To Clara's surprise, the conversation had little to do with committee activities, but instead took a philosophical turn, including subjects related to legal ethics. She wasn't sure, but she got the distinct impression Mrs. Fairfax was familiar with the law review article she had written about some ethical issues related to attorney-client privilege. One thing Clara felt sure about, though, was that Mrs. Fairfax had been sizing her up and had finally decided she was trustworthy.

"I've been thinking about making some changes in the disposition of my estate. I understand your firm does that sort of thing."

"Yes, Katy MacLeod is one of the partners, and she's certified by the state bar as a specialist in estate work. I'm sure she would provide excellent legal services."

"These are actually rather simple matters, and since it's so convenient to work with you, I'd like for you to handle them."

"Of course, I'd be happy to. If there's anything I feel unsure of, I'll confer with Ms. MacLeod to make certain everything is handled expertly."

"That's fine. Here is the first assignment." Mrs. Fairfax gave Clara some papers about adding a rather simple codicil to her will and an amendment to her family trust.

Clara had no difficulty carrying out those tasks and various others that followed. She kept Travis informed about her progress, and they discussed Mrs. Fairfax's demeanor at length. Clara was sure there was more to this than appeared on the surface.

"After all, Mrs. Fairfax has no reason to use me for these legal services, which could easily be handled by the firm she normally uses for stuff like this."

"I think you're right, Clara," Travis said. "Mrs. Fairfax will tip her hand, but only in her own sweet time."

The time finally came. Following a meeting one afternoon, Mrs. Fairfax suggested she and Clara go for a drink at a posh watering hole. Clara made no attempt to keep up with the Manhattans Mrs. Fairfax was downing at a surprising rate. Clara wondered if her waiting chauffeur was accustomed to handling Mrs. Fairfax after the proverbial "tee many martoonis," or in this case, too many Manhattans.

Of all things, they began discussing Shakespeare. Mrs. Fairfax somehow knew Clara had been an English teacher, although she was certain she had never mentioned it.

Clara assumed Mrs. Fairfax had been checking on

her at the same time she had been researching Mrs. Fairfax.

"You know, don't you, my dear," Mrs. Fairfax said with a theatrical flourish, "that quote they found at Bernard's murder scene about killing all the lawyers is grossly misinterpreted? You lawyers really ought to straighten that out. Which play is the source of that line?"

"I'm impressed you know about that, Mrs. Fairfax. Most people take the line at face value and don't realize it really reflects a would-be dictator who would do away with law and order. Actually, the character in *Henry VI,* who says it is one of the rabblerousing followers of Jack Cade, a loutish rebel who responds that he intends to kill the Clerk of Chatham for the monstrous crime of knowing how to read and write. So the line about killing lawyers is really wonderful irony."

Mrs. Fairfax abruptly shifted the subject. "Who is your favorite Shakespearean character?"

Clara couldn't imagine where this conversation was headed, but she wanted to keep it going. "I guess I've always had a particular fondness for Portia in *The Merchant of Venice.* Would you also choose a woman as your favorite character, Mrs. Fairfax?"

"Of course. I adore Lady Macbeth as much as I deplore her wimpy husband. Don't you love it when she tells him to screw his courage to the sticking place? What she should have done is give him a few Manhattans."

"Would that help to inspire courage?"

"Yes, I'd say so. Take me, for instance. I can't remember when I've had this many Manhattans at one sitting, and I feel like attacking windmills. Oops, I guess I'm mixing my literary metaphors along with the drinks."

"I'm not exactly sure about what metaphors you're mixing, but I do have the feeling there's something you'd like to attack."

"You're a very astute young lady. And a very discreet one, too, I think."

"Well, we all know that discretion is the better part of valor. That's Shakespeare, too, you know."

"Ah, but do you agree with it?"

"Under the appropriate circumstances, certainly. Lawyers, of course, are ethically bound to be discreet."

"Not all lawyers. Some of them are scoundrels."

"Do you have anyone in particular in mind?"

"Let me put it in the form of a question. How would you classify your former employer, the charming Bernard?"

"Perhaps the discreet way to answer your question is to tell you I left his employ a month before he was killed. At the time, my opinion of him was low, and it has continued to descend ever since. Why do I have the feeling you already know that?"

"I don't generally do things haphazardly. Yes, I do know quite a lot about you, Clara, and I've come to believe I can trust you."

"Am I correct in assuming your concern about trusting me is more than just whether I'm capable of adding a codicil to your will?"

"I think it's time for me to stop beating around the bush. Yes, there is a very special reason. I need a job done, and I think you're the one to do it. I can pay you well."

"Tell me about the job. Then we can discuss payment. If you've checked me out as thoroughly as I suspect, you already know that money isn't a big motivator for me."

"Yes, I know. All right, here goes." Mrs. Fairfax took a large gulp of her drink, the last one she had for the duration of what turned out to be a remarkable conversation. While Mrs. Fairfax had seemed to be succumbing to the effects of the alcohol, suddenly she appeared to be quite lucid. "What I want you to do is find something for me. It's a set of negatives. There may be some prints, too, but I doubt it. I think he'd have found it easier to hide just the negatives."

"Are you planning to tell me the subject of the negatives?"

"I'm going to tell you the whole thing. You may need to know in order to find what you're looking for. I also think it's only fair to tell you, so you won't be totally shocked if you find it."

"I gather it's pretty bad. Would I be correct in assuming the negatives had something to do with blackmail?"

"I guess it doesn't take much of a leap for you to figure that out. What's so stupid is I didn't have to stand for the blackmail, as it turned out."

"Why so?"

"Let me start from the beginning. I met Bernard Kahn at a cocktail party I gave for one of the First District appellate justices when he was appointed. Kahn wasn't even invited but managed to tag along with someone else. The crowd was large and noisy enough to carry on a conversation without anyone overhearing. Kahn cornered me and soon began a coy repartee that led to the subject of unusual sexual proclivities. He asked if there was anything I had never tried. I was intrigued, but I told him that this was no place to discuss such things. Foolishly, I gave him my private phone number. He called in the wee hours of the morning, and we had a long conversation. I'll spare you the embarrassing details, except the pertinent ones. We discussed sexual fantasies, and I told him one of mine, which placed me in the role of dominatrix with two well-built young men to do my bidding. Kahn said he could arrange it. I laughed at him and said it was only a fantasy. He asked me why I should stick with fantasy when it could be reality. There were several more such conversations before the meeting was arranged. It was to be in a certain room at the Ritz-Carlton Hotel.

"When I entered, the room appeared to be empty, but on the bed, there was a skimpy black leather outfit for me, which exposed strategic parts of my anatomy, along with a whip, handcuffs, and other paraphernalia. He had instructed me that when I was properly attired, I should pick up the whip and my fantasy would appear. Something appeared, all right, but it was hardly my fantasy. Instead of two muscular young men, from the bathroom emerged a puny runt of a man with a slight paunch, completely naked except for a black hood over his head, his face totally covered except for small eyeholes. It was the most disgusting sight I've ever seen. I knew it was Kahn, not just from the physique, but also from the nauseating lavender cologne I'd smelled on him at the cocktail party. He started gyrating around me. At first, I was disgusted. I told him to get out of my sight, and when he kept circling around me, I hit at him with the whip. After a few blows, he made a hasty retreat into the bathroom. I dressed with the speed of light and got out of there just as fast. To this day, I can't bear to attend a function at the Ritz-Carlton."

She paused and slumped, as if fatigued from telling about it, then continued. "That night Kahn called me and told me if I didn't want the local tabloids to know about my afternoon fantasy I'd better meet him the next day. To my horror, he had eight-by-ten glossies that would've raised my mother from the dead. He gave me the pictures as a 'memento' of the occasion, but said the negatives were readily available for publication unless I decided to retain his legal services at an exorbitant sum to be paid regularly in cash."

Clara noticed she used almost the same words Miguel had used in describing Bernie's blackmail proposition.

"I took the pictures with me only to destroy them, and I was about to that afternoon when my maid came in with my afternoon tea. It was routine for her to bring my tea and lay out my clothes for the evening. So I quickly stuffed the envelope in the back of the desk drawer and locked it, intending to destroy the pictures later. As it turned out, they stayed there for weeks because I couldn't bear to touch the filthy things. I was getting pretty sick of my payments to Kahn, and one night I decided to look at the pictures again before destroying them. I had some vague hope that maybe they weren't as bad as I thought, and maybe I'd just take my chances.

"When I first saw the pictures, I barely looked at them, but this time I scrutinized them and found something important. In one of them, Kahn had his arms crossed over his chest to protect himself from the whip. On the spot where he normally wore his Rolex wristwatch was the tattoo of an eye. It was clearly visible and unmistakable with a magnifying glass.

"The very next morning I went to Kahn's office and insisted on seeing him. He was surprised but naturally didn't object. I gave him a bunch of gibberish as I sidled close to him and pretended to admire the garish diamond ring he was wearing. Then with one quick wrench, I grabbed his watch and ripped it off his wrist—and there it was—the tattoo of the eye! I never laughed so hard in my life. When I caught my breath, I said, 'You just dare publish those pictures, you filthy bastard! The world will know who was on the receiving end of that whip. You have as much to lose as I do, and you'll never get another cent out of me.' His face was white with fear, and I never heard from him again."

Mrs. Fairfax no longer looked exhausted, but instead exhilarated. She smiled tentatively. "I know this must all be a shock to you, Clara."

"It's less of a shock than you might think, Mrs. Fairfax. I knew Bernie was despicable. I just didn't know it had taken this particular form."

"Don't you think you should start calling me Pamela, my dear? You now are in possession of my deepest, darkest secret. I haven't even told my shrink, can you believe it? But then I didn't have a reason to tell her, as I have with you."

"Of course, I appreciate your trust, Pamela, but I've been wondering about your reason for telling me."

"Quite right, it's time to get to the point. You see, I never did get those negatives back, and I'm still afraid they might surface. I certainly wouldn't want them to wind up in the wrong hands. I want you to find them for me."

"But what can I do? I have no access to Bernie's house."

"I don't believe he'd ever have hidden them at home. There's too much chance that his wife might discover them. I think if they exist, they must be at the firm somewhere."

"I'm almost certain they're not in Bernie's office because the police searched it thoroughly. I can't imagine he'd hide them anywhere in the common areas."

"All I can ask is that you try. I don't think I'll ever rest easy until I know those negatives are destroyed. I'll pay you anything you want."

"You mentioned that before, and we need to address it. Actually, if I can find them, I don't want payment, but there is something I do want. I want you to give your legal work to Grimaldi and MacLeod. But there's an essential caveat—you needn't stay with them unless you are genuinely satisfied with the quality of their legal work."

"Done. I'll do that anyway, whether you find the negatives or not. I like your style, Clara. But please try to find the negatives."

"Don't worry. I'm intrigued by a bit of detective work anyway. If the negatives are there, I'll find them. Do you mind if I ask you just one question?"

"After what I've already told you? Of course not. Fire away."

"I saw you at Cypress Lawn expressing your condolences to Bernie's widow. Why did you do that?"

Mrs. Fairfax laughed so raucously, a couple of heads turned in their direction. Then she said in a low, malevolent tone, "Can't you guess, my dear? I wanted to see Kahn's wife. I just wondered who normally wielded the whip!"

🙰🙰🙰

Clara could hardly wait to tell the latest fantastic tale to Travis. He roared with laughter at Mrs. Fairfax's comment about Charlotte and thoroughly enjoyed the whole story. "There's nothing quite like seeing the dirty linen of the upper crust to make me satisfied with being a plain old Oakie."

"Okay, Travis, I'm glad you find this all so amusing, but I really do feel sort of sorry for her. I don't like to see anybody duped by Bernie, even among the privileged class."

"You're a softy, Quillen, but I guess it's one of the things I like about you. You haven't forgotten about the possibility of Mrs. Fairfax being a killer, have you?"

"Of course not, but I don't think so. She'd already gotten herself out from under Bernie's blackmail. If anything, killing him would put her in more danger of having the negatives discovered. And if so, they'd not only be ugly publicity, but they'd also implicate her in his murder."

"But what if she murdered him and now wants you to find the evidence of her motive so she can destroy it? What would she do to the only person who knew her motive, namely you?"

"Uh, yeah, I see the problem," she said uneasily. "But it's hard to believe she'd have murdered him and then counted on someone finding the negatives for her. And what about the other two victims? You haven't found any motive related to them, right?"

"Not yet. That's what keeps throwing a monkey wrench into this thing. The truth is, I'm starting to think it may not turn out to be anyone on Kahn's blackmail list. That is, assuming we ever do find out who did it."

"Are you having doubts, Travis? I thought you Oakies always got your man. Oops, no, that's the mounties."

"Now don't get smart with me, kid. This is just one of those points in an investigation where it all starts to seem impossible. We've sifted through mounds of stuff as carefully as a paleontologist, but we still don't know how to piece the bones together."

"Sorry, Travis. I guess this is tougher on you than it is on me. After all, you're the pro. I'm only an amateur."

"Yeah, but what a team. We're not licked yet."

"Okay, coach, what do I do now?"

"Find the negatives."

"Just like that—find the negatives? Like where?"

"Come on, Quillen. Think like a detective. See what you can come up with."

"Does that mean you have no idea, but you'd rather not admit it?"

"Hey, you're not supposed to figure that out. Just keep your mind focused on the problem, okay?"

"You're a tough guy to work for. Okay, I'll see what I can do."

☙∽☙∽

She could think of little else that night besides where Bernie might have hidden an envelope of negatives. Travis assured her nothing had been found in Bernie's office in the search by the woman detective he considered the absolute best at uncovering physical clues. It was unlikely to be in anyone else's office or even a cubicle because there was too much chance of untoward discovery by the usual occupant, and even the files wouldn't be really safe from discovery. It would also have to be somewhere not frequented by the cleaning crew.

She also thought of secret compartments, like the false bottom of the black box that had yielded the notebook. But there weren't any other boxes like that in the office. Of course, there was the firm law library, but even the oldest case law books were sometimes consulted. Bernie wouldn't have taken the chance of creating a hiding place in one of the books.

That night her dreams were a cross between Alice in Wonderland creeping through shadowy passages and Miss Marple snooping around with a flashlight. When she awoke, she fleetingly hoped her subconscious had somehow miraculously solved the puzzle of the hidden envelope, but she didn't feel any closer than the night before. She just felt as if she'd been on a treasure hunt all night and was a little tired from the effort.

All day at the office, she created excuses for examining every bit of the common areas of the firm and surreptitiously checked everywhere she could think of. She would go back into her own office and contemplate, then do a bit of work, hoping some idea would bubble to the surface when she was concentrating on something else. By the end of the day, she was beginning to think that if the negatives existed, they were not in this office. She decided not to stay any later and search because she didn't want to arouse any suspicion, even though everyone had already left for the day except the attorneys and Francis. Maybe if she reflected more after taking a break, something would come to her.

Just as she was about to go out the door of the office foyer, she noticed a cluster of framed Oriental prints with a mirror in the center, so ordinary she had never paid any attention to them. They were just cheap prints, and even Charlotte hadn't bothered to take any of them in her sweep of the office.

Clara guessed that was exactly how Bernie's mind worked. He knew anyone passing those prints would be on the way out, distracted by other thoughts. Then there was the mirror, a very commonplace mirror, about nine by twelve inches, with a pseudo-bamboo frame. Like others, Clara had often glanced at herself in the mirror before going out the door, but she had never actually thought about the mirror itself. She was sure this was it.

She started to breathe a little faster as she took down the mirror. The back was covered with plain brown paper. She took out her key ring that had a small Swiss Army knife Jake had given her, opened the blade, and made a long vertical slit, just deep enough to slice the paper. There it was—a sealed brown legal size envelope. On the outside, in handwritten red letters, were the words BERNARD C. KAHN—PERSONAL.

She quickly dropped the envelope into her briefcase and hung the mirror back up. The whole process had taken less than a minute, although it felt more like an hour to Clara. No one had passed her while she performed the surgical procedure. She went back to her office, opened the envelope, and looked at the negatives with a magnifying glass. She could make out just enough of the shapes to be assured she had found what she was looking for.

She called Travis to fill him in. Rather than meet to get the photos, Travis told her to mark it for him and leave it with security in the building. He'd pick the envelope up after she left.

"Do we really need all this cloak and dagger stuff, Travis? Sometimes I feel a little silly playing sleuth."

"That note on your car is enough to put you on notice."

"But there hasn't been anything since then. The killer probably thinks his note scared me enough not to worry about me anymore."

"Don't be too sure."

"Okay, now I'm scared again. Thanks a lot. Anyway, back to the subject. What happens after you get the photos?"

"I'll do the analysis unofficially myself for now. Jo Anne can make prints for me; photography is one of her hobbies. I don't think there's any need to check this into evidence unless I decide Mrs. Fairfax is a serious suspect. I'll hang onto it for now, and you just tell Mrs. Fairfax you're still looking. We'll see how things develop, if you'll pardon the pun, and decide where to go from here."

"What will you do with the pictures and negatives if you decide Mrs. Fairfax didn't have anything to do with the murders?"

"It's easy enough to destroy the prints, and I see no reason why she shouldn't get her negatives back. Even the idle rich deserve some peace of mind, especially after dealing with a sleazeball like Kahn."

"That's what I was hoping you'd say."

"Now it's about time to tackle another subject, Clara.

Is it possible you've been reluctant to follow through on AH—Andrews, Hershel? He's the last one on the list, except for the one we still haven't identified, HA."

"I've been pretty busy you know," she said, somewhat defensively. "Okay, maybe I have been inclined to put off Dr. Andrews. At first, it was awkward when I started seeing his son, but then it was awkward because I wasn't seeing his son. Don't you think I have a conflict of interest?"

"Probably, but don't let that stand in your way. Remember, part of any investigation is exculpating the innocent as well as implicating the guilty."

"Despite the self-serving nature of that little aphorism, I have to admit you're right. Okay, Travis, I'll see what I can do. Any suggestions for an approach?"

"You've been doing amazingly well without my suggestions, Quillen. You're beginning to actually think like a detective. If you keep this up, you can give up lawyering altogether and get a respectable job."

"Cheap shot, Travis. That's no way to treat a lady lawyer. Some of us are honorable, you know."

"Yeah, I do know. You'd be surprised how many decent lawyers I meet in my business, on both sides. I might even be willing for my son to marry one. Speaking of lady lawyers, we may have a break soon in the case of the DA who was killed."

"So when were you going to get around to telling me? I thought you were going to keep me posted on that."

"Don't get testy. I'm not holding back. We just got some promising DNA evidence from the lab this afternoon. It looks like it may tie in with a guy she prosecuted. As soon as we pick him up, we're gonna use the DNA to get a confession. He was locked up at the time of the other murders, so it doesn't look like they're connected. But we've gotta line up all our ducks in a row."

"So are we back to square one with the three murders when Bernie was killed?"

"More or less. But that doesn't mean the guy who left the note on your car didn't threaten you. You've still gotta take that seriously and not take any chances."

"Don't worry. I've never really been much of a risk taker—but especially not with my life."

CHAPTER 12

Good Doctor

C lara couldn't think of any good excuse to put it off any longer. She had tried to ignore her reluctance to follow through on Dr. Andrews. It had been nagging at her all along. Many times in her life she had tried to avoid unpleasant tasks, hoping they would go away, but she knew they rarely did. She had also tried to ignore those niggling little feelings, the ones that just make you feel off-kilter, like trying to get gum off the bottom of your shoe on a hot day. No matter what you do, it's just sort of a sticky mess.

She didn't like feeling that way about Heath. Things seemed to have started off so well and then just didn't go anywhere. In part, it was because she had real questions about trusting him after seeing him in a restaurant with an attractive woman when he said he'd be working. She didn't even have the nerve to confront him about it, afraid of what his response might be. And as if that weren't bad enough, now she had to face up to using Heath to find out about his father. She just couldn't feel very good about it.

As she wondered what approach to use, on her desk, she noticed two tickets for *A Fabergé Fantasy* that had been sent to the Westgate Trust to preview the special exhibit at the MH de Young Memorial Museum in Golden Gate Park. This was as good an opportunity as any. When she called to invite Heath, he said he would like to go, but had to see if he could get out of a commitment. She wondered about the commitment then wondered if he was interested in her company or just wanted to see the Fabergé exhibit before the big crowds expected when it opened to the general public. Then she wondered why all of her old insecurities were raising their ugly little heads. Then she wondered why she kept wondering.

He called back to say he could go, but since he wasn't sure when he'd be able to get away from a meeting at UCSF Medical Center, they decided to meet at the museum. Clara knew Adrian and Blake were planning to go, and she could ride over with them anyway. At the last minute, Adrian begged off because of a migraine, but even then he was good humored. "I'd go anyway," he said, "but these little white spots I see when I get a migraine would make all the Fabergé eggs look speckled."

The exhibit was fairly good, although she'd seen finer Fabergé eggs in Russia and elsewhere, but the hors d'oeuvres were barely adequate and the champagne even less so. Was she being picky or just edgy about seeing Heath again? Probably the latter, she thought. After all, it was hard not to be impressed with the exhibit that included the Chanticleer Easter Egg, made of gold, diamonds, pearls, and a stunning shade of blue enamel, with a rooster that emerges from the egg, flapping its wings to crow the hour. Of course, it was much more elaborate than the exquisite little gold egg pendant Jon had hidden in a basket along with chocolate eggs on their first Easter together, but no other egg would ever seem as beautiful to her as Jon's gift.

She didn't want to think about things like that, and

Blake was a pleasant diversion, as well as an engaging escort.

When she caught herself looking around for Heath, she tried to control her anxiety. It was eased because of Blake's affable company, and she felt a little smug when Heath first spotted her with a man only slightly less imposing than a Nordic god. She could have sworn his brown eyes showed a hint of the green-eyed monster of jealousy. She introduced them, and he seemed to relax slightly when Blake said it was nice to have met him and parted company.

"Who's your friend?" Heath asked, with an edge to his voice.

"He's both a friend and a neighbor. He lives across the hall from me with his significant other, a lovely man named Adrian."

Heath smiled, and his jaw muscles lost most of their rigidity. For a moment, he hesitated, as if standing on the edge of a high diving board, then decided to take the plunge. "I saw you with another man a while back, but instead of tall, fair, and handsome he was tall, dark, and handsome."

Instantly, Clara realized he had seen her in the restaurant that night with Miguel Fuentes. She remembered all too clearly seeing him with another woman. "Is that by chance the night you told me you had work to do, but you were having dinner with an attractive woman?"

"Oh," was all he could say at first. "That was no woman. That was my research associate. You thought we were a couple?"

"The thought did occur to me."

"Let me dispel that notion without delay. There are two distinct reasons we're not a couple. First, I never get romantically involved with people I work with, and second, she's devoted to her husband and two kids."

It was Clara's turn to say, "Oh."

Then he had the nerve to ask, "But while we're on the subject, who was Mister Tall, Dark, and Handsome?"

"Let me put it this way. 'There are two distinct reasons we're not a couple.'" He laughed at her quoting him. "First, I never get romantically involved with a client, and second, he's completely devoted to his wife and four kids. In fact, I like to think my good counsel helped him with his family concerns when they were having some difficulties."

"Sounds like noble work. You know, as stuffy as it is in here, suddenly the air seems a lot clearer. By the way, I happen to be famished—I haven't had any dinner."

He scarfed up some hors d'oeuvres and agreed with Clara that the champagne left something to be desired. After they went through the exhibit, in which he seemed to take only polite interest, he suggested they try to find some better champagne.

Once they were in his car, he turned into Jimmy Stewart again, full of awkward, boyish charm. He fumbled with his keys, took a wrong turn out of the park, and finally said, "I know this sounds like a come-on, but I'm not much on nightlife. The only place I really know for good music and decent champagne is my place. Do you have any other suggestion?"

"Aha," she said with a mock sneer, "the old my-place-or-yours routine, eh?" He squirmed a little, but she could see he was glad when she said, "I've already been to my place. Let's try yours."

When they entered, she was pleased to discover he obviously wasn't planning on a visitor. The coffee table was strewn with books and papers, as was the surface that probably was a dining table somewhere under the piles.

The rest of the place was stark modern decor and gave the distinct impression that the occupant did not pay much attention to his surroundings. The one exception was a wall of shelves, floor to ceiling, that had books from about waist high on up.

The lower portion was a well-organized collection of vinyl records and a large newer section of CDs. It was mostly classical but had more jazz than Clara's collection, as well as an eclectic batch of things that must have just struck his fancy at various times: some folk music, soundtracks of musicals, various ethnic selections, and a few other odds and ends. The sound system was excellent, as good as her own.

She stood at the door of his kitchen and watched him take out a bottle of 1985 Diamant Bleu champagne from Reims. The refrigerator was nearly empty, but he managed to find some very ripe brie to go with a baguette that was more like a briquette.

"You just happen to have this bottle chilled?" she asked.

"The one thing I always have in the fridge is a bottle of champagne. I'm not sure how good this one is or how long it's been here. There's something reassuring about keeping champagne on hand, just in case there's a good reason to celebrate something."

"Are we celebrating?"

"I managed to lure you up to my bachelor pad, didn't I? Old Hef would be proud of me."

"Really? I didn't know anyone still used the term 'bachelor pad.' Is that what I have to expect from you? You're really a playboy in doctor's clothing?"

"I guess that's why it's easy to be flippant about it. I'm about as far from a playboy as you can get. Of course, I hit the big four-oh this year, so I'm probably due for my midlife crisis any day now. But you're too young to understand."

"Compliment accepted. I'm only two years from forty myself. But I already had my midlife crisis. It was called law school."

"You'll have to tell me more about it," he said as he swept the coffee table clear enough to make room for their glasses and the champagne bucket. Instead of personal subjects, Clara steered the conversation to music, when he gave her the choice of where to start in his extensive collection. She decided on jazz, and the cool jazz went well with the cold champagne.

The music and conversation continued until they reached the awkward part of the evening, the inevitable where-do-we-go-from-here stage. Was she ready to go to the next level or not quite comfortable with the idea yet? She couldn't remember ever being so ambivalent. Her physical desire was clearly long overdue. But she knew her real reluctance toward intimacy was because of her objective to follow up on Heath's father and any possible connection to Bernie's murder.

That determined the limit she felt she had to set, and she knew he would comply. It was simpler than she anticipated, with a little string of exchanges:

"I think I'd better be getting home now."

"Are you sure you have to go."

"Yes, let's save some music for next time."

"Okay, as long as next time is soon."

"Is tomorrow too soon?"

"I can't tomorrow. I'm going to see my daughter in LA. Is Sunday okay?"

"Sunday's fine."

He took her home and made no effort to invite himself in. He was rewarded as she let herself be folded into his arms with a lingering goodnight kiss. It took sheer effort of will for her to extricate herself. But nothing after that required any effort because something had repealed the law of gravity—she was floating.

"Sunday, sweet Sunday," Clara was half humming, half singing the words of one of the songs from *Flower Drum Song* as she got ready for the day. They had decided on a picnic at Point Reyes lighthouse. She would bring the food, and Heath would provide gourmet coffee and champagne. She had spent part of Saturday selecting delectable goodies for the picnic basket she hadn't used in years.

It was a gray day, but for them, it seemed to glow. After they crossed the Golden Gate Bridge, they continued on Highway One, past Tamalpais Valley, Muir Beach, Stinson Beach, and Bolinas Lagoon, then along the edge of Point Reyes National Seashore. The shadows, the deep green forest, and the gray sky were only a backdrop for the radiance inside the car as they drove along. They turned at Point Reyes Station, taking Sir Francis Drake Boulevard, past the small community of Inverness and foggy Tomales Bay on down to the Point Reyes Lighthouse. Inverness reminded her of being in Scotland, where he had never traveled, and she told him about her sojourn in the lovely land of bagpipes and lochs, the closest she ever came to feeling ethnic identity.

They spoke of many things, even cabbages and kings—literally. "You'd be surprised at some of the unusual rewards of teaching high school. One student brought me the largest cabbage I've ever seen when he came back from a summer working on his uncle's farm."

"I'll see your cabbage and raise you a king," Heath said. "I was working in Chicago at Northwestern Hospital once when the king of Norway happened to have a heart attack while visiting the hospital. Somewhere, I have a letter on his highness's royal stationery expressing thanks to the staff for saving his life."

In the course of it all, she began to learn more about the elder Dr. Andrews. Heath practically idolized his father.

"I really admire Dad, not just as a doctor, but for the kind of man he is. He had a distinguished career before accepting the position of administrative head of Golden Gate Hospital in his last years before retirement. He's a superb diagnostician, and his former colleagues still sometimes consult him. He never made me feel I had to live up to him, but my greatest source of pride is that my father is proud of me. I know down deep that he'd have been just as proud if I'd been a good plumber or forest ranger. Dad still works one day a week at a volunteer clinic for people with AIDS. It was mostly my work in blood research that got Dad interested in AIDS, and he started the volunteer work while he was working full time. I don't know how he ever had the energy to do all the things he did. My mother always said he never lacked energy, and the only thing that ever limited him was time. I think he had a tendency to shortchange my mother in that department. But she was of the generation of women who accepted that as their lot in life. She has always busied herself with good works, and she has a whole scrapbook full of awards for volunteerism."

"It sounds as if you've been lucky in the parent department."

"Yes, I'm one of those rare specimens of people who had a happy childhood. Oh, I missed a lot of my father's attention growing up, but my mother always tried to make up for that. As adults, though, Dad and I have become close. Well, I admit it's more like being professionally close. I can't exactly say we share our deepest, darkest feelings with each other."

"Do you both have deep, dark feelings?"

"Doesn't everyone?"

"Maybe so. Mark Twain said, 'Everyone is a moon and has a dark side which he never shows to anybody.' What's your dark side?" she asked.

"I guess Mark Twain's response would be that it would hardly be a dark side if it's revealed. Anyway, it's against the law of the great outdoors to talk about dark things on a gray day. That picnic basket looks very enticing. Is it about time to check it out?"

"Sure. Let's find the perfect spot to spread our blanket."

His changing the subject had not escaped her notice. As she reflected, Clara wondered if it was for any particular reason, and if so, what it might be. Perhaps it was nothing more than an attempt to be a bit mysterious. She had played that game a few times, back in her youth when she was experimenting with ways to attract men. But she had given up games a long time ago and couldn't quite see Heath in that role.

After lunch, they went out to Limantour. Standing at the tip of the point, they gazed at the white cliffs. They saw traces of the great Point Reyes fire, new vegetation where once the bushes behind the dunes had been curling black stakes, but now with lupine blooming next to them. They could see seals at play on the ocean side, and sand dollars and horseshoe crab shells dotting the sand. The things they saw were of this earth, but it seemed they were suspended in space and, at least for a short while, the only inhabitants of their own little planet.

As they returned to the city, the spell began to dissipate, even as the fog thickened. With solemn apology, Heath said he had to get home and finish some work for the next morning that he had not gotten to because of going out Friday night and to LA on Saturday. Both anticipating a busy week, they made their next date for the following Saturday night, which was to be a very special occasion. It was the forty-first wedding anniversary of Dr. and Mrs. Andrews, the occasion for a large party at their home in the Berkeley hills.

ↄ⌘ↄ

On Saturday, as they wound their way up the narrow road to the party, Clara realized it was not so far from the little cottage she and Steve had rented when they first came to Berkeley. But when she entered Dr. Andrews's house, it seemed like a different world. There was a magnificent sweeping view of the bay, with the Richmond Bridge off to the right, Mount Tamalpais in the distance, then the Golden Gate, the Bay Bridge and city beyond, and the bay fading off into the distance southward. The house itself was a masterpiece of Craftsman architecture filled with a fine collection of Arts and Crafts furnishings.

They arrived early, before the guests, but everything was in readiness. It was clear Heath's parents were expecting her, and she was warmly welcomed.

"It's so good to see you again, Clara," Dr. Andrews said, as he introduced her to his wife.

"Are these lovely Arts and Crafts furnishings all of your choosing, Mrs. Andrews?"

"Some of the pieces were already in my family, but I filled in the rest," she replied with obvious pride. "But please call me Margot, and do let me show you a few of my favorite things."

They had only a few minutes to talk before others started to arrive. Most of the guests were doctors and their wives, mainly of retirement age, but some younger ones as well. Several would surely qualify for any list of who's who in the Bay Area medical community. There were a few other professional people, including a judge, a professor, and an architect, who was the current head of the firm that had designed the house.

It was a gracious occasion, filled with goodwill and appropriate toasts, but Clara could see it was tiring for Heath's mother. She was a lovely woman, pretty for her age and with a sparkling intelligence, but she gave an impression of fragility, like translucent bone china that would break if it were not handled with care. She was delicate and thin, but it seemed to be more than that. Everyone was particularly solicitous of her, and Clara learned why on the way home.

"Your mother is everything I expected, Heath. She would have to be a very special woman to be married to your father."

"Hey, how about being special enough to be my mother?"

"That, too. But did I sense she may not be entirely well?"

"Yes, she tries not to show it, but she has to really rest up to get through occasions like this. She's had several bouts with cancer and a lot of chemotherapy. She's remarkably strong, even to still be alive."

"How's her health now?"

"Touch and go. That's one of the reasons for the party tonight. She wasn't well enough for a party last year on their fortieth anniversary, and they aren't sure if she'll make it for their golden anniversary. I hope you weren't too bored with all the tiresome medical conversations tonight. It seems that all doctors can talk about is their work and their investments."

She noticed his change of subject and followed his lead. "Actually, I find the work talk interesting, but the investment stuff is generally a bore. Most doctors seem to be so bad at it, and they're always getting taken in by poor advice."

"Yes, I think there are two important areas of study not provided in medical school. One is bedside manner, and the other is how to spot a phony investment. In fact, Dad almost got sucked into that one by your former boss."

"What investment was that?"

"I assumed you knew about it. It was some sort of elaborate scheme to set up funding to treat AIDS patients. When Kahn first told Dad about it, he made it sound like a panacea for helping people with AIDS. It turned out to be more of a pyramid scheme that would really benefit the initial investors, mostly Kahn. I understand they had a big fight about it, and Dad pulled out."

"I'm glad to hear that. As far as I'm concerned, any investment scheme proposed by Bernie Kahn would've been suspect."

"I gathered you didn't like him much, but I didn't realize it was that strong."

"Somebody must've felt very strongly about him— the guy who decided he no longer deserved to live."

"Do you have any idea who that might be?" he asked.

"A lot of people apparently had reasons to dislike him. But it's hard for me to relate to the idea of any reason strong enough to put a bullet into somebody's head, to say nothing of putting three bullets into three heads."

"You never know what will push somebody over the edge. My guess is that even if most killers are despicable, there may be some who'd be nice people under normal circumstances. When I did the psychiatric part of my medical training, I saw some pretty strange behavior, sometimes by people with seemingly normal case histories."

"Do you think this killer is a psychopath?"

"I have no idea. I really haven't given it much

thought. I guess that's insensitive of me. It must have been preying on your mind a lot. Even if you didn't like Kahn, it must be unnerving to have known a murder victim."

"Yes, a bit. I'll feel easier about it when they find the killer."

"I haven't seen anything about it in the news lately. Do you know if they have any serious suspects?"

"I don't really know. We don't even talk about it much at the office anymore. It was the main topic of conversation for a while, but nobody seems to want to think about it now. I'm sure we'd all be more comfortable to see the killer brought to justice. Unfortunately, the more time passes, the more remote that seems."

ひとつ

When Clara arrived at the office Monday morning, there was already a message to call Dr. Andrews. She knew from the number that it was the elder Dr. Andrews, not Heath.

"Thank you for returning my call so soon, Clara. We enjoyed having you for our anniversary celebration."

"It was a wonderful occasion, and I feel very privileged to have been there. I especially enjoyed meeting your wife. She's a lovely lady."

"She is indeed. She said the same thing about you. I know you modern women don't necessarily consider that a compliment, but it was meant as such."

"Don't forget I was reared as a Southern lady. My mother would be very disappointed if I didn't live up to her careful training."

"You may tell her for me that you turned out admirably. Now, I realize you must be busy, and I did call for a reason. I wonder if you can spare time for lunch with a boring old doctor."

"No, I'm afraid not, but I would love to have lunch with you, Dr. Andrews."

"Your mother did teach you good manners, didn't she? So when's a good time for you?"

"Any day but Wednesday. We have a staff lunch here at the office on Wednesdays. I'm even free today, if you are."

"Perfect," he said, and they made arrangements to meet at Yank Sing restaurant in nearby Rincon Center.

℘℘℘

As she walked over from the office, Clara was wondering why Dr. Andrews had called her for lunch. Was he going to try to find out if her intentions with his son were honorable? She, of course, had not been able to get out of her mind what Heath had said about his father's bad investment with Kahn. She realized she was experiencing some symptoms of denial. For the first time, she hadn't even made a prompt report to Travis. She told herself there was no reason to, as she didn't really know anything yet. But she knew she was avoiding it, hoping it didn't amount to anything.

Dr. Andrews was waiting for her when she arrived, right on time. They had a lovely lunch, making small talk about a variety of subjects while they sampled the dim sum dishes. She wanted him to get to the point when he was ready for it, but when it came time to consider dessert, she was beginning to think she would have to initiate something herself—but what?

They passed up dessert but continued sipping tea. "Dr. Andrews, this has been really lovely, but I can't help wondering if you had any specific purpose in asking me to lunch."

He took a sip of tea and sighed. "I've been trying to

figure out how to broach the subject. I never thought I'd have to discuss this with anyone, but I get the impression that things could get involved between you and Heath. He told me about your conversation the other night, and I feel I really must clear the air. You know about the AFF, the AIDS Funding Foundation, Bernard Kahn's so-called investment opportunity to set up a foundation for AIDS patients to get funding for treatment."

He didn't phrase it as a question and was clearly surprised when she said, "No, I didn't know about it. I never even heard of it until Heath mentioned it."

"I suppose I shouldn't really be surprised. It would be like Kahn to keep quiet about it around people who might have been in a better position to check up on him. It was apparently a crooked pyramid scheme right from the start, but I swear I didn't know until I'd already signed some papers and given him a rather large sum of money. I felt so utterly stupid when I realized it. We had a big row about it."

"Is that what you two were arguing about the night when I happened to see you in the parking garage?"

"Yes. I wondered if you'd remember that. We went on back to the office then, and the argument escalated. I told him, in no uncertain terms, I would not support his dirty scheme any longer. He then informed me I had no choice, as the papers I'd already signed were evidence of my involvement. Needless to say, I hated the thought of having my reputation ruined, but even more, I hated the thought of what it would do to my wife. She was very ill then. I was worried, too, it would have ramifications for Heath's career. I didn't want him tainted by my stupidity."

"I'd hardly call it stupidity, Dr. Andrews. I know how persuasive Bernie could be, and he fooled a lot of people in a lot of different ways."

"There's even more to it, though, I'm ashamed to say. I wound up allowing myself to be blackmailed. Kahn said if I made substantial payments to him, he wouldn't expose my involvement. So I paid him off regularly until he was killed. You can imagine that I wasn't exactly grief-stricken when I learned of his death. The only emotion I felt besides relief was curiosity about who had a strong enough reason to kill him."

"I hate to even suggest the possibility, but what about you? Did the thought ever cross your mind?"

For the first time since he'd raised the subject of the investment scheme, he smiled. "The funny thing is, the amount Kahn extorted from me was a mere pittance by my standards. I know he viewed me as a prosperous doctor and probably thought he was really gouging me. But he had no idea of the wealth I have access to because of my wife's fortune. So the only consolation I had was that Kahn so greatly underestimated the value of his dupe."

"Well, it's over now. You must feel very relieved."

"Yes, I do in a way, but I can't say I really feel very comfortable about the way my problem was solved. Still, it's good to know that, in the end, the bad guys don't always win."

"Yes, but it's better if they get their comeuppance in more legitimate ways. I would have preferred seeing Bernie exposed for what he was. But, unfortunately, it might've hurt a lot of nice people in the process."

"Maybe that's what the killer thought."

એજ્બજ

As soon as she got back to the office, she called Travis. He wasn't in, but she left a message, and it wasn't long before she received a call from "Mr. Powell."

"So what's up? Any luck?"

"Yes, I think so. Sort of, anyway. Shall we meet at Take Five after work, and I'll tell you all about it?"

"Sure. Six o'clock okay with you?"

"Let's make it six-thirty."

"Okay, Clara. I'll be sure to arrive earlier, so we're not seen together. And Andy will let us use his office in the back to talk. See you then. Take care."

"Always. 'Bye till later." She realized she could've told him over the phone, but she missed seeing him. The feeling was mutual, she suspected, though he'd probably never admit that to her.

He was waiting eagerly, and she told him all about Dr. Andrews and the pyramid scheme. "Please tell me you don't think that's enough motive for murder. I don't want it to be Dr. Andrews."

"I understand. If everything checks out, I'd say the chances are good that it's not him, especially if his assets turn out to be as extensive as he says. But this could be important. I remember seeing something about this AFF somewhere in the investigative file, but I didn't pay much attention to it at the time. We've learned a lot more about Kahn since then. It could give us a lead on someone else, maybe even a tie-in with the other two victims."

A phone rang, and Travis fished it out of his coat pocket. He didn't bother to look at the caller ID and answered with his usual gruff, "Travis." He listened a moment, and his tone immediately softened. "It's for you," he said.

"For me? Who—" she started to ask, as he handed her the phone.

"Jo Anne?…Oh, sure…I could hardly turn down fettuccini Alfredo, and I haven't had my once in a blue moon allotment of it yet!…Okay, if you really want me to bring him along." She smiled as she handed Travis the phone.

"What was that all about?" he asked his wife on the phone. After a pause he said, "Yes, ma'am, we'll be right there."

Clara hadn't realized Take Five was only a few blocks from Travis's home. He gave her directions and left by the back entrance before she went out the front, the same way she had come in. She arrived just a few minutes later at the neat, cream-colored house with a profusion of roses growing in the tiny front yard.

Jo Anne answered the door and greeted her warmly. Travis was setting the table. Jo Anne took both of Clara's hands, pulling her to the sofa. "You're even prettier than I expected," she said.

"So are you. Your husband tends to speak of your stronger qualities."

"Yes, I know. When I met his first partner, he was shocked. He expected some sort of battle-ax, I think. No telling what Roy had told him. But I'm actually quite nice, except when he really gets out of line."

It was the first time Clara had heard anyone call him Roy, and she was amused at his pretending to pay little attention to their conversation as he opened a bottle of wine. She was also surprised Jo Anne was slightly shorter than her own five feet two inches.

"You have a lovely place. It's really homey. And your roses out front are gorgeous. You must have quite a green thumb."

"No, I prefer working indoors. Roy is the gardener. That's how he clears his mind."

"That's a talent he never told me about. In fact, he hasn't told me much about himself. For example, I'm curious—how did you two meet?"

"I was teaching at a junior high school in East LA, and Roy came to speak to the kids about drugs. He was just a rookie then and quite dashing in his uniform. I was a little afraid of going out with a cop, but he was so cute, I couldn't resist."

Clara could have sworn she saw Travis blush.

"I know what you mean. I had the same problem. That's how I got into this detective business. He can be very persuasive."

"Let me go put dinner on the table. Then I want to hear all about it."

Dinner was a delight, first talking about what Clara had been doing in connection with the murder case, then turning to the subject of education and other mutual interests.

Jo Anne was especially interested in Clara's travels, as she had rarely been able to lure Travis into a long trip, and Clara was interested in Jo Anne's hobby of photography. Excellent examples of her work decorated the walls, and Jo Anne promised Clara a copy of one she particularly admired, a spectacular display of blossoms and a pagoda in the Japanese tea garden in Golden Gate Park.

The evening passed quickly, and as it ended, Clara said she'd love to have them for dinner at her place soon. Before she left, she and Travis talked again about the possible importance of Kahn's AFF investment scheme.

"I'll dig out the information on it first thing in the morning and get it to you," Travis said.

"Great. Let me know what you find out. Do you really think there's still hope of cracking this case?"

"You're starting to sound like an old Raymond Chandler mystery, Quillen. But yes, there's always hope. In fact, I never totally give up hope until I've solved a murder. I only have a couple of unsolved homicides hanging around from years past, and I still haven't given up on them. But I'm getting a good feeling about this one. I think we may be getting close."

"God, I hope so. I'm about ready to take down my

sleuthing shingle. It's been a lot more nerve-wracking than I ever imagined."

"I hate to tell you, but the closer you get, the worse it is. That's when it starts to get really dangerous. When you start sniffing around the right suspect, he often gets a whiff of you. I'm not kidding, Clara. Now you have to be extra careful."

"But I thought my part was essentially done. I've followed up on everybody on Bernie's list except for the one we haven't identified."

"Remember, it ain't over till it's over. We still have to hear the fat lady sing. And we really have to stay in close touch now."

"I don't mind that. But I still think you're being overly protective."

"Indulge me, okay?"

"Consider yourself indulged."

CHAPTER 13

Murderer Unmasked

Her dreams that night dredged up the worst scenes from all the mystery stories she had ever read, with a few anxieties from old Hitchcock films thrown in. They all involved vulnerable young women in dire danger, but she always woke up before anyone came to the rescue. After each disturbing episode, Clara felt anxious, with the uncomfortable sensation that someone was watching her. She did deep breathing exercises to get back to sleep, only to have another bad dream.

Finally, at five a.m., she decided she might as well get up. She deliberately avoided the reflection of her tired face in the mirror, made coffee, and went out onto the balcony. The fog was still as thick as the cobwebs in her head.

At six, she thought about calling Travis, or Heath, or maybe Maura or Katy. The only person she felt certain not to disturb, though, was Adrian. He was always up early to squeeze fresh juice for Blake, who left in time to be at the office before the stock market opened on the east coast.

Adrian answered immediately. "Clara, what a nice surprise. You've never called this early in the morning before. I always feel like Robin without Batman after Blake leaves for the office."

"I knew you'd be up, and I just wanted somebody to talk to."

"Is anything wrong, luv? You don't sound quite like your usual cheerful self."

"I just had a restless night. No, nothing's really wrong. I just seem to be a bit on edge."

"Why don't you take a day off? We could go play in the park. The Martha Stewart-type projects I had planned for today can just as well be done tomorrow. That's one of the advantages to being a housefrau."

"Thanks, Adrian. Just thinking about the option makes me feel better. I actually have some work I really need to do at the office. In fact, that's probably the best remedy for my malaise, to do some work and get my mind off disturbing thoughts."

"Now what disturbing thoughts have been troubling you?"

"Well, I thought I had put Bernie's murder aside, but I guess I've let it prey on my mind without realizing it. I just wish they'd find his killer. It's unnerving to know there's a killer who doesn't like lawyers still running around loose."

"You haven't gone back on your word about sleuthing, have you, luv?"

"Well, I—" Clara almost started to say something when she remembered how vehemently Travis had admonished her not to tell anyone, no matter how trusted. "No, of course not," she went on hastily. "It's just that the more time goes by, the more I wonder if the murders will ever be solved."

"Until they are, you should heed your own advice. Get your mind on other things. Are you sure you won't change your mind about taking a day off? We could go to

Golden Gate Park and take a picnic to Stow Lake and climb Strawberry Hill. We had such a nice picnic there with Blake last fall."

"It's tempting, Adrian, but I think I'm ready to face the day now. I can always count on you to cheer me up. I think I'll get myself together now. Have a good day."

"Okay, luv. Don't hesitate to call again if you're feeling down. 'Bye for now."

Eye drops helped her bloodshot eyes, and a little more make-up than usual camouflaged the circles under them. She put on a camel-colored pantsuit with a yellow blouse. She added a marvelous Hermes silk twill scarf woven with yellow and golden butterflies. For good measure, she wore the butterfly earrings Adrian and Blake had given her for her birthday. By seven-thirty, Clara was absorbed in her work at the office.

But before that, Adrian had already called Blake at work and mentioned his conversation with Clara.

❦❦❦

Midmorning, Clara received a call from "Mr. Powell."

"Hi, Travis, what's new?"

"I've been digging into the AIDS Funding Foundation. I have a list of about a dozen investors and some other stuff. All the signs indicate a dirty scheme, but so far none of it points me toward any particular suspects. None of the initials match up with Kahn's blackmail list except for Dr. Andrews. Can you look over everything and see if anything rings a bell?"

"Sure. I need to feel I'm doing something to get this thing solved. It's starting to get to me."

"Bad dreams?"

"How did you know?"

"It's pretty typical for a neophyte detective. After the first ten years or so, you learn to sleep like a baby."

"That's a big help. I plan to make this my last detective job, thank you very much."

"We'll see about that. Believe me, it's easier when you don't know the victim. Anyway, why don't you say you're going to run an errand and meet me at the bookstore just down from your office? I can be there in fifteen minutes, if that's okay for you. Just browse until you find me."

"Sure, I'll see you there."

Clara couldn't help thinking about that scene in *Double Indemnity* when Barbara Stanwyck meets Fred MacMurray in the market. But they were the bad guys, not the good guys.

When she found Travis behind a tall shelf in the travel section of the bookstore, he handed her a large manila envelope so fast she hardly knew she had it. She glanced down, noticed there was no writing on the envelope, and turned it over to see it was sealed and also fastened with brads. When she looked up, Travis was nowhere to be seen. She had to smile at the Raymond Chandler routine.

Back in her office, Clara went through the contents of the envelope. Superficially, the documentation for the AFF looked on the up-and-up until she got to the figures. She didn't feel entirely competent when it came to deciphering accounting tables, but she had little doubt that close analysis would show the plan to be a phony pyramid scheme. What interested her most, of course, was the list of names. It had last names, with only a first initial. Travis was right. The only initials that matched the blackmail list were AH for Dr. Andrews, Hershel. There was still no match for HA, the only initials that they had not yet identified.

Clara had a sick feeling in the pit of her stomach. *What if HA really stands for Heath Andrews? What if Bernie left the initials in that order because he already had AH?*

She was desperate to find another answer. She looked at all the other names. There were a couple of other prominent physicians she knew only by reputation and some totally unfamiliar names.

The only other familiar name was Erikson, B. It reminded her of the name on the mailbox in her building, for Blake Erikson. But this couldn't possibly be Blake. Surely he would have said something about it to her if he was going to consider any involvement with Bernie.

That is, unless devious Bernie had somehow managed to convince him otherwise. Clara had watched Bernie manipulate intelligent clients into doing things against their better judgment time and again.

Much as she didn't want to admit it, it made some sense that Blake might have invested in the AFF. Both Blake and Adrian had worked long hours on political projects in support of AIDS research. They had had so many friends who had succumbed to AIDS. They were empathetic, and they felt very fortunate they'd had a committed relationship for such a long time that they didn't fall within the group of gays at high risk for AIDS.

If Erikson, B. was indeed Blake, Clara wondered if Adrian had also known about the AFF. She thought he must have, because Adrian had often told her that he and Blake always discussed major decisions. Sometimes they disagreed, like any couple, but they seemed to resolve their differences.

Then it hit her full force—HA—Holt, Adrian. No, it just could not be. Adrian and Blake would never have become involved in a crooked investment scheme, especially on a matter so dear to their hearts. But could they have been fooled the same way Dr. Andrews had been duped into thinking they were helping to achieve the much-needed funding for AIDS treatment?

No doubt, that was a distinct possibility. Clara's mind pulled and stretched and twisted, like taffy in a machine she had seen at a county fair when she was a kid. She thought it over and over again, trying to reach some other conclusion. Of course, the most hopeful answer was that Erikson, B. simply wasn't Blake.

She did a quick Internet search and found references to four Eriksons with a first name beginning with B in San Francisco. She didn't recognize any of the names but Blake's, which popped up in connection with the investment firm he worked for. There could, of course, be other people named Erikson, B. who just didn't come up for some reason. Besides, this was only San Francisco and didn't include the surrounding Bay Area. And she didn't even know whether all the names on the list of investors were from the Bay Area.

She knew she was grasping at straws. Her gut told her it was Blake. After all, that didn't mean he had anything to do with the murders. And it said nothing about Adrian. Still, her gut also told her it was something she just couldn't ignore.

What had Travis once told her about paying attention

'You can do all the investigating in the world, Quillen, but a lot of crimes wind up being solved by your gut.'

'That sounds slightly disgusting, Travis.'

'Maybe so, but I've been doing this stuff for a long time. Once you've followed every lead, collected every fact you can lay your hands on, and then analyzed the facts to a fare-thee-well, at some point, you have to sit back and let your gut take over. When it starts to knot up, you know you're onto something.'

Clara's gut was knotting up right now. She thought

about all the times Blake and Adrian had quizzed her about the case. She winced as she recalled her conversation that very morning when Adrian had asked her if she had been sleuthing. She shuddered at how close she had come to telling him she had been doing some detective work.

She reached for the phone to call Travis and then pulled back. How could she implicate two of her dearest friends on such a tenuous connection?

Why was she hesitating? She'd told Travis everything about her other good friends. Why was this different? Maybe it was because the others were already at least in the ballpark as suspects. Maybe it was because Clara got so tired of hearing about gay bashing in other parts of the country that she felt protective of her gay friends, even in San Francisco. That wasn't a reason to give a pass to a murderer, but what really scared her was that her gut was telling her something she just didn't want to believe.

That was it, she admitted to herself. If either Adrian or Blake was a murderer, he had to be brought to justice. Friendship or no, that principle was absolute. If it was Blake or Adrian, which one was capable of murder—or were they accomplices? Could she really be so wrong about people she thought she knew, two men she had thought were truly gentle men? She reached for the phone again, but pulled back again and reached for her shoulder bag.

For the first time ever, she forgot to speak to the receptionist as she went past.

"Off to lunch, Clara?" the receptionist asked.

"Um-hmm," Clara mumbled over her shoulder and kept on walking.

こうこ

Blake's office was only three blocks away. Clara wasn't sure what she was going to say to him when she got there, but she knew she had to see his face when she talked to him. A phone call wouldn't do.

It had been quite a while since she had been to Blake's office, but she and his secretary remembered each other. She told Clara that Blake was in with his boss, but should be out soon and asked if she could get her some coffee. Clara declined and took a seat near the secretary's desk.

Clara looked idly at the *Wall Street Journal* and a few other investor publications on the table beside her. She began to look around the room until her gaze focused on the nameplate on the secretary's desk: Shirley Sheldon. Shirley's eye happened to catch Clara's.

"Did you notice the name change? I went back to my maiden name after my divorce was final."

"Yes, I was just trying to remember what it was before."

"Well, don't bother. I'm trying to forget everything about that jerk. Pardon me, I mean my dear ex-husband."

"It sounds like the divorce was not an amicable one."

"The divorce was even worse than the marriage, and that was lousy. After all his affairs and with all his money, I wound up with next to nothing except the kids. But that's all I really care about anyway, so I can't totally complain. Still, it's rough being a single mom."

"Didn't you at least get your share of community property and child support? California divorce law is usually very fair."

"No offense, Ms. Quillen, I know you're a lawyer. But some lawyers are really scum, and my ex's lawyer was the scummiest. He used that guy Alvin Hanks who does all the big-time divorces, the one somebody killed. I could've killed him myself, but he was only second on my list after my ex-husband. They hid assets, and that shyster pulled every dirty trick in the book. I just wanted out with as little damage to my kids as possible. We'll be okay."

"I'm sure you will," Clara said automatically. But her mind was racing, thinking about Alvin Hanks. A chill had run through her the instant she heard the name. She halfway expected to hear the name Rinko, the third victim. She thought of those three dead men that fateful night in Marin, each with a bullet hole in his head.

She wondered if there were as many people who hated Hanks and Rinko as she knew despised Bernie Kahn. There could be all sorts of people who wanted them dead. There must be connections they just hadn't discovered yet.

Maybe her gut was getting in the way of her brain. She needed to keep thinking this thing through. She just didn't want to accept that the murderer could be Adrian or Blake.

She tried to focus on what Travis had said about part of the process being to eliminate the innocent, not just implicate the guilty.

That's it. She had to eliminate Blake and Adrian as suspects. Then she'd tell Travis all about it. He would be impressed that, even as a novice, she was already doing solid detective work.

Just then, Blake emerged from his boss's big corner office and spotted Clara. He looked ever so slightly bewildered and then smiled broadly. "Hi, Clara, what a nice surprise. What are you doing in this neighborhood?"

Clara managed a friendly smile. "I thought maybe we could have lunch. There are some things I want to ask you about. Can you spare the time?"

"Come on into my office. I just need to clear a couple of things, then we can take off."

While she waited, Blake sent an e-mail and did a couple of cryptic things on his computer. "Now, to what do I owe the unexpected pleasure of your company?"

"I wanted to talk to you about an investment matter I ran across, the AFF."

Blake's face blanched almost imperceptibly, but his expression didn't change. "I was hoping it was more social than business, but, of course, I'll be glad to give you any investment information I can. How about a quiet place for lunch while we talk."

"Yes, that's what I had in mind. Someplace very private, as this is a somewhat sensitive matter."

"I have a terrific idea. Let me surprise you," Blake said.

On the way out, Blake's secretary reminded him that he had a two o'clock appointment. "Don't worry," he replied. "We're just going to the deli, not a three-martini lunch."

They stopped at the deli and bought lunch, then headed to the parking garage for Blake's forest green Jaguar. Soon they were traveling west toward Golden Gate Park.

"Where are we going, Blake? Isn't this a bit far from the office?"

"It's good to get away once in a while. Spontaneity is good for the soul." Blake turned into the park, heading in the general direction of Stow Lake.

"How funny that you should choose this, Blake. Only this morning I was talking to Adrian, and he mentioned our outing here last fall."

"Really? That's a coincidence. I just thought this might be a nice quiet place for a talk, and a picnic away from the office seemed inviting. Are you game for a short hike up Strawberry Hill?"

Clara had been feeling apprehensive twinges all

morning, and now they were growing in intensity. But she smiled gamely. "Of course. Our jobs are much too sedentary anyway."

Blake parked the Jaguar on a side road near Stow Lake and asked Clara to take the bag from the deli while he got a blanket out of the trunk of his car.

As they approached the bridge to the path that led up the hill, Clara began to feel panicky. What if she was walking up to an isolated spot with a murderer? *Don't be silly*, she told herself. *This is Blake, your friend. But what if your friend is a cold-blooded killer?* Blake was a foot taller and about a hundred pounds heavier than she was. What could she possibly do to protect herself if he decided to harm her? Why hadn't she taken those self-defense lessons she had always meant to take?

The only thing she could think of to do was to call for the cavalry. Her phone was in the bag that dangled from her shoulder. As they climbed the hill, she chattered about the lovely nasturtiums blooming beside the path while she reached into the bag and pressed the button where she had programmed in Travis's number. She hoped to cover any sounds that might emit from the phone, but simultaneously could not tell whether there was any answer.

She made references to how pretty Stow Lake looked even on an overcast day and how much steeper Strawberry Hill was than she remembered. If Travis was listening, she hoped he could hear what she said. She had seen a maintenance truck pass before they started climbing, but she was well aware that she didn't see another soul once they got to the top of the hill. This was one of those days when the fog didn't lift by midday, as it usually did. With the fog and the trees and the thick foliage, it was hopeless to try to find a visible spot, where they might be seen by passersby below.

Blake spread the blanket behind a large tree in a place so dense it was like a grotto. After they set out the sandwiches and coffee from the deli, Blake asked, "Now, what is this investment you want to know about, Clara?"

"I think you already have some familiarity with it, the AFF, a foundation to fund treatment for AIDS."

"What makes you think I know something about it?"

"Your name was on a list of investors involved with my former boss, who was murdered."

"I can't tell you how sorry I am that you became aware of that information, Clara."

"Why are you sorry?"

"It's embarrassing for someone in my profession to admit he was taken by a shark like Kahn. I really should've known better."

"Bernie fooled a lot of people, Blake. That was his specialty. You really shouldn't take it personally."

"The affront was not only to me for my stupidity. It was also the idea that something that might've been of real benefit to so many was nothing but a scam to make money for the investors, especially Kahn."

"Were all of the investors in it for the money?"

"No, Kahn was clever about that. He got a few legitimate people to go in on it so he could use their names to validate the deal. Adrian and I were known as activists in AIDS causes. Some of the others were doctors who really cared about AIDS patients."

"Was Adrian an investor, too?"

"Not directly. We treat our assets like community property, but I handle all the finances in our family."

"Then why was Bernie blackmailing Adrian?"

Blake choked on his coffee and sputtered, "What do you know about that?"

Clara watched him as he carefully blotted his Armani tie and avoided looking at her.

She waited until he finally looked up before going on. "I stumbled on some papers. But I don't really understand why Adrian was being blackmailed."

"It was for me, of course. When I found out the AFF was a scam, I first tried to conceal it from Adrian. He has such faith in me to handle our money, and he's obsessive about people living up to their commitments. He thought this was a genuine opportunity to help AIDS patients. He was absolutely furious with Kahn when he found out. He told me I should expose him and take him to court. I explained that I could hardly sue Kahn without implicating myself as well. It would ruin my career. We had a lot of arguments about what to do."

"So how does the blackmail come in?"

"Well, you know how impulsive Adrian can be at times. He just couldn't stand to see a guy like Kahn get away scot-free. On top of that, he didn't like the way Kahn treated you. So, without telling me, he confronted Kahn and threatened him with a lawsuit, but that only made matters worse. Kahn turned the tables on him and said if Adrian didn't cough up ten thousand dollars, he would implicate me and ruin my career. Adrian borrowed money from his mother and paid him off. Then Kahn came back for more. That's when Adrian finally came to me. He knew it had gotten out of hand. I told him we couldn't possibly continue to let Kahn control our lives."

Clara waited a moment, then asked quietly, "Is that when you thought about killing him, or was that Adrian's idea?"

"Don't be absurd, Clara. How could you ask such a question? Not that the bastard didn't deserve killing. Thank God, someone else thought so, too. I don't know who killed Kahn, but whoever it was did us a great favor."

"Was it also a favor to kill Alvin Hanks at the same

time? Did you hate him, too, for what he did to your secretary?"

"How did you know about that? No, of course I didn't hate him enough to kill him, even if I knew about his odious representation of Shirley's ex-husband. That's hardly motive for murder. Where do you get these ideas, Clara? You read too many murder mysteries."

"What about Rinko? What did you have against him?"

"Nothing. I never met the man."

A voice then seemed to come from nowhere, and even though the tone was not like the usual sound of Adrian's voice, they recognized who it was before Adrian stepped from behind the tree.

"But you did know he was secretly giving legal advice to Kahn to avoid malpractice liability, didn't you, Blake? I told you about that the day I confronted Kahn, the day he laughed in my face when I threatened a malpractice suit. He said he had all the bases covered, and Rinko made sure he had no exposure."

When he came into full view, Adrian looked as if he might burst into tears any minute.

"Where in the world did you come from, Adrian? How did you know we were here?" Blake asked.

"A little deduction and a bit of luck. Clara seemed so down this morning, I decided to surprise her and take her to lunch. But when I got to her office, she was out. So I thought I'd have lunch with you and went over to your office. Shirley told me you had gone to the deli for lunch with Clara, but the deli man said you'd just left with sandwiches. You weren't in the little park nearby, so I went to the parking garage and saw that your car wasn't in your reserved parking space. I'd mentioned this spot to you on the phone this morning, so I decided to try it—and here we all are."

"How long have you been listening behind that tree?" Blake asked. "It isn't like you to be an eavesdropper, Adrian."

"It's about time I listened to some things I haven't wanted to hear. There are a lot of questions that have been preying on my mind for a long time, but one has been uppermost. Now I have to ask. I have to know if you killed those men, Blake. I've been dreading finding out, but I've suspected it ever since the day after the murders. You told me you were working late that night, but I called the office, and you weren't there. I was afraid you might've had a rendezvous with someone else, but the next day that thought paled beside the fear that you might've killed three human beings. I went looking for that old .38 we used to keep in the back of the closet. When I discovered it was no longer there, I was afraid of what you had done. I've been in denial ever since, but in my heart of hearts, I knew."

"Be quiet, Adrian. There's no proof of anything. You're just giving Clara ideas that could get us both into a lot of trouble."

"Blake, I've promised to stay with you in sickness and health, till death do us part. But I didn't take murder into account. I thought I knew you, your moral fiber, but I don't know you at all. Even if Kahn was a scoundrel, how could you do such a thing?"

"Don't you see, Adrian? It was for you as much as for me. We couldn't keep on living under the cloud of Kahn's threats. It was undermining our relationship, and we would've lost everything. And besides, I rid the rest of the world of those slimeball lawyers. I didn't want them to be in a position to hurt anyone else."

The momentary silence was broken only by the sweet chirp of a bird high in a tree, until Clara said quietly, "That all sounds noble, Blake, but nothing justifies coldblooded murder."

As soon as she spoke, she realized her mistake. There was such a delicate balance already, a fragile tension between the two men, and her intrusion had upset the balance.

Adrian and Blake turned and looked at her. She knew instinctively that life-altering decisions were about to be made. She was the only one who would point to Blake's guilt, and she could not count on the man who loved him most in the world to protect her.

Her only real chance was to stall long enough that Travis might get to her, if Travis had even gotten her message. Was he on the way? She could try to play on Adrian's sympathies, but her best hope was to hold out for Travis.

"Blake, I don't really blame you for hating Bernie Kahn. A lot of people had good reason to hate him. But help me understand—I need to have some justification that I can really accept. I never knew you to do anything violent to anyone."

"Don't think you're fooling anyone, Clara. I know your self-righteous attitude about murder. You couldn't possibly understand that your precious legal system is a dismal failure. There's no justice in this world when the so-called officers of the court are allowed to cheat the very people the system is supposed to serve."

"But we're not all like that, Blake. You know that. Most of us are honest and hardworking, just like most doctors and mechanics and stockbrokers. It's the bad ones who give the rest of us a black eye."

"Well, I made sure the three I killed deserved it. Of course, it was Kahn who was really my main target. The other two were mainly to cover up. I figured three unrelated lawyers would take the focus off Kahn and make it impossible to connect me, especially when I left the Shakespeare quote about killing lawyers. I never even met the other two until that night."

"How did you do it, Blake? You must've been very clever in arranging it." Clara was still trying to stall, but in an odd, detached way, her question was genuine. She had always wondered how the murders had been contrived.

Blake was still sitting near her on the blanket, and Adrian had slumped down on another corner. She tried to watch them both but kept her line of vision focused on Blake, with a peripheral view of Adrian. Now she saw the distinct reflection of arrogance in Blake's eyes.

He hesitated, at first, as if deciding whether to answer. When he began to speak, though she was looking mostly at him, she could make out a contortion of pain on Adrian's face. They both seemed to know there was no way Blake would let her go on living, knowing what she now knew, and even more so once she knew the details of how the murders were carried out. And Blake somehow felt compelled to explain how cleverly he had formulated and executed his plan.

"I suppose the beauty of the plan was really its simplicity," Blake began. "I focused first on Kahn and decided how to do it, then planned the others. If anything had gone wrong with Kahn, I wouldn't have gone ahead with the others. The plan for Kahn fell into my lap when he once bragged to me about his fancy borzoi and how they went for their nightly walk in his fancy neighborhood. I decided that was the time and place for him.

"Then I set up an appointment with Hanks. I used a phony name and said I needed some advice about how to hide assets from my wife, whom I planned to divorce. I arranged to meet him in the parking lot of the Lark Creek Inn. It seemed like a beautiful spot for a murder, nestled in the redwoods. He didn't hesitate to meet me when I promised him big bucks under the table in addition to a hefty retainer to handle my divorce. I used another phony name and set up a meeting with Rinko in the parking lot of the Marin Civic Center and told him I'd bring a ten-thousand-dollar retainer in cash to consult him about a legal malpractice matter."

Clara was fascinated and repulsed at the same time by how matter-of-fact Blake was with regard to taking human life. He might as well have been making a decision about a stock investment.

"I'd bought a silencer for the .38. Until then, it hadn't been out of the box for years. I'd already made three copies of the page from *Henry VI* and discarded the book in a random trashcan. I took our plain second car, the brown Honda, and splattered enough mud on the license plates to make the numbers illegible. That was probably an unnecessary precaution because I don't think anybody but the victims ever saw the car."

Adrian remained immobile, his face a mask that betrayed no emotion.

"The rest was amazingly easy. I drove along until I spotted Kahn and the dog. I stopped right in front of him and got out. At first, he didn't recognize me in the dusk, and then he said, 'Blake, what on earth are you doing here?' I handed him the page from Shakespeare, smiled, pointed the gun at his head, and said, 'I'm just making sure your brain will never again come up with a scheme to harm anyone.' Then I pulled the trigger. Kahn fell, and the dog just whimpered. I got in the car and drove away.

"I'd already scouted out the kind of cars Hanks and Rinko drove several days before. When I got to the parking lot of the Lark Creek Inn, I spotted Hanks in his car and just waited long enough to make sure no one else was around. Then I walked up to his car, spoke to him through the window, and handed him the Shakespeare quote. When he looked down at the paper, I put a bullet through his head. When I got to the civic center, it was almost the same with Rinko.

"As I drove back across the Golden Gate Bridge, I threw the gun into the bay. I was home well before the eleven o'clock news."

Clara was amazed at how cool and collected Blake was as he described the murders. Now his cool demeanor became frigid, as his ice-blue eyes focused on her.

"What about the woman DA who was shot? Did you have anything to do with that murder?"

He smiled. "No, that was just fortuitous. And by then I knew you were working with that detective. The way you talked about him made me suspicious. I followed you a couple of times and saw you meet him at that shabby bar. Adrian had mentioned your penchant for sleuthing."

Adrian winced.

"But you did leave the threatening note on my car, didn't you?"

"Of course. After that lady lawyer was killed, I thought the note might scare you into quitting the detective business. It's a shame it didn't. I followed you a few more times, but I didn't see you with the detective again. I thought I'd scared you enough."

Blake paused and inched a little closer to her. "I really don't want to do this, Clara, but you know I can't allow you to turn me in."

She knew her time had run out.

"That's the end of story hour, Clara. I'm sorry, but now it's time to turn out the lights and go to sleep."

She lashed out and tried to knee him in the groin, but he grabbed hold of her leg before she could hit her target. She tried to reach his eyes with her fingernails, but his long arms kept her from making contact. She tried to bolt away, but he held her ankle and kept her from rising. As he jerked her back, she caught only a flash of Adrian, who seemed frozen on the far corner of the blanket.

She tried again to break away, but somehow Blake's powerful arms managed to pin her arms behind her. She struggled with all her might and tried to kick, but she couldn't get any leverage with her legs.

The pain in her arms subsided and then gave way to another pain far more frightening—she could feel her own silk scarf being tightened around her throat. When she tried to pull away, the scarf became even tighter, so she shrank back, trying somehow to make her neck smaller and less vulnerable. But the scarf tightened in Blake's strong grip. She heard her own gasps, then no more sound.

Her last sensation was her own eyes seeming to bulge as she caught her last glimpse of Adrian, still immobile, with a look of mournful anguish. Then all was black, as the scarf continued to tighten around her neck.

&ℭ&

The only one who observed what happened next was Travis, who had come bounding up the hill with his heart pounding like a pile driver. He broke into the grotto just in time to see Adrian leap across the blanket and cry out, "No, Blake, no!"

As Blake turned his head abruptly toward the sound, with the force of a lightning bolt, Adrian's knee came up under Blake's chin with a blow that sent his whole body back. There was an audible crack as Blake's head struck the large rock behind him.

Travis instantly appraised the scene. All three players were motionless, but he only cared about one. He threw his body over Clara's and began CPR. The only sounds were those of his convulsive efforts, which he continued while he ignored his own blurred vision, distorted by tears.

Then Travis heard the sweetest sound he had heard since the birth-cry of his last child. It was the sound of life. It was a sound from Clara, gasping for breath.

EPILOGUE

C lara tried to say it wasn't necessary to go to the hospital, but she couldn't make her voice utter a sound. Travis would have overruled her anyway. Heath was at the hospital by the time they arrived. Travis had called him to meet them at the emergency room. He made an effort to conceal his annoyance when Heath took charge and made him wait outside while the head of the ER conducted the examination and ordered follow-up tests, then a sedative.

It was dark outside when Clara finally opened her eyes and saw Travis sitting beside her hospital bed. She felt his big hand over her small one and gave it a weak squeeze. She smiled at him, but when she tried to speak, the first sound was more of a croak than a word. It came out vaguely as, "Thanks."

Travis blinked away the tears in his eyes. "Don't talk, kid. The doc says you need to give your throat a rest for a couple of days."

"But I have so much to tell you," she whispered.

"Shush...it can wait. I already got the whole story from Adrian. And he's fine, by the way, at least physically. I think he's still in shock."

"What about Blake?"

"Those are your last words for the day, young lady. I

guess you might as well know now as later. Blake had a concussion and a broken jaw. It was really Adrian who saved your life. I'm sorry...I tried, but I didn't get there in time. The important thing is, at the crucial moment, Adrian knocked Blake away from you. It was a powerful blow, and Blake's head hit a rock. He was still unconscious when he arrived at the hospital. They were going to perform surgery, but he was dead before he got to the operating table. The official cause of death was cerebral hemorrhage."

"Oh," was all Clara said before sinking back to sleep.

This time it was peaceful.

❦

When she woke early the next morning, an unfamiliar but smiling face greeted her. It belonged to an affable black male nurse who was just about to wake her for a lukewarm liquid breakfast. She could barely swallow, and it burned going down.

"How do you feel this morning—don't answer that. Just smile if you're okay."

Clara smiled groggily. "What time is it?" she asked, mainly to try out her voice. It was still more of a croak than a voice, but it was audible at least.

"Time to see your doctor. He said to call him as soon as you woke up. You must have some clout because you've really had the royal treatment around here."

The nurse disappeared. Clara barely had time to look around the flower-bedecked room before Heath appeared. For a tall man, somehow he looked like a small boy at first. Then he adopted a professional tone.

"Your prognosis is excellent, Ms. Quillen. I predict you'll be going out with an eligible doctor within a week. Meanwhile, you need a lot of rest and a prescription of

TLC. You have to get the rest, and I'm in charge of the TLC."

"Sounds like a deal," she whispered. As she tilted her head to receive his kiss, she winced from the pain in her neck. "Maybe we'll have to go easy on that for a while."

ᘓᘔᘓ

Of course, she had no idea how difficult it was going to be to go easy in her relationship with Heath. In the next few weeks, they talked, seemingly ad infinitum, about recent events. First, he was concerned that he had not been there for her in a life-threatening situation. Then he was annoyed with her for not trusting him enough to tell him what was going on. Then he was proud of her for her role in solving the murders. Then he was irritated that she had put herself in danger. Then he was angry at Travis for involving her in the whole mess. At each stage, he was diverted by patients and other professional obligations.

Meanwhile, Clara was physically and emotionally recuperating, while trying to cope with Heath's concerns. She was also trying to come to terms with her relationship with Adrian. She made several efforts to talk to him when she first got home from the hospital, but he wouldn't see her. She knocked on his door and left messages on his voicemail.

Finally, after seven days, Adrian called and asked her to come over. She found him hunched in the corner of the sofa. Although it was a warm day, he was wearing pajamas and a robe and was wrapped in an afghan.

"I really don't know how to begin, Adrian. I'm just so sorry about everything."

Tentatively, she reached out to touch his hand, and they both began to cry. That opened a floodgate of emotion for them both. They had many long talks after that.

In the end, Adrian decided to go back to New York, where he had worked as a young man and still had good friends. Staying in San Francisco, in the penthouse he had shared with Blake, was just too painful. His financial assets were sufficient, as he and Blake had reciprocal wills and owned the penthouse in joint tenancy, and they also had substantial life insurance on each other.

Under California law, a person who feloniously and intentionally kills another cannot benefit economically in any way from the death. In Adrian's case, there was never any serious question about whether the killing was justifiable to protect Clara. Travis made sure Adrian was not unduly hassled by law enforcement, and he had little difficulty in winding up his affairs. He put the penthouse on the market, made one final farewell dinner for Clara, and departed for New York.

Clara was still in touch with Travis, but he was busy finishing up the case of the murdered deputy DA, making sure the prosecutors had enough evidence to convict the killer. Clara still did some work for Maura and Katy, but they began to need her less and less, even though the firm was doing quite well.

They had hired another woman attorney, who was a real crackerjack, and they expected to add more as the need grew. The publicity following the killings had generated some business, but mostly they were getting a lot of referrals from satisfied clients.

Clara wanted to keep ties with the firm, but she still preferred not to make a full-time commitment. She wanted to leave herself time to do some pro bono work on her own and think about other interests she had neglected.

And the most neglected part of her life—her love life—now had someone in it, as she allowed her feelings for Heath to grow. They had eased into an intimate relationship, and Heath was all Clara could wish for in a lover. Well, not quite, when she really thought about it. Physically she could ask for nothing more, but emotionally he wasn't always there for her. All too often, their time together was subject to the professional demands on him. Even so, they were developing a much fuller relationship when outside forces intervened again.

Their time together tended to be casual and spontaneous because his schedule was so often unpredictable, but one day he called and asked her to dress for a special dinner that night. He took her to the Carnelian Room, with its fabulous view of the city. It was an unusual choice because most often when they went out to dinner, it was some interesting little ethnic place. Clara couldn't help wondering if the fancy dinner was to be the setting for a proposal.

As it turned out, it was, but not quite what she expected.

They had evolved into a comfortably familiar relationship, but there was something strained about the way the evening progressed. And no ring fell out of her napkin when she put it on her lap or appeared at the bottom of her wineglass. Conversation seemed superficial rather than romantic. Finally, Heath broached the subject that was really on his mind. His whole demeanor changed, and his excitement was almost palpable.

"Clara, I have something important to tell you. I've been offered the professional chance of a lifetime. A grant has just come through for a team to do AIDS blood research at UCLA Medical Center. I've been asked to head the team, and it's a fantastic opportunity. It's the best-financed research of its kind to date, and the support facilities are excellent. I've known about it for a while, but I didn't want to say anything till it was certain. There's only one drawback. They need my answer right away. They actually want me there next week to begin the preliminary planning."

Clara didn't know quite how she should react, but it was clear this was something Heath wanted to do. "That's terrific, Heath. Do you have any hesitation about doing it?"

The excitement in his voice faded slightly. "None professionally, and personally it has the advantage of giving me a chance to spend more time with my daughter. But the obvious question is what about us? This is a three-year research project, and it will be very time-consuming." He paused and took her hand. "Will you come to LA with me?"

"Is that a proposition or a proposal?"

"It's whatever you want it to be. I just don't want to lose you, Clara. What do you say? Please tell me we have a future together."

The waiter arrived to offer the selections for dessert. Clara was grateful for the intrusion. She found herself asking the waiter to describe the dessert selections in detail and wound up ordering only espresso. After he went away, Heath asked again, "What do you say, Clara?"

"I don't know what to say yet. I've been through a lot of emotional turmoil recently. I need a little time to think. Meanwhile, I don't think there's any doubt in your mind about what you want, is there?"

"No," he admitted. "I really want to do this."

"Then, of course, you'll accept. We can figure out what to do about us later."

"I guess when you come down to it, that's one of the things I love about you. You understand how important my work is to me."

"Yes, I do understand." *All too well*, she thought.

∽∼∾

That night, they made love with their usual passion, but in some ways more tenderly than ever before. Instead of staying, though, he went back to his place for some sleep before an early morning meeting. She lay awake thinking about Heath and, more pointedly, about her with Heath. Was this what she really wanted? Was she ready for a real commitment again? Did she want a commitment with a man who was already so committed to his work?

These and other questions were running through her head when she finally fell asleep. She dreamed of Heath, but it was all mixed up with dreams of Steve and Jon, and somehow she wasn't quite sure who was who in her dreams. She kept reaching out to someone and taking his hand, but she could never quite make out his face.

The only thing she knew for sure when she woke the next morning was that there was no reason she had to decide right now. Just because Heath had to begin his new project the next week didn't mean she had to make an immediate decision. She could pull a Scarlett O'Hara and think about it tomorrow. There had to be some advantage in having been reared as a Southern belle. She simply decided not to decide—at least not right away.

Therefore, she was feeling somewhat relieved as she started her day. She read her *San Francisco Chronicle* in more detail than usual, more leisurely than she did when she was pressed for time. She was intrigued by a small story about a suspicious death the day before. The story described the victim as a young woman who had graduated second in her class the year before Clara graduated from Boalt law school. Clara recalled the name, although she didn't know her. The body had been found on the rocks in the bay, near Fort Point.

She was interrupted by the telephone and was glad to hear the familiar voice of Travis on the other end of the line. But she could hardly believe what he said.

"Clara, how'd you like to snoop around some people connected to your old law school? I'll stop by and fill you in on my way back from Fort Point."

About the Author

J. E. Gentry was a lawyer and law professor until she decided to devote herself full time to writing. She earned a bachelor's and a master's degree in English before going to law school and then earned a Juris Doctor degree. She has traveled extensively and now lives with her husband in the San Francisco Bay Area. She enjoys classical music and classic movies, and also show tunes and cool jazz. She is somewhat like her central character, Clara Quillen, but, in the book, Clara is better looking, nicer, younger, and much wealthier.

CPSIA information can be obtained
at www.ICGtesting.com
Printed in the USA
LVHW08s0104130918
590003LV00009B/121/P